If Jane hadn't misread [ ] murder suspect.

"Am I under arrest?"

"No, but we'd like to search the cottage."

"What for? More bodies?"

Toussaint's glance was impersonal. "It's a matter of procedure. We need to eliminate you from the investigation."

She knew how the police worked; he would have a warrant. Her permission was a courtesy only. Her stomach cold and tight, she rummaged in her bag, withdrew a set of keys and handed them over. As the other policemen disappeared in the direction of her cottage, Toussaint held the passenger door for her. He was polite, even solicitous, but the easy warmth and charm of their previous evening together was gone.

When she stepped forward to get in the car, his jacket flipped open in the breeze. She saw the butt of a gun, and Toussaint suddenly fell into context. For years he'd been a frustrating, missing link to her past—now he was larger than life, more male and difficult than she'd bargained for...*and* a cop.

Toussaint was a cop, and somehow she had ended up on the wrong side of the law.

"*Body Work* is the kind of book that sucks you into the pages and won't let you go until the end. It's edgy and different, with a strong hero and heroine who don't fit the usual mold."
—*New York Times* bestselling author Linda Howard

Also by FIONA BRAND

TOUCHING MIDNIGHT

Body Work

FIONA BRAND

MIRA

ISBN 0-7783-2289-0

BODY WORK

www.MIRABooks.com

Printed in U.S.A.

ACKNOWLEDGMENTS

Thank you to Susan Lowe, a former lieutenant with the Columbus Division of Police for help with the forensic and procedural details, and to Claire Russell of the Kerikeri Medical Centre, New Zealand, for supplying the medical information.

To Linda Howard, for years of inspiration,
unfailing support and friendship.

Part 1

The Seeds Are Sown

One

Forty-five years ago

Throat tight with panic, ten-year-old Etienne Dexter launched himself off the veranda, bare feet thudding on sun-hot dirt, kicking up dust as he ran. Lurching around the corner of the house, he cut through a ragged mass of weeds that had once been a rose garden, eyes blind to the velvety shimmer of acres of uncut hay and the hot, arching perfection of the Louisiana sky.

As he barreled through the open doors of the barn a nesting swallow arrowed past his head. Heart pounding, he skidded to a halt, the breath shoving in and out of his lungs so hard it felt as if his chest was trying to turn itself inside out.

Agony scored him as he dodged around the

skeletal remains of ancient harvesting equipment, although he was neither cut nor burned. Rounding a stack of drums that filled the barn with the thick reek of machine oil, he crouched down, thin shoulders taut as he lifted the trapdoor in the wall, put there instead of a regular door in Prohibition days to hide the fact that Grandpa Dexter had a moonshine still situated practically on top of the storm cellar. Ducking through, he held his breath against the instant need to gag. Crawling into "the pit"— a windowless shed tacked on to the rear of the barn, with a storm cellar beneath—always made him want to throw up.

A shudder of reaction swept him as he leaned against the trapdoor, preventing it from closing fully and shutting him into the dark before he'd had a chance to switch on the flashlight he'd stolen from the kitchen.

Tears ached in the back of his throat and hazed his vision as he fumbled at the button. His fingers, which were normally deft, were shaking and, instead of turning on, the torch popped from his grip, hit the dirt floor and rolled. He grabbed for it, lost his balance and sprawled forward, skinning the palms of his hands. Simultaneously, the trapdoor banged shut behind him, plunging him into darkness.

A sharp, metallic rap told him that the flashlight had rolled through the open cellar hatch and hit the rungs of the ladder. Raw panic spasmed, making him feel physically sick. If he took the flashlight back to his stepmother, Eloise, broken…

The flashlight hit the floor with a clunk and, miraculously, turned on. Light washed up through the hatch, turning the pitch-blackness soupy.

Relief flooded Etienne. He had to find Charles, but there was no way he could go any further without a light, even knowing that his twin was down here somewhere.

Holding his breath against the acrid smell that permeated the wood floor, he got to his feet and started down the ladder, gripping each wooden rung with his bare toes and keeping his gaze fixed on the burning incandescence below. Even though he could breathe, he felt like a diver descending. Logically he knew that the only difference between down here and outside was the lack of light, but a part of him still wanted to bolt. The heavy blackness reminded him of the Lassiter River after a storm, the water thick with mud and so murky it was like swimming in black tea.

Once he had the flashlight in his hand he felt steadier. He would never admit it to either his stepmother or his brothers, but he had always been scared of the dark, and not just ordinary scared. He would rather be beaten black and blue than be locked down here. In the old days, when the Dexter family had had money, the cellar had been used to store blocks of ice in summer and apples in winter, but after the original shed that had been built on top of the cellar had blown down, nobody much had bothered with it. Nowadays the only things the cellar stored on a regular basis were worms and mice and a whole lot of darkness.

He swung the light around, orienting himself. The walls were lined with stone blocks, apart from one section at the rear, as large as a small doorway, where the blocks had been systematically removed and placed to one side. He aimed the beam down the tunnel his twin brother had spent the summer excavating. Distantly, he could hear scraping sounds.

As he started down the narrow tunnel, Etienne's eyes widened with shock when he saw how much Charles had done. The last time he'd ventured into the cellar, Charles had only just begun digging; now the tunnel stretched out, straight as an arrow until it hit a boulder and took an abrupt turn to the left.

He rounded the corner and saw Charles standing in a pool of light cast by a kerosene lamp, ankle deep in mud and perched on a mound of dirt, systematically scraping. Filled buckets of dirt were lined up against one wall, ready to be taken outside and dumped.

For long seconds, disbelief drowned Etienne's

fear and the shock that had sent him running in the first place. "What are you doing?"

"Heading for the river."

Etienne blinked at the sheer scale of the project. The river was more than a quarter of a mile away; it would take Charles years to dig that far. He stared at his twin. "You're crazy."

Charles's gaze was oddly blank. "You'll see. The tunnel's going to be way cool."

"What if Eloise finds out?"

He shrugged. "She won't do anything. Haven't you noticed? She's scared of the dark. That's why she thinks it's such a big deal locking us down here." He smirked. "I like it."

Cold gripped Etienne's spine. Even though they were identical twins and looked as alike as two peas in a pod, there had always been differences between them. He liked apples, Charles liked oranges. He was fascinated with models and construction, and it was a fact that Charles was more interested in breaking what Etienne made than in building anything himself. At school, Etienne achieved good grades, but the only thing Charles seemed interested in was making trouble and trying to lay the blame on Etienne.

When they'd been five, switching places and bamboozling people had been fun; now, the way Charles played the game, it had become a nightmare.

Eloise had always picked on Charles more than any of them. Unlike Etienne, Charles hadn't learned the art of being invisible; he always had to answer back. He seemed to delight in pushing Eloise into a rage, especially when she'd been drinking. Lately, he had become her main target.

Once Eloise had locked him down here for a week, feeding him pig scraps every second day. The first two days Charles had gone crazy, clawing at the trapdoor and screaming until he'd lost his voice. Then he had gone quiet. When she'd finally let him out, he had been different in a way Etienne couldn't define. Charles used to be as scared of the dark as he was, but not anymore. Now he seemed to like being under the ground better than being outside in the sun, and he cared even less about upsetting Eloise.

Charles dumped another bucket beside the wall and brushed a lock of black hair out of his face, leaving behind a smear of dirt. "What're you being so prissy about, anyway? This is our way out."

Reality reasserted itself, and with it a heavy dose of dread. "You've got to come now."

"Why?"

The scorn in his voice was biting. Once Charles wouldn't have argued, he would simply have fallen in with Etienne's plans, but now it was almost as if Charles had turned on him.

Misery squeezed at Etienne's chest, along with a replay of the numbing shock he'd felt when he'd found his father lying face down at the kitchen table, his eyes half open, his skin cool to the touch. "It's Dad—"

A high-pitched voice echoed down the tunnel.

Charles's mouth curled. "Well, whaddya know? It's that little worm, Stephen. C'mon." He slipped past Etienne, taking the lamp. "We can't let him see the tunnel."

Etienne followed. As they emerged from the tunnel entrance into the cellar, he turned off his flashlight, and hid it behind his back. He noticed that as Charles went up the cellar ladder, he didn't bother to conceal the lamp. Lately he was becoming increasingly cocky. When Eloise hit him, he began to laugh.

Charles pushed the trapdoor wide and stepped through, deliberately shouldering Stephen. When the younger boy reeled back, a mud-coated hand shot out to steady him, leaving a large smear on his shirt. Charles leaned in close. "What do you want, *worm?*"

Stephen shrank from the contact, his gaze sliding nervously to the mark on his clean shirt. Despite the heat, Etienne noticed Stephen was dressed in long pants, with socks and shoes, his hair neatly combed as if he was going to church— only Eloise never took them to church.

Stephen stared into the pit as Etienne stepped through, his eyes wide. He was too scared to venture beyond the cellar hatch, and there was no way he could see the tunnel entrance, but Etienne didn't trust him an inch. Charles might be weird about a lot of things, but he was right about Stephen. The kid was only seven, but already he was a snake and a snitch. He was Eloise's son; and her pet. When Stephen did something wrong—which wasn't very often because he was so busy sucking up—Etienne and Charles usually got to pay.

As the trapdoor fell shut, a shadow slid through the sunny door of the barn. A split second later, Eloise appeared, the thick outline of her body visible through the cotton of a shapeless sundress, blond hair tangled and trailing around her shoulders, her face bloated and red, as if she'd been sitting in the sun drinking.

She blinked, adjusting to the gloom of the barn, and her expression sent a shiver down Etienne's spine. Her mouth was curved in a smile that people in town never got to see, and her eyes almost seemed to glow in the shadows.

She crossed her arms over her chest, and her smile grew. "Your father's dead."

Two

Eloise Dexter surveyed her husband's casket through the dark film of her veil and tried to summon up an appropriate expression of grief.

Burton Dexter had been a handsome man in his day—big and strapping, with the remnants of the Dexter wealth cushioning his existence—but drink and disappointment, and yes, the demands of his nasty wife, had all taken their toll.

The priest finished intoning, the interminable ceremonies were completed, and finally Burton's coffin was pushed into his slot in the swanky Dexter crypt.

As the stone that sealed the hole was lifted into place, Eloise slipped a tiny silver flask from her purse and celebrated the moment with a surreptitious swig of Burton's best—and, for that matter, *only*—brandy, then almost spat the mouthful on the floor when she saw that he was interred next to his first wife, Helene. There were only two other slots left in the crypt, both at floor level, which meant when she was buried, that was where she would go.

Over her dead body.

Hazily, Eloise decided there was something not quite right about the statement, because if she needed a slot in this expensive piece of stone junk she *would* be a dead body, but…

Fury sent a flush of heat through her as she shoved the flask back in her purse. She had specifically forbidden this burial arrangement, but that scrawny spider of a lawyer Burton used, Andre Poche, must have vetoed her instruction.

Craning around, she spotted Poche, who was lurking at the entrance to the crypt. One thick gray brow lifted in acknowledgement, his thin mouth curved in barely veiled contempt.

She swore beneath her breath. The hushed buzz of conversation ceased, and the priest's head whipped around on his skinny neck.

A tide of red flowed up Eloise's face, making her feel even hotter and sweatier. She must have said the words more loudly than she'd thought, or else it was the good acoustics.

Her mouth flattened at the disapproval, which was palpable. Not for the first time, she felt gauche and ungainly in the company of Burton's peers. Not that she knew any of these people on an intimate basis. Despite the fact that she was his wife, Burton had been insultingly careful about keeping her out of both his social and his business life.

An hour later, the social niceties of a wake waived on the basis that she couldn't afford one—and even if she could, she wouldn't waste her precious time mixing with Burton's snobby friends—Eloise was uncomfortably ensconced on one of the lumpy horsehair sofas in her front parlor.

If the funeral had taken most of the day, the reading of the will took no time at all. Burton had kept things simple. He had left everything to his three sons. Eloise was left with nothing but the clothes on her back and the bill she'd run up at the liquor store. She was allowed to stay in the house for the length of time she was guardian to the boys, but the second the youngest child—her own son, Stephen—either left home or turned eighteen, she was out.

Poche and some other fossil were the executors of the will and trustees of the assets. She would be paid a monthly allowance and that was it. She could fight it in court, but according to Poche, the will was ironclad and fair. Financially she was cared for, and Burton had looked after the rights of his sons. If Eloise wanted to contest the will, she would have a battle on her hands, which, of course, would require money she didn't have.

With a grim smile, Poche packed up and left, leaving her a copy of the will, his movements neat and precise—the thin curl of his mouth insolent enough that she itched to slap him.

As the sound of his car receded, Eloise eyed the boys, who were sitting quietly on a sofa in the corner, her temper simmering. She hadn't wanted them in on the reading of the will, but Poche had insisted. Since they were beneficiaries, he had claimed, it was appropriate they were there, but that didn't make Eloise like having them witness her final humiliation any better. Charles and Etienne both had smirks on their faces, and Stephen looked suspiciously blank.

One of the twins stared directly at her, his gaze insolent, and a snarl erupted in Eloise's throat. She had long since ceased to try to tell them apart, and lately her vision had gone blurry, making it even more difficult, but it scarcely mattered.

Reaching into the bodice of her dress, she pulled out a thick silver chain from which dangled a key. Lifting the chain from around her neck, she swung it in front of the three faces, enjoying herself for the first time on what should have been the best day of her life.

Eeny, meeny, miney, moe. "Who's going in the hole today?"

The round-eyed shock was gratifying. None of them had expected a punishment on the day of their father's funeral.

With an imperious gesture, she pointed at Stephen, almost chuckling when his face went paper-white. With jerky movements, he got to his feet and crossed the faded carpet to stand in front of her.

Instead of directing him to the pit, Eloise handed the key to him. *Her* child. "From now on, you're in charge of the key."

Stephen's eyes went huge. She could see that he immediately knew what that meant. He never had to go under the ground again.

"Yes, Mama."

Warmth flooded Eloise. "Since you've lost your daddy, you get to choose." Heaving herself to her feet, she snatched up the cane she habitually carried in the house, gripped his shoulders and turned him around. Her face went hard as she surveyed the two older boys. "Which one goes in?"

The fact that they had lost not only their father but their mother was of no consequence to her. They might be orphans, but they were still looked after—still cushioned. Burton had seen to that.

Fury ate at Eloise as she considered the implications of the will. Her husband had left her *nothing*. In death he had had his revenge; he had done what he had never succeeded at in life. He had out-

witted her. She'd had no idea he had a heart condition, or that he had quietly made a will, that ex-
cluded her.

He had made his plans, then dropped dead,
using that weedy solicitor to do his dirty work
both before and after he'd stopped breathing.

She stared at Charles and Etienne. They were
both tall and handsome—revoltingly like Burton—and now independently wealthy. She was little more than their housekeeper. The only bright
spot was that Burton hadn't been able to cut her
out of her role as guardian to his sons. They had
been married; she was the mother of his youngest
child, and stepmother to his two eldest boys. Try
as they had, Burton and Poche hadn't been able to
oust her completely.

Helene's boys now belonged to her.

Hatred welled, and she made no effort to stop
it. Burton had had no idea of real grief, no idea of
what she had suffered.

Ten years ago she had lost her first baby. Within
minutes of her child being delivered, stillborn, Helene Dexter had given birth to twins.

Two live, squirming babies, while she had given
birth to a deformed corpse.

If that wasn't bad enough, on top of the grief of
losing her child, she had had to watch her ex-lover
shuffle out of the ward—relief on his face because,

with the death of the baby, his responsibility toward Eloise was gone.

For the next two weeks, owing to a flu epidemic and a shortage of beds, she hadn't been transferred to a general ward but had to remain on the maternity ward, next to a woman who had received more than Eloise had ever hoped for. She had watched the oh-so-fragile Helene, who also suffered from a heart condition, whispering and cuddling with Burton, watched the gifts and flowers pile up around her bed until that corner of the ward had looked like a shrine. Worst of all, she'd had to watch her cuddle and feed her babies, their tiny mouths latched on to her breasts as she'd settled back against the pillows with a mindless, contented expression that had made Eloise want to scream.

She had daydreamed of stealing one of the babies.

She had even considered taking them both. If she took one, then why not both? But what was the point in stealing Helene's babies when she no longer had a boyfriend to support her?

The corrosive bitterness had eaten at her until she couldn't bear to watch either Helene or the babies. She couldn't eat, couldn't stand the taste of food, which she ordinarily adored. Even water was sour in her mouth, and her round plump belly with its puckered folds of skin shriveled up.

Concerned, one of the nurses had tried to force-feed her oatmeal just as the twins were brought in for breastfeeding, and a black rage had exploded inside her. With a guttural cry she'd knocked the bowl of oatmeal from the nurse's hand and surged upright in the bed. A hot pain had sliced through her abdomen, as if something inside had burst, and warmth gushed down her thighs. Blackened clots of blood that looked like chunks of rotted meat and bright red arterial blood, had erupted from between her legs, splattering the white sheets.

Things had gotten a little hazy then, but she could remember doubling over and vomiting—long, wrenching convulsions that had hurt her stomach and her throat—and she could remember the stuck-up look on Helene's face. Eloise had spoiled the right royal Mrs. Dexter's precious feeding time with the twins.

Doctors had arrived then. Not one, but four, all male, clustering protectively around her, treating her as if she were made of bone china.

Alternately sweating and shivering, she had been removed to a private room with soothing blank walls and the luxury of her own television. Her head pounding, body limp, she had lain on a fresh bed while she'd been prepped for surgery and heard the murmured comments the medical staff had made.

Someone had made a mistake. The clean-up operation after the "thing" had slid from her body hadn't been comprehensive enough. A piece of the placenta had been left behind, decomposing in her womb and causing an infection. That was why she had become progressively sicker instead of getting well—why she had felt so depressed and had stopped eating.

Heads would roll, she was assured, and the room and the surgery were on Lassiter General. She could stay as long as she liked at no charge.

A peculiar satisfaction had uncurled inside Eloise. She hadn't cared about the pain or the fact that she had almost died of blood poisoning. For the first time in years, she was actually happy. In a lifetime that had seen no discernible pampering beyond the fact that her mother had allowed her couch space so long as the welfare checks kept arriving, the treatment and consideration were astounding. Eloise had felt like a princess.

She had stayed three months. By the time she had left, she was glossy and plump again, her womb surgically repaired, but, contrary to what the doctors had promised, the dark bouts of depression hadn't left her.

She still couldn't get over the shock of what she'd given birth to. It hadn't looked even remotely human. The misshapen fetus had seemed symbolic of what life continually dished up to her. Not second or third best, but absolute garbage.

When she'd finally made it home to her apartment, she found that her ex-boyfriend had left town, sold all her belongings and sublet the apartment. Standing on the doorstep of the shabby little building, her bitterness had condensed into a hard knot. Childbirth had taken almost everything from her—the child, her boyfriend and almost her life—and yet it had made Helene Dexter a queen.

Viciously, she'd kicked at a plant and broken the flap on the letterbox on her way past. As hard as the medical staff at Lassiter General had tried to make amends for their shoddy treatment, it was a fact that while she had been rotting from the inside out, they had been clustered around Helene like bees to a honey pot, attending to her every whim and fussing over the twins.

She could have *died*.

To her way of thinking, Helene Dexter owed her.

In the end, Eloise hadn't had to think or scheme about how to get her own back. Two years later Helene had died, ironically enough, in childbirth. Not contented with everything she already had, the silly cow had been trying to have a third baby and had paid the price.

Burton had been grief-stricken, easy pickings when Eloise had called. She had gotten him drunk, waltzed into his bed, and made herself indispens-able as a nanny and a housekeeper—perfect wife material. She had also made sure she got pregnant immediately.

Burton had delayed proposing, but when she had sickened the way she had with the first child, he had finally come up to the mark. Lassiter was a small enough town, and the Dexters a prominent enough family, that everyone at the hospital had known she was carrying his child. And if they hadn't, she had made sure they did.

They had been married from her hospital bed a month before Stephen was born, and this time the pregnancy had stuck. The baby had been small but perfect in every detail. When he had taken his first look at the child, the sick, grieving look had finally left Burton's face. Even he had realized that as a newlywed with a new baby, he couldn't continue mooning after Helene.

Eloise's gaze swept the three boys in the parlor. She had dressed them in suits for the occasion, and the money had been well spent, even if she had be-grudged the expense. The funeral had been large; even the mayor had been present. In all their mar-ried life, it was the grandest occasion she and Bur-ton had ever attended, and the fact that Burton had to be dead for it to happen hadn't escaped her.

Her mouth thinned. Helene had been taken to

balls and on trips abroad. *She* had been hidden away like a guilty secret.

Her bitterness condensed as her gaze settled on the twins. Even from the grave, Helene had managed to take from her, and Burton hadn't been much better. When she had insisted that her son carry the name that she had chosen, Stephen, Burton hadn't argued, nor had he bothered to tell her that Stephen was the English version of Etienne, and that she was recycling a name Helene had already used for one of her twins.

Eloise regarded her son. Stephen wasn't as tall and physically strong as Helene's boys, but, in her opinion, and in the opinion of the teachers at school, he was a lot smarter.

She jerked her head at Charles and Etienne. "Choose."

Etienne watched Stephen's fingers close on the key. His half brother had a healthy fear of both Charles and himself. When Eloise's back was turned, they didn't hesitate to pound him into the ground, but Stephen was more afraid of Eloise.

He didn't want to choose, but he knew that if he didn't, Eloise would put them all in the ground.

"Worm," Charles muttered, his stare malignant.

A low, hissing sound escaped from Eloise. Her hand struck out, and Charles's head snapped back.

When his head flopped forward, blood slid down one cheek where her nail had caught him.

Etienne swallowed, his spine rigid, his gaze straight ahead. The silence thickened. The heat in the parlor had become so intense that the sweat oozed from his pores and turned cold on his skin. He could smell the fresh blood trickling down Charles's cheek and the choking sweetness of Eloise's perfume, and feel the decision being balanced and weighed. If Stephen didn't choose right, he would get the next backhander.

Stephen's Adam's apple bobbed, his gaze locked on Etienne's, and his head jerked.

"Good boy," Eloise purred. "I knew you would get it right."

With a jerk of her head, Eloise indicated the door. Stephen might be holding the key, but it was Eloise calling the shots. Briefly, Etienne considered running, or even fighting back, but the cane at her side convinced him not to try. His father had been a big man, but Eloise was almost as large, her shoulders broad, her arms thick. He didn't make the mistake of underestimating the soft layers of fat. Eloise hit harder than his father ever had.

Miserably, he led the way out to the shed, ducked down and stepped into the pit. The trapdoor banged shut, plunging him into darkness, and he heard the bolt being shot on the other side and the grating metallic sound as the key was inserted into the padlock.

Stoically, he waited for his eyes to adjust, so that he could make out the dim light that seeped around the edges of the trapdoor. When the faint edge became visible, he lowered himself to the floor, keeping his gaze pinned to the outline and his mind blank. If he didn't think, he wouldn't get scared, but it was hard not to think today. When he'd watched his father's coffin disappear into that hole in the crypt, he had finally understood that he was never coming back.

The priest had assured him that his father had passed on to brighter and better things, but Etienne couldn't get it out of his mind that his father's body was in a place just like this, only smaller.

Silence closed around him. Time passed, and he began to feel not only thirsty but hungry. Gradually, the light faded.

Etienne squeezed his eyes shut, trying to tell himself that the difference between light and dark was still there, that he'd been staring at the sliver of light for so long that his eyes simply couldn't see it anymore, but when he opened his eyes, there was no outline.

Panic coiled. His heart raced, and for a raw moment he couldn't breathe. With an effort of will, he forced air into his lungs, then expelled it, repeating the process until his heart slowed down.

The reason the light was gone was explained by the rumbling in his belly. It was night.

Panic grabbed him again, and Etienne struggled with the painful need to urinate. Eloise had never left him in the ground for so long, except for that one occasion when his father had been away on business for a week, and Charles had been locked in.

But then, his father had usually come home from work, and, sober or not, he had expected to see all his sons at the table. Eloise had had to let him out.

Now his father was gone, and she didn't have to do anything she didn't want to.

The implications of his father's death sank in and, with a sharp pain, his bladder loosened.

Excruciating seconds later, he inched forward, moving away from the wet patch, although there was nothing he could do about his pants. He came up against the rough surface of the stones and pressed his forehead against the cool rock. He couldn't see a thing; he couldn't even remember which way was up. The blackness was absolute, pressing in on his throat and chest so that it was hard to breathe, but as long as he could touch something he would be okay.

Closing his eyes and focusing on the rough texture of the stone biting into his skin, Etienne crouched in the dark and waited.

Part 2

Roots Go Deep

Three

Twenty-five years ago

The first body was found in Atlanta. Stab wounds, bruising, ligature marks, rape—the usual, if the destructive pattern of a pathological rapist/murderer could be considered in any way routine. What wasn't usual were the traces of hydrated calcium sulphate, commonly known as gypsum, found on the victim's skin and in her hair, and the fact that the killer had cut off most of the victim's long blonde hair and taken it with him.

Speculation was rife. Gypsum could be used to make plaster of Paris, as an ornamental material, and as a fertilizer, which left the location of the killing, and the occupation of the killer, wide open. But whether they had a sculptor or a farmhand committing the crime, the result was no work of art and made Burton Coley throw up—thereby "busting his cherry" in homicide, providing a moment of grim humor for the other members of the Atlanta PD—and making him determined to solve the case.

The second body, found a month later twelve miles from the location of the first, exhibited the same "signature," with one difference. The victim had had short hair, and this time the killer had removed her entire scalp, complete with skin, with surgical precision. Either the fact that she'd had short hair had enraged him, or he simply hadn't wanted to be bothered with cutting off such short tufts.

Coley, who'd thought he was thoroughly hardened by the first body, threw up again. When he'd cleaned himself up, he flipped his notebook open and entered the details. Despite his psych major and twelve-week course at the FBI National Academy, there wasn't much more to add except *Conclusion: he wanted the hair.*

The third body confirmed that the Atlanta PD had a serious problem on their hands, and the only conclusion Coley had come close to reaching was that in the midst of a rash of petty crimes characterized by felons who were hot-headed and just plain stupid, they had finally been stumped by a smart one.

Two weeks later, in the middle of a heat wave that carried its own killing power, four bodies were uncovered in Florida exhibiting the same distinctive signature.

Coley made the trip to liaise and share information. The killer was no longer confining his activities to Georgia, but he apparently liked the East Coast, and it seemed the hotter and stickier the summer got, the more active he became. That theory got a little skewed when the lab work from the FBI finally arrived on Coley's desk, matching the signature with bodies that had been discovered in Los Angeles, Seattle and New York. Some of the cases—fourteen in all—dated back ten years. At that point the Atlanta PD stepped up the investigation and formed a task force, promoting Coley to second-in-command. With the FBI working in an advisory capacity, the task force picked up the thread of twenty-one linked, unsolved murders, and the press went ballistic.

Their boy liked his women young and defenseless. He preferred long hair, and he traveled, moving from state to state on a killing spree that had spanned almost eleven years...and counting. There was always the possibility they hadn't found all the bodies or connected all the cases. Then an agent on a study tour in England took time out from researching Scotland Yard's methods to see the sights: Buckingham Palace, the Tower of London and Madame Tussaud's Wax Museum.

The mystery of the presence of hydrated calcium sulphate at each crime scene was solved. The killer was using plaster of Paris to mold his victims' faces: he was making death masks.

The psychological profile of the killer became more complex, and the focus on the hair as the prime trophy was dropped. The only reason he wanted the hair was to complete the masks.

One of the members of Coley's task force became so upset at the gruesome turn the case had taken that he had to be reassigned. Another—a transfer in from Louisiana named Stephen Dexter—simply went AWOL.

At 2:00 a.m., Stephen Dexter parked his car at a motel in downtown Berkley, Michigan, just outside Detroit. It had taken two days, and he had driven all night, but he had finally tracked down Etienne. It hadn't been as difficult a task as it should have been, given that his brother had changed employers and locations approximately five times since he had last checked. Once his mind had fastened on the possibility, no matter how remote, that his brother could be involved in the killings, all he'd had to do was check the most recent trail of bodies and, bingo, guess who had been resident in each city, for each death?

Sliding his Smith and Wesson from the glove compartment, Stephen chambered a round and holstered the weapon. Shrugging into a sports jacket, he adjusted the fit so the shoulder holster was concealed, checked to make sure he was carrying his badge, then locked the car and walked into the motel office.

The badge wasn't necessary; the lights were on, but the desk wasn't manned. Either the clerk was taking a break, or he had fallen asleep out back.

It was a simple matter to turn the register around, check the occupants listed, then go through the various cupboards and drawers until he found where the keys were kept. When he'd selected a key, he studied a map of the units, which was conveniently tacked to the wall, then strolled along to 15A.

After carefully sliding the key in the lock and turning it, he stepped into the room and gently closed the door behind him, allowing himself time to adjust to the darkness. He flicked on a small penlight and played it around the room. The units were standard in layout, designed for the constant flow of a mobile workforce: one main room, which included the bed and a kitchenette, with a small bathroom off to the side.

Sliding his gun from its holster, he crossed the room, flicked on a lamp and simultaneously shoved the barrel of the Smith and Wesson against his brother's throat. "It's you, isn't it?"

Etienne's eyes flicked open. The stare wasn't friendly, but then, there had never been any love lost between them.

Stephen worked to control the fury that had driven him ever since he had found out about the waxworks gimmick. It had taken years, but he'd hauled himself up out of the dirt of that backwoods Lassiter farm and made a *life*. If what he believed was true, his brother was on the brink of destroying everything he had ever worked for. His jaw clamped. "You've got to stop. Now."

"Stop what?"

"Don't act dumb."

With a contemptuous movement, Etienne shoved the barrel aside as if it was one of the plastic water pistols they used to play with. Pushing the covers back, he surged to his feet, the movement fluid and controlled, and Stephen couldn't repress a small spurt of fear.

Dark brown eyes locked with his. "You're losing it, Stephen. If you've got an axe to grind, why don't you leave your badge and your gun out of it?"

Dismissively, Etienne walked to the bathroom. The toilet flushed, and pipes gurgled as water was run. Long seconds later he reappeared, a towel in his hand, and Stephen studied his older half brother. Etienne was lean and tanned, his face pleasant—even handsome—and it was difficult to judge whether he was lying or telling the truth. Normally Stephen was very good at reading people, but lately he was reassessing. It was possible that his half brother, who had always been at the bottom of the Dexter food chain, along with his twin, was smarter than anyone had ever dreamed.

He centered the gun on Etienne's chest, but, for the first time in his law enforcement career, the rush that went with using the weapon was absent. He studied Etienne's face, waiting for a reaction. "We know about the masks."

Etienne slung the towel over one muscular shoulder and ambled to the kitchenette. "What masks?"

Belatedly, Stephen realized that that was one detail that hadn't been released to the public.

"That's what the killer is doing. Not collecting hair, *making masks*." Stephen stared with fascination at Etienne's lithe, tanned back as he began making coffee. His movements as he spooned grains into the filter were meticulous—precise. Stephen had a sudden vivid image of his brother messing around with lumps of clay and, later on, sculpting, and his stomach tightened. As a child,

Etienne had always been secretive and withdrawn, with an artistic bent. His room had been filled with modeling materials.

Cold eyes eerily like his own fixed on his. "Get a grip, Stephen. Are you sure it isn't you?"

A moment of disorientation sent Stephen spiraling back to a childhood that could politely have been called dysfunctional and that had bordered on nightmarish. For a moment he actually entertained the thought. What if it *were* him? Some kleptomaniacs stole, then couldn't remember, and got off in court because they were mentally ill.

Stephen shook his head, abruptly angry at the distraction—at the way he'd been manipulated. *He* hadn't done anything wrong.

He was fascinated with crime—fascinated with law and order. He had studied the subject intensively. It wasn't possible for a mentally ill and disorganized person to have perpetrated such an elaborate network of crimes. The pressure of carrying out perfect crime after perfect crime was too intense; a mistake would have been made and, so far, none had been. The cleverness of the killer was stunning.

The coffee machine began to gurgle. The room filled with a delicious aroma.

Cold dark eyes met his again. "You know," Etienne said, setting mugs on the bench and reaching for packets of sugar, "for a moment you actually considered that you could have done it. Ever thought of booking yourself some couch time?"

Stephen ignored the insult as he followed the mundane movements. As abnormal as his family had been, he had always been unutterably aware of his own normality. He had been a straight-A student. No kinks, no vices—and none of the weird artistic crap his half brothers had been into. With a mental shrug, he loosened his grip on the gun and holstered it. Unless he was prepared to fire it, the Smith and Wesson was superfluous.

He watched as Etienne leaned against the bench and folded his arms across his chest, ostensibly relaxed, and the reason he'd driven through the night reasserted itself.

Etienne was too calm, too collected. If Stephen had been woken by a gunman at two in the morning, he would be climbing the walls.

Tension ate at his stomach, the acid hot and corrosive as it burned into an already inflamed ulcer. "So where are they?"

"Where are *what?*"

"We've got the bodies. We want the masks."

"You're serious, aren't you?" Etienne shrugged. "*Where are the masks?* Now, let me see…" He vacated the kitchenette and did a slow circuit of the room, mockingly lifting cushions on the couch, ending up mere feet away from Stephen. "You're the cop," he said softly. "If I'm the killer, I guess that would be for me to know and you to find out."

Stephen had a split second to consider that his brother hadn't moved out of the kitchen until the moment he'd put the gun away. In a reflexive movement, he went for the weapon. A hand punched out, snake-fast, clamping his throat with machine-like strength. Stephen reeled back, the gun sliding from his fingers. The back of his head bounced off a wall, and a lamp crashed to the floor in a shower of blue electric sparks, throwing the room into semi-darkness, but the choking grip on his trachea didn't ease.

Dazed, he stared into cool, slitted eyes, their rock-solid calmness telling him that while his world might be shaken, Etienne's was perfectly intact—and a tiny, inane fact clicked into place.

Panic squeezed at his guts as he struggled for breath; bile burned the back of his throat, and he felt the moment his stomach started to bleed.

He *knew.*

Four

Four days later
Lassiter, Louisiana

The small hand wrapped around Emily Mathew's fingers tugged, the grip firm, the dark gaze that went with it resolute. "Come on, Mom. Last one today."

Emily stood firm, a hot breeze whipping dark strands of hair around her face as she stared at the long winding drive, and at the shimmering pattern lacy shade trees made on the pitted, weed-infested gravel.

The farm didn't look promising. The faded name—Dexter—painted on the mailbox matched the rest of this down-at-heel section of Lassiter, but a chance to walk in that deep, inky shade instead of slowly roasting beneath the Louisiana sun was a powerful enticement.

Jane tugged at her hand again, and Emily dug her heels in to avoid being pulled down the shabby drive before *she* had a chance to come to a decision. With an effort of will she dragged her gaze from the mesmerizing play of light and dark, the effect like water rippling on a slow-moving river. Unexpectedly, the urge to paint again hit her like a tidal swell, the power of the need swamping her.

She stared blindly at Jane, for a moment not seeing her small daughter at all. "I've got to rest first."

And think. She stared into the dark, cool tunnel of the driveway again, arrested by the shimmering light and the shattering knowledge that, after years of blankness, she was finally ready to paint again.

Jane let go of her fingers as if granting a reluctant reprieve. "Okay."

Shoving a damp strand of hair out of her face, Emily moved off the road into the shade of the first tree, where the twisted, graceful boughs arched across a wooden fence. She eased out of the heavy canvas pack that held most of their possessions and let it drop to the ground. Dust puffed up around her legs, coating her sandals and jeans with another layer. Sinking down, she propped herself against the pack.

Dimly, she was aware of Jane darting around

her, picking daisies, and of the fact that something else had changed. For over two and a half years they'd been on the move, running and surviving, shifting from town to town and job to job, always a bare half step ahead of Jane's father, Ray. It had been more than two months since she had last seen him, a fleeting glimpse as he'd walked out of the diner where she was working. Now the fact that he had simply eaten and left without bothering to make inquiries took on a new significance. Usually he checked out the staff and asked questions. Sometimes he even had the nerve to walk out the back, searching for her and Jane.

She decided that in all probability he had been on his way back to Cleveland—he had given up on the hunt—but even if he hadn't, it occurred to her that what Ray wanted no longer mattered: they were free. Something inside her had shifted. She wasn't running anymore. If he ever tried to come after her and Jane again, she would simply walk into the nearest police station and press charges. The bruises had long since faded. There was no physical evidence, and no witnesses to support her claims—it would be her word against his—but she would win.

Letting out a breath, Emily tilted her head back and stared at the sky, blinking at the translucent purity.

Legally, Ray couldn't touch them.

He was down on Jane's birth certificate as her father, but that was all. He didn't own them, and he had no rights to them; he had lost those the first time he hit her.

The relief of that knowledge settling inside her and finally taking root was immense. After years of allowing herself to be kept off balance and pushed around, she had finally found her center of gravity—and she had found a part of herself she'd thought she would never regain.

Minutes later, her hands full of tiny flowers, Jane dropped to the ground and sat cross-legged, instantly absorbed with the daisies, her face as still and serene as a Botticelli angel as she constructed a chain, link by careful link.

Emily stared at Jane, not for the first time startled at the child she'd given birth to. In the middle of the chaotic storm of her life, with all of its mistakes and muddles, had dropped this small, exquisitely calm being.

Practically from conception, Emily had been aware of the difference of the child she was carrying. When she'd been pregnant, she'd been calmer and more settled than she could ever remember. Everything had changed—even the way she'd painted. Some days her emotions had bordered on ecstatic—as if the new life forming at the center of her body had permeated every part of her, even transmitting itself onto canvas, so that her paintings lost their jagged edges and became subtler and more serene.

When Jane had been born, the labor had been difficult, the process utterly and exhaustingly physical, but when it was over, she had felt a sense of wonder and achievement that had surpassed any painting she had ever done.

A child.

Jane had been perfect in every detail, and as changeable as the sea—one minute red and squalling, small fists bunched, the next as calm and pale as a doll. And so still that Emily had held her breath, listening, certain Jane had stopped breathing.

But starting when Jane was about six months old, the quiet, reflective period had changed. Emily's boyfriend, Ray, worried about her continuing distance from him and her fascination with the child he had fathered, decided to move in.

From the first day there was strain. Ray didn't like having his sleep disturbed, and he didn't like Emily breastfeeding the child. As if the escalating tension had somehow filtered into her consciousness, Jane had changed from a placid baby who slept all night to something scarily precocious. She had refused to crawl, pulling herself upright on sofas and chairs for weeks until she could finally stand unaided. Seconds after she had managed to stand, she took her first steps. By the end of the week, at the age of eight months, Jane had been steady on her feet.

In hindsight, Emily realized she had been ready to leave. In the strange, intuitive way of small children, Jane had picked up on the cues, but, mired in the complexities of a relationship that had always been demanding and difficult, it had taken Emily another four years.

She had literally woken up one morning and seen how the poison of the relationship had infected every part of her life, paralyzing her mind and her emotions. She had stopped painting, and Jane never smiled. The decision to leave was unequivocal, but then, when she'd packed their things, Ray had locked her in a room and gone out for the day.

Emily had pounded at the door in desperation, and then, when Jane began crying, had broken a window to get out. Unfortunately, Ray had returned at that point and had locked them in again. This time the window was boarded up and he didn't leave the house. Shocked, and frightened that he might harm Jane, Emily had stayed quiet, but desperation had eaten at her.

Two weeks later, when he had finally let her out, Emily had been quiet and docile, but the experi-

ence had changed her. She felt as if she was operating on two levels, one the surface survival mechanism that replied and complied, the other a
savagely angry mother protective of her child.

It had taken a month to gain Ray's trust enough
that he stopped locking her in every time he left
the house—and at night—and a further two weeks
to execute her plan.

As soon as Ray was asleep, she had emptied his
wallet, taken his car keys so he couldn't come after
them and woken Jane. They had gone out through
Jane's bedroom window, collected the pack Emily
had left ready in the bushes and walked to the bus
station. They had been running ever since.

Long minutes passed now as her gaze followed
the deft movement of Jane's fingers. Her lids
drooped, and the landscape swam. Smothering a
yawn, Emily resisted the urge to let her lids close.
It didn't seem right, sleeping while Jane was
awake, but some days sleeping was all Emily
wanted to do. When she slept, she didn't have to
think, and when she didn't have to think, she
wasn't afraid of all the things that had gone wrong
and could still go wrong.

The daisy chain finished, Jane rose to her feet,
dropped the chain around Emily's neck, then lowered herself down on her stomach in the shade,
her body almost instantly still. Automatically,

Emily put a hand on her daughter's back and came fully awake, alarmed by how thin Jane had become. Carefully, so as not to wake her, she peeled back her T-shirt and found another beneath…and another. Jane was wearing three T-shirts-in this heat.

Fear struck through Emily as she pushed the fabric up and bared the knobbly line of Jane's spine. She stared at the soft pale skin, the downy hair and the angular shape of her shoulder blades. Jane had lost weight, and she was hiding it.

She'd had the jeans she was wearing for over a year. They were faded and frayed at the bottoms. She'd already outgrown them—her ankles were poking out—but the waistband was actually loose. She had lost weight when she should have been putting it on.

Jane didn't stir as Emily rolled her over and pulled off the top two T-shirts, her body limp and pliable, her arms as flexible as spaghetti.

Fierce tenderness formed a lump in Emily's throat. When Jane's eyes were open—calm intelligence radiating from them—Emily forgot that she was barely seven years old. Asleep, Jane was little more than a baby.

She studied her face—the high cheekbones and fine-drawn skin, the dark hollows beneath her eyes, the small crescent-shaped scar where she'd opened her jaw up on a piece of broken glass—and finally saw what she should have seen weeks ago if she hadn't been so absorbed by her own misery. Jane was slowly, quietly, starving to death.

Etienne Dexter surged to his feet, chafed by the overstuffed, narrow confines of Adele Toussaint's parlor and rubbed raw by the old lady's attitude.

Adele met Etienne's glare, her gaze chilly. "What have you done with Mary?" she asked bluntly.

The question bordered on a demand. After fifteen minutes of stifled conversation and veiled insults, the gloves were finally off.

Etienne stared at the old couple seated in the parlor. Adele was thin but elegant in tailored pants, a fine-knit sweater and pearls. Her husband, Sidney, was dressed in his usual gray: gray trousers, a gray shirt and vest, his stringy hair plastered back from a widow's peak as he sat, shrunken and emaciated, in his wheelchair.

Grimly, Etienne repeated the explanation he'd already given for his presence. He was contracted to supervise the maintenance of a bridge in Beaumont, just over the state line in Texas. He had taken the job because it was the closest he could get to working in Louisiana. The reason he was back was so that he could make a last-ditch effort to find Mary and clear up the adoption issue of

Mary's son—his stepson, John—which had been in process when she disappeared two years ago. He didn't want to hurt the Toussaints; he just wanted their cooperation.

Unfortunately, cooperation was the last thing Adele was offering. She hadn't seen Mary since he had reported her missing; apparently nobody had. And she didn't care that John was little more than a baby and living with the only father he could remember.

Frustrated by the couple's blank hostility, he paced to the window and lifted the thick curtain of lace to check on his truck sitting out by the curb. Plaisance was one of Lassiter's better streets, but he had reason to be careful. John was ducked down in the passenger seat, munching his way through a candy bar and flicking through a picture book while he waited.

When he saw the top of John's head, he relaxed slightly. The kid might only be five, but he was hell-on-wheels to watch. The wonder of it was that in the last fifteen minutes he hadn't either figured out how to hotwire the truck, or broken out of the vehicle and found the nearest dog to pet. Usually, if Etienne had to be on the move, he paid someone to look after him until he could collect him, but after a two-week absence, he had wanted John with him.

Etienne hadn't told Adele her grandson was outside in the vehicle. If she knew John was actually in Lassiter, she would go ballistic, and he could end up with exactly what he wanted to avoid: a legal battle.

Turning his back on the shady street, he decided to try one more time before he dropped the idea of dealing with the Toussaints any other way than through his law firm. "The reason I've been shifting from job to job, moving around the country, is so I can look for Mary. The last two years haven't been easy."

Adele's expression was dismissive. "Liar. You know where she is. I've already told the police all about you." Her gaze narrowed. "I had my suspicions when Eloise died, and now I'm certain."

Etienne's stomach hollowed out. Just the mention of his stepmother was enough to make him break out in a cold sweat when little else could. She had died almost thirteen years ago, but it seemed that in death, as in life, Eloise still had the power to create havoc. "Eloise died of natural causes."

"At age fifty?" Adele's gaze was arctic. "Eloise was as strong as an ox. I don't believe all that nonsense about a stroke, and I don't believe you're a fit father for John. I told Mary not to have anything to do with a Dexter."

Etienne's jaw tightened at the entrenched hatred. He had lived away from Lassiter for the better part of twelve years and would happily never return. The Toussaints were old money, as were the Dexters—once—but the Dexters came with Irish blood and a propensity for drink. For Adele, the taint of being linked to the Dexter reputation had always been too much.

"Believe what you want," he said coldly, "but try and take custody of John, and I'll pay a visit to the White Moons. John's half Chippewa. His father may be dead, but the family connection is strong. You'll have a battle on your hands."

Adele Toussaint's expression changed from icy hauteur to frustration. He caught the glitter of tears and experienced a moment of compassion, but he couldn't afford to soften. She'd never made any bones about the fact that she didn't like him, but she actively feared the White Moons. Adele knew that if John stayed with Etienne, they could maintain contact with their grandson, but if Etienne lost custody to the White Moons, she was convinced she and Sidney would never see the boy again.

It wasn't true. The White Moon family were good, decent people—they were just poor. They would fight a battle for John's sake if they had to, but with two unattached daughters living at home—

with a total of seven grandchildren between them, and counting—one more stray child was the last thing the old couple needed.

Sidney Toussaint lifted his head and stared directly at Etienne, his gaze milky with cataracts. The old man was practically fossilized, his face frozen after the last stroke. One eye flickered as if he was winking, the fingers of his right hand twitched spasmodically, and a pungent smell filled the room.

Adele's nostril's pinched, the affront profound. She muttered something sharp in Cajun, but the bowel motion now passed, the old man's chin dropped to his chest. He was already asleep.

Etienne's jaw tightened. "John stays with me."

No way on this earth would he allow any child to come into this house. It was no mystery why Mary had run away from home at age fifteen. Locked up in this mausoleum with Adele and Sidney, she could have gone crazy.

Seconds later, Etienne breathed the clear, warm air of the autumn day as he climbed into the cab of his four-wheel drive and put the vehicle in gear.

John popped up into his seat, fastened his safety belt and stared out the window as Etienne drove, his head constantly moving as he identified the cars streaming toward them. He spotted a six-wheeler truck with a crane on board, but instead of reciting the model and year of the truck, his face grew pensive.

Etienne spared the small boy who had become the center of his world a glance. "Yeah, Daddy's got to go to work."

Somehow. In ten days' time. And until they left for Beaument, he would be busy with the search.

Etienne had known Mary since they were both kids, and even in all the years she'd flitted from relationship to relationship before they'd gotten married, she had never been gone so long.

He had a bad feeling about the disappearance, and so did the police. Mary had loved her son; it was unusual for her to leave him for any length of time. The last time she'd been seen had been when she'd visited her parents after old man Toussaint had a massive series of strokes and they'd thought he was going to die. Mary had stayed with her parents for a few days and then left to come home—only, she had never made it.

Etienne had checked every known relative and friend, including the White Moons, against the remote eventuality that she had decided to stop off in Mississippi for a visit and had come up with zilch.

The police had already interviewed him, but without a body, they couldn't charge him, or anybody else, with murder. His wife remained a missing person, and he and John remained in limbo.

Dust billowed up behind the truck as he passed the cemetery. His father, Burton Dexter, was buried there, along with the two women he had married, Etienne's mother, Helene, and his second wife, Eloise.

His jaw tightened as a raft of memories surfaced. He could remember his mother—just. He would never forget Eloise.

Minutes later, he turned onto the long straight stretch of road that had once been a busy hub when the sugar plant had been operating and all the plantations around Lassiter had been in full production. What had once been a thriving part of the community was now little more than a dead husk.

He couldn't wait to leave, and once he left, he wouldn't be back.

He didn't trust Adele an inch.

At the moment she had her hands full looking after the old man, but once he died, she would turn her attention to her grandson, and when that happened, Etienne wanted John well away from Lassiter.

He slowed for the turn into the Dexter drive and noticed a woman and a small girl on the roadside—the child lying down, the woman sitting propped against a pack.

Automatically, he checked her appearance: long dark hair, medium height, slim. The long hair fit, but the height was wrong. Mary had been tall, close to five ten; this woman was lucky if she made five foot five. Braking, he made the turn, frowning as dust billowed around the pair.

There was something about them...

Shaking off a vague presentiment, he glanced at John, who had settled himself against the passenger door and promptly fallen asleep. Over the past two years he had checked out literally thousands of women who bore even the remotest resemblance to Mary. He had flashed her picture at roadside diners, bus stops, airports—anywhere he thought she might possibly have passed through. In that time he had spoken to more people than he could count and heard a lot of hard-luck stories. The woman and the child looked lost and tired, but he couldn't allow that to distract him. John was his priority, and to keep John safe, the only woman he needed to find and help was his wife.

Five

Emily shaded her eyes and squinted as dust from the truck swirled and was just as quickly snatched away on the freshening breeze. The sound of the engine faded, drowned out by the rush of air sifting through the treetops. The truck had been driven by a man, which automatically made her wary, but there had also been a child with him, which meant a family lived down the drive.

Decision made.

They had been running for over two years, and now they were running on empty. They didn't have enough money to afford a campground fee, let alone a motel, and they had no food other than the bread and peanut butter in her pack. It was time to settle down and get a grip on life.

Rising to her feet, she inhaled. The air was hot

and dry, laced with the aromatic scent of crushed grass and the all-pervasive dust. Turning in a slow circle, she examined the country she'd been walking through, which previously had looked so down-at-heel, and felt a bubble of excitement expand inside her. The land was poor but interesting, with undulating fields, colorful belts of oaks, their leaves beginning to pile up in drifts, and clumps of wild roses sprouting through the fences.

She could have been in the middle of the Kalahari Desert and she wouldn't have cared. Lassiter looked just fine.

A lump in her throat, she crouched down beside Jane and called softly. When Jane didn't move, she gave her a gentle shake. "C'mon honey, time to go."

Jane's lids flickered. Finally she stirred, but she was slow to wake, which was alarming. For the first time Emily noticed the dark circles beneath her eyes and the fact that Jane's face wasn't just pale, it was waxen. Fear squeezed her heart tight. She'd gotten used to seeing shadows beneath her own eyes, but she was an adult; Jane was a child. Jane didn't just look tired, she looked sick.

As Jane sat up, for the first time in months Emily reached out and took Jane's hand, and not the other way around. She had been like a bird with a broken wing, allowing Jane to shoulder the burden, but that was all over. She was the mother and Jane was the child—finally she was going to get that part right.

Rearranging the loops of the pack so they were easy to hook her arms through, Emily shrugged into the pack, then rose to her feet, adjusting to the weight.

She would get a job. She could do anything that required manual labor: scrub floors, weed gardens, clean windows, paint houses. This time she wouldn't take no for an answer.

The drive was unexpectedly long, and the shadows were lengthening by the time they reached the house, an impressive old mausoleum that must have been one of the prime plantation houses before the bottom had dropped out of the sugar market.

Jane was flagging as they walked up an overgrown path bordered by clumps of grass and a snaking creeper that had covered most of the garden and a section of lawn, and Emily was forced to go slowly; she couldn't carry Jane as well as the pack. Frowning, Emily examined the house. Aside from the pick-up truck parked outside, the place looked derelict. Most of the paint had peeled off, and the windows were bare of curtains.

The truck confirmed that they had come to the right house, but it didn't look like a family home. There was no laundry on the line, no toys on the lawn—no sign that children lived here at all.

She flipped Jane's bangs, fluffing her hair around her face, and a memory of her mother doing the very same thing sparked off a sense of time merging.

She forced a smile. "Look pretty." That's what her mother had always said. Only some days, pretty was more trouble than it was worth.

Apprehension tightened her stomach as she mounted the steps to a veranda, its roof sagging under the weight of an ancient wisteria, the gnarled stem as thick as a tree trunk. Taking a deep breath, she lifted the heavy brass knocker. The house was more isolated than she'd bargained on, and a lot creepier.

At first she didn't think anyone was going to answer, and relief warred with fear. Jane needed to rest—they both needed to rest—and it was getting late, the air developing a definite nip. By the time they made it back to the road, it would be dark.

The muffled sound of footsteps alerted her. Seconds later a tall, pleasant-faced man answered the door, his features lean, his skin darkly tanned, as if he spent a lot of time outside.

Emily's hand tightened on Jane's. She checked over the man's shoulder, hoping to see his wife in the dim hallway. "I'm looking for work."

His expression was impassive. "There's nothing here. The plantation hasn't operated for years. It closed down when the sugar mill went bust."

Something hit her leg with a small pinging sound. Distracted, Emily inspected her jeans, expecting to see that a small insect had attached itself, but saw nothing. "I can cook and clean." She gestured at the weed-infested borders. "I can fix your gardens. Look. Mr.—"

He stared at her throat. Startled, she glanced down. Heat warmed her cheeks when she discovered she was still wearing Jane's daisy chain, the flowers lying limply against her T-shirt.

His gaze went sideways. "Dexter. Etienne Dexter."

Emily studied the sharp, clean line of his profile, and swallowed. She hated to beg, but their situation was desperate. "I *need* a job."

"Ouch," Jane muttered, and jerked free of Emily's grip.

Etienne Dexter's gaze locked with hers, surprising her with its intensity. "Okay."

Emily blinked, confused, sure he'd been about to turn her down.

Something pinged on her leg again. Jane marched down the steps just as a small shadowy form launched itself across the overgrown lawn and rolled into a patch of lilies. A peashooter appeared over the crushed stalks.

Jane snatched the peashooter from the small

boy's hand. "That's rude," she said flatly. "You don't shoot guests. Ever."

"You're not guests," a belligerent voice said.

"We are now." Jane turned on her heel.

"That's the job," Etienne Dexter said, an ironic note in his voice. "I need someone to mind John when I'm away. I'll give you room and board. And the kid gets danger money."

Etienne led the way through the hallway and up the stairs, apologizing for the cobwebs and the film of dust that coated the furniture. "We only arrived yesterday. We're here for two weeks, max, then we're heading north."

He showed her to a room, which contained a single bed, a dresser and a shelf that housed a collection of intricate architectural models.

"It used to be mine. I'm sleeping down there." He jerked his thumb toward a room at the end of the hall.

Emily set the pack down, feeling suddenly vulnerable and wondering—desperate as they were— if she had made a mistake. So far there was definitely no sign of a woman in the house.

Her gaze fastened on a box of oil paints. She crossed the room and picked up the carton of neatly arranged tubes. "Are these yours?"

"Used to be. I don't paint anymore."

Absently, she set the paints down, trailing her

fingers across them. In the corner she spotted a canvas poking out from behind the dresser. Crouching down, she slid the canvas free. "If you don't paint, what do you do?"

"Fix bridges, mostly. Sometimes I design them."

She stared at the canvas, which was blank, abruptly curious about Etienne Dexter—and reassured. He was an artist, a designer and a father—and so far there hadn't been the tiniest hint of the sexual byplay she'd gotten used to fending off when she'd been waiting tables. He simply seemed...nice. "Why didn't you use this?"

He shrugged. "Painting wasn't my best talent. I preferred sculpture."

She set the canvas back behind the dresser, loath to let it go. "Do you mind if I use it?"

"Be my guest. You're welcome to the paints *and* the brushes." He opened a wardrobe and pulled out an easel. "There's a drop cloth in here. It was more than my life was worth to get any paint on the floor."

A thudding on the stairs heralded the arrival of the children.

Jane had the room next to Emily's. John was down the hall, next to Etienne. The next hour was spent cleaning the rooms and making beds. The sun had set and the air was filled with an autumnal chill when Etienne called them down to eat.

The kitchen was unexpectedly cheery, with a

small potbelly stove blazing, a casserole bubbling on top of it. The table was set with a salad and a fresh loaf of bread.

It was an odd situation. A weird old house, a strange man and his son, but sitting down to dinner, Emily was reminded of her own childhood. It felt almost as if they were a family.

Emily stared dreamily at her canvas, which she'd set on the easel in the garden. The shape of the trees lining the driveway was right, but the shadows weren't quite there. They needed... She closed her eyes and tried to remember that day a week ago. The light had been clear, the sky high and arching, a translucent blue without a cloud in sight, and the shadows had been...

A sound disturbed her train of thought, and the now familiar little flip-flop that her stomach did told her the visitor was Etienne.

...purple. "Just a minute."

She could feel him watching, which was distracting, but if she didn't mix the color right now, she would lose the sense of what was *exactly* right. Once she allowed herself to become indecisive about a color or a line, the process became muddied and difficult.

Etienne was silent while she worked, and

though he wasn't intrusive, he was hard to ignore. This afternoon he had been busy fixing the roof, and, shirtless, he was impressive.

Emily had tried hard to dismiss the fact that, legally married or not, with his wife gone for two years, Etienne was to all intents and purposes single. She was about to give up.

When she stepped back from the easel, Etienne took his time surveying her work.

"Don't paint the house in," he said abruptly. "The trees are fine."

Emily wiped her brush off on a cloth. She understood perfectly why he didn't want the distant roofline of the house included. From what she'd gleaned, when Etienne's mother had died, his father had remarried, and things hadn't been happy. All three of the Dexter brothers had chosen to leave the family farm—none of them willing to live here full-time. Apparently it had been tenanted off-and-on, but now Etienne wanted to sell.

"Roger that," she murmured. "No house." She dipped the brush into a glob of burnt sienna and painted in a stick figure right next to her shadow, labeling it "Etienne."

He grinned, shook his head and walked back to his ladder.

Emily sat down in the shade and fanned herself

as she watched Etienne at work on the roof. She decided that now might be a good time to switch from landscapes to nudes.

Six

Etienne found a space in the confusion of the fair-ground car park and, when they were all out, locked the truck and dug in his pocket. He went down into a crouch beside Jane. "Understand he's slippery. He needs watching all the time."

Jane eyed John Toussaint. He was small, but fast as a snake. She'd been on her toes ever since they'd moved into the Dexter house. "He won't get away from me."

"Here's that danger money I was talking about."

She eyed the dollar bills he handed her. It was more money than she had personally held in her entire life. "You don't have to pay me." She glanced at John, who was already checking out the rides. As far as little kids went, he was what Emily would call predictable. She would bet he wanted to go on all the fastest, most sick-making rides at the fair. "He's not that tough."

He shrugged. "Then it's hush money. You take care of John, feed him and get him around the rides, and I get some peace and quiet."

Emily laughed, and Jane eyed her mother. Emily was wearing a sundress and looked...different. She couldn't put her finger on what exactly was different, but it didn't matter. The tired look had gone, and for the first time in as long as Jane could remember, she looked happy.

John watched, his gaze sharp as she tucked the money in her purse, and Jane decided as they walked into the fairgrounds that the best way to make sure he stayed with her would be to hang on to the money.

They went on the rides first, then they ate, munching through hot dogs and letting themselves be carried along by the crowd, eyes roving the colorful stalls until they ended up directly in front of a cotton candy stall.

Jane stared, transfixed, at the swirls of spun sugar, her nostrils filled with the sweet scent, her mouth watering so powerfully she had to swallow. The sign said that the bags were a quarter. She didn't have to dig around in her purse to know she had exactly a quarter left.

She turned to check if John wanted any and

found herself staring at clear space. Disoriented, her gaze darted around the milling crowd. She tried to calculate how long she'd been staring at the cotton candy and when, exactly, she'd last checked that John was beside her. Panicked, she threaded her way between knots of people, the heavy flow of traffic impeding her at every turn. John could be just feet away and she wouldn't be able to see him.

She was supposed to be looking after him—she had promised Etienne—and he had slipped away.

The stalls widened out, the crowd thinned. Her gaze was caught by a tall dark man in a shabby overcoat and a ridiculously colorful hat crouching down talking to a child—John. Frightened, Jane sped across the trampled grass as the man lifted a camera and took John's picture.

Jane snatched John's hand and began pulling him away.

The man with the camera followed. "Where are your parents, kid?"

Paper slid out of the bottom of the camera and he brandished it in front of John's face. "Hey! Whaddya know? Look at that."

John pulled against Jane's hand, his gaze riveted as the photo magically appeared on the blank paper, becoming stronger and more defined by the second. "That's me," he declared flatly. "I want it."

The man's gaze slid to her hand. Automatically, her fingers closed on the coin.

"You can have it for a quarter."

He showed his teeth, and all the hairs on Jane's nape prickled. She didn't like the man, and he didn't like her.

She stared him down. "It's not worth that much."

The man's gaze was hard. "You don't pay, you don't get the picture. Simple."

He dangled the snapshot in front of John, just out of reach of his fingers. He made out that it was a game, but Jane could see the meanness. The picture was worth nothing to him, but he wasn't going to hand it over until he was paid.

John's face took on a stoic cast, and Jane's fingers tightened their grip on the coin. Now she knew *exactly* how Emily felt when she asked for things they couldn't afford.

Jane handed over the money, and John took the snapshot, his hands reverent.

As they walked through the grounds looking for Emily and Etienne, John found a quarter glinting in the grass and blew it on a throwing game at which he was unaccountably accurate. Dazed, the stallholder handed over a set of Matchbox cars, a bag of candy and a chocolate bar.

"How did he do that?" she muttered. "What is he? Four?"

"Five," John said flatly, examining the prizes with a cagey eye.

They walked around, chewing on candy, until Jane got tired of the heat and the constant tide of people pressing against her, and began to actively look for Emily.

She spotted Emily and Etienne sitting beneath a brightly striped marquee drinking what looked like lemonade.

John started toward his father, but Jane blocked him. "Leave them." Jane stared at Emily. Her chest swelled tight, and she knew what had changed: Emily liked Etienne, and he liked her.

She shrugged. "It looks crowded and hot in there. Why don't we sit here?" She patted the ground beneath a tall oak.

John gave his father a hard stare, shrugged his shoulders and sat down to examine his winnings. He played with the cars, ate some more candy, stared at the photo, then slipped it in his pocket and simply lay down in the shade and fell asleep. Jane sat beside him, keeping watch, her gaze automatically drawn to Emily and Etienne until her own lids began to droop.

A firm shake of her shoulder jerked her awake.

"There you are." Etienne handed her a cellophane bag bulging with candy cotton, and she stared at him dumbstruck, too shocked to say thank you. Sitting up, she brushed a loose strand of hair out of her face. First the dollar bills, now this.

He flicked her bangs and smiled, and for once she didn't mind, enchanted by the swirling pink and white spun sugar. It occurred to her that she *liked* Etienne.

He leaned down, scooped up John's pile of cars and candy, and slipped them in his pockets. With a practiced movement, he picked John up and slung him over one shoulder without waking him.

Emily made a production of peering at John's upside-down face, then linked her fingers with Etienne's and laughed. There was something sparkly in their eyes, a fizzy warmth that tugged at Jane's mouth and made her want to smile.

As she trailed along behind them, she opened the cellophane bag, careful not to rip it or damage it in any way, and almost floated away on the rich scent. Transported, she pinched off a small chunk. The first mouthful exploded across her tongue, almost painfully sweet; the second tasted even better. The sugar went straight to her head, making her feel hot and flushed and a little dizzy, but she didn't care, she had never tasted anything so good.

A cloud slid over the sun as they reached the car, bringing with it a fitful wind and the first cold scattering of rain. Etienne opened the door for Emily, then buckled John into the car seat in the rear. Jane couldn't help noticing that Emily didn't do it, *he* did it. When Ray had lived with them, Emily had had to do everything.

Jane settled into her own seat, shivering as the rain thickened, running in rivulets down the window and obscuring the fairgrounds.

After carefully placing the bag of cotton candy on the floor, she buckled her seatbelt and surreptitiously watched as Etienne got behind the wheel. His hands were tanned and strong, the nails clean, and not for the first time, she noticed his hair was nice—short and neatly cut.

He caught her watching him in the mirror as he put the car in gear, and winked. Jane winked back, and he grinned, and something inside her relaxed. For the first time since she and Emily had sneaked out of Ray's house, she decided that everything was going to be all right.

A strange vehicle was in the driveway when they got home.

A man walked out of the house, and Emily froze in the act of helping Jane out of the truck. For a moment she wondered if she was seeing double, then Etienne walked up to the man and she realized there was nothing wrong with her vision, there *were* two Etiennes. The other man was a perfect image—Etienne's identical twin.

Emily had seen twins before, plenty of times, but they were usually only identical when they were young. As they aged, the difference in personality showed up in their physical appearance and the way they dressed. Despite the fact that Etienne was thirty, his twin could have been his double. He was perfect down to every last detail, including the tan and the haircut.

"What are you doing here?" Etienne said grimly.

"I could ask you the same question." His gaze flicked to Emily. "You going to introduce me?"

"No."

"Shame. She might like me better than you."

Etienne stepped between his twin and Emily, blocking his view of her. "I don't think so."

"Maybe you should give the lady a chance?"

"Leave, Charles."

"Or what? You'll go to the police?" He slipped dark glasses on the bridge of his nose. "Maybe I'll beat you there, do a little confessing."

"Confess to anything and I'll beat you to a pulp."

"Hey! I'm just leaving." He slid behind the wheel of his car. The door closed with an expensive thunk. As he started the ignition, the electric window slid down with a whine. "By the way, the cops called about an hour ago, asking questions about Eloise. They wanted to know what your relationship with her was like. Apparently some old biddy's been making accusations."

"What did you tell them?"

"Nothing. Relax." He grinned as the car pulled away. "I told them I was you."

Emily rubbed her arms and watched as Etienne collected the still-sleeping John from the car. In the space of an hour the warm weather had evaporated, blown away by the icy northerly, and that wasn't all that had changed.

Etienne's expression was grim as he took John inside. Concerned, Emily followed. Somehow Charles Dexter had spoiled their day—the last day she and Etienne had together for at least a week, because he had to leave tomorrow. Feeling let down and unaccountably tense, she watched as he set John down on a couch and pulled a blanket over him.

"What does your brother do?"

Etienne's gaze was wintry. "He's a computer geek. He designs software. Apparently he specializes in game systems."

Seven

Etienne placed his suitcase in the truck, gave John a hug, ruffled Jane's hair, then turned to Emily. Two weeks had passed so quickly he couldn't believe it.

"I'll be back from Beaumont Friday night."

"Make it early."

Emily linked her fingers with his, and he pulled her close, enjoying the feminine feel of her against him, the smell of her skin and hair, and the simple happiness that poured through him whenever he was with her. He had no idea what had happened between them. It was too sweet to be called a fatal attraction, and too sudden and powerful to be labeled either friendship or a fling. Whatever it was, he was drowning.

Technically, he was still married, but when he

left, if he could convince her, he was taking Emily and Jane north with him.

John gave him an assessing look that said he could only stand so much of the soppy stuff; Jane simply observed. Etienne was aware that while Jane had accepted him, she was also still very protective of Emily. Every night, at some point, Jane had gotten out of bed and walked through the house, checking on Emily. The first time it had happened, he had thought they had an intruder. She'd stood in the doorway like a shadowy little ghost, checked where Emily was, then gone back to bed.

Half an hour later, the sun setting, Etienne did a U-turn in town and headed back in the direction of the farm, his mood grim. Turning in at the cemetery, which was less than a mile from the house as the crow flies, he parked the truck behind a hedge, which provided the best concealment from the road, and sat, waiting for full dark.

He was due in Beaumont tonight—his motel was booked—but he couldn't leave Lassiter just yet.

Fifteen minutes later, he retrieved a flashlight and a bag from the back seat. After locking the truck, he stood for long moments, waiting for his night vision to improve, then skirted the newer part of the cemetery and headed for the moss-encrusted crypts that formed a row at the rear and housed Lassiter's oldest, most affluent dead.

As he walked, a chill breeze rustled through the dried leaves of an ancient oak, and, just to add to the atmosphere, an owl hooted, sending a shiver up his spine.

Grimly, Etienne eyed the way the moonlight made the stone and alabaster monuments glow. If there was one place on earth he never wanted to be, this was it.

The crypt was elaborate, built by his great-grandparents with the last of the sugar money, and now almost fully occupied—with room for only one more.

Etienne, for one, wouldn't be putting his name in the hat for the privilege of resting here. He doubted an expensive stone crypt guaranteed peaceful rest if it meant lying next to a monster like Eloise.

Setting the bag down, he extracted a crowbar, a stack of newspapers and a can of gasoline. Crypts were a prime target for vandalism. Tonight the Dexter family crypt would become just another statistic.

What he had to do didn't sit easily with him, but he couldn't find any other solution. His mind ran on logistics and facts. His expertise was in building bridges, not in dealing with emotions or the nightmare of the past.

Thirteen years ago, Eloise had died. He hadn't killed her; it just looked like he had.

He had made a mistake, the kind of stupid mistake he still couldn't believe, because he was meticulous about detail. Eloise had suffered from a number of ailments, including depression and high blood pressure. One night she had demanded Etienne get her medication, and Charles, who had been in the kitchen helping himself to Eloise's rum, had offered to hand him the pills, which were kept in the cupboard he was leaning against.

The fact that Charles had voluntarily offered to do anything should have made him suspicious, but he had been seventeen, pumped and ready to leave for college. He had simply taken the pills Charles had counted out and handed them to Eloise.

After taking the pills, instead of dozing off in her chair in front of the television, she had sat bolt upright and flushed a deep shade of red. Eyes bulging, she'd gasped for breath, tottered to her feet and vomited a dull brown stream of fluid. Seconds later, she had fallen to the floor, convulsing. She had died within minutes.

When old doctor Carlton had finally made it to the house, he had skirted the mess, shaken his head at the overpowering reek of rum and pronounced Eloise dead. The bottles cluttering the room and piled around the sink were enough to verify that

Eloise had committed the cardinal sin of mixing alcohol with her medication. The pills she had taken had been innocuous in themselves, but when mixed with large quantities of alcohol, the effect had proved fatal.

A week later, at the inquest, the official cause of death was noted as heart failure.

The day of Eloise's funeral, Charles had informed him that the reason Eloise had died was because they had murdered her. The pills Etienne had handed Eloise had been a fatal dose of cyanide—rat poison that Charles had taken from the barn and hung on to until the opportune moment.

Innocent though he'd been, Etienne had felt guilty. It didn't matter that he knew Charles had replaced the pills with his own homemade version, mixed and shaped to look like the tablets Eloise had been taking. He'd carried the guilt for years, and somehow Adele Toussaint had picked up on it, enough that—spurred on by her anxiety about Mary—she had gone to the police.

With careful precision, he crouched down and pried loose the stone covering Eloise's final resting place, then placed it to one side. Taking a deep breath, he dragged the coffin out, frowning at the lightness of it. Even after thirteen years, he had expected the coffin to be difficult to move.

Lowering the coffin the few inches required for

it to rest on the stone floor, he unlatched the lid and lifted it, and all the hairs at his nape stood on end.

Eloise was gone. Someone had been here before him.

Jane's eyes flipped open. The moon was shining directly into her bedroom, the light as cold as ice. Seconds later, the heavy edge of a cloud slid across the bright crescent, plunging her into darkness.

"Mama?" she whispered, certain someone had just been in her room.

Sliding out of bed, she grabbed the flashlight she'd commandeered from the kitchen and hidden beneath her bed, flicked it on and checked the door. It was closed, but the small piece of ribbon Emily had taught her to wedge between the door and the jamb was on the floor.

Crouching down, Jane examined the small shred of pink and repressed a shiver. The days were still warm, but the nights had grown icy, and the cold flowed up through the floorboards, chilling her bare feet as she straightened and stood absolutely still, listening.

Something was wrong. She couldn't explain what exactly, but when something was wrong with Emily, she *knew*. She had known it when Ray had beaten her and locked her in that room, and she had known it when a man who had employed Emily to pick apples had broken in to the small cabin they were renting. That time Jane had pretended to sleepwalk into the room, and that had stopped him—but she had never been able to stop Ray.

A shudder swept through her at the thought of her father.

He wouldn't find them. They had traveled too far and hidden too well for him ever to track them, but that didn't mean they were safe.

An image of Etienne's twin, Charles, flitted into her mind. They had seemed so alike at first that she hadn't been able to tell them apart, until she'd looked closely. Etienne's eyes smiled, but Charles's eyes didn't do anything; they were like marbles.

Another brother, Stephen, who had come by to see Etienne later that very same day, hadn't made her feel much better. He'd smiled a lot when he'd walked into the kitchen, but Etienne hadn't been any happier to see him than he had Charles—and neither had Emily.

Stomach churning, driven by an urgency she couldn't explain, she padded across the room to the dresser and unlaced her duffel bag. Wherever they stayed, no matter how safe it seemed; she always kept everything in her duffel. That way, if they had to leave in a hurry, she wouldn't leave anything behind. She dressed, choosing her darkest clothes: jeans and a blue T-shirt beneath an oversize navy sweatshirt. Pushing her feet into sneakers, she picked up the flashlight, turned it off and eased her door open a crack. Seconds later, she checked Emily's room. The bed was rumpled, but Emily wasn't there.

Heart pounding, she began searching the house, checking Etienne's room, even though she knew Emily wouldn't be there—Etienne had left that afternoon. John was in his bed, a lump beneath a tangled mound of quilt. After carefully closing his door, Jane crept downstairs.

Minutes later, after completing a circuit of the downstairs rooms, she stepped outside, her stomach knotted tight.

Moonlight shafted between ragged clouds as she stood beneath the tangled wood of the wisteria vine, her breath pluming on the air as her gaze skimmed over the lawn. A line of footsteps cut through the dew.

Gripping the flashlight, but not turning it on, Jane followed the line of trampled grass until it ended at the doors of the barn, which were usually locked. Heart pounding, she laid her ear against the boards, and the marrow froze in her bones. Emily was in there, and so was someone else: a man.

Inching along the side of the barn, she peered through an uncovered section of a boarded-up window just in time to see the glow of lamplight abruptly swallowed by darkness as a door closed. She stared at the spot where the light had been just seconds ago and debated what to do. This time, pretending to sleepwalk wouldn't work.

Shivering, her fingers stiff with cold, Jane inched the barn door open and slipped inside. Instantly the wrongness of what was happening hit her. The air was dank, heavy with the smell of machinery and foul with stale air and mold—and something else that made her stomach turn.

She could smell rotting meat.

Swallowing, Jane flicked on the flashlight and inched across the room, her gaze locked on the place where she'd last seen the glow of light. Her sneaker landed in something slippery. Clamping her jaw against a shriek, she backed up and directed the beam at the floor around her feet. For a wild moment she thought she'd stepped into blood; then the color and density of the liquid registered. The barn was full of rusting equipment and barrels, wreathed in cobwebs and gleaming dully in the light. One of the barrels had leaked a dark, viscous puddle of oil, which had coated the sole of her sneaker, and which also clearly marked the prints of whoever had just walked through the room.

Letting out a breath, Jane followed the prints to the wall and examined it. At first glance there was no door, but she'd definitely seen one open.

Placing the flashlight on the floor, so its beam

illuminated the wall, she flattened her palms against the boards and pushed. She could feel a faint give, but not in the direction she expected. Shifting her hands lower, she shoved, and tumbled headlong into a gaping hole as the entire section of wall flipped open, then just as quickly flipped shut, enclosing her in pitch blackness.

Heart slamming in her chest, Jane got to her knees and felt around until her fingers scraped against the rough boards of the trapdoor. Seconds later, she located the metallic curve of a handle—and pulled it toward her. Instantly, light flooded the space she'd fallen into.

Heart pounding, she reached through and grabbed the flashlight. Struggling to her feet, she stared around at the windowless, cobweb-infested space. A cold breeze sifted against her face, and she directed the beam at an opening in the floor—the hatch door of a cellar.

Moving silently, she eased down the ladder and examined the room. The cellar was the entrance to an underground tunnel. Chills running up and down her spine, she began walking, following a glimmering trail of oil.

A faint scraping sound outside the crypt jerked Etienne's head around. Adrenaline pumped. Heart hammering, he fitted the lid of the empty coffin back into place, ghosted to the door of the crypt and opened it a bare few inches. Outside, clouds were building, but there was still enough moonlight for him to make out the shabby lines of crypts and memorial stones, and the strips of weedy grass in between. A cold breeze sifted in the door and sent desiccated leaves rattling against the sides of the crypt.

Long minutes passed while he continued to keep watch. Shaking his head, he closed the door at last and returned his attention to what had to be done—regardless of the fact that Eloise's body was missing. If Adele managed to push the right social and political buttons, she just might get the autopsy she wanted. If it was discovered that Eloise's body was missing, regardless of who had taken it, the police would be knocking on his door. Whichever way he looked at it, he was going to lose—and so was John. A man who was suspected of murder wasn't going to get custody of a child.

Gritting his teeth, he maneuvered the heavy oak box back into place, refitted the stone plate, then studied the seam. He was no cop, but now that he knew what to look for, he could plainly discern the faint marks he'd made prying it loose and another set made by whoever had removed Eloise's body.

Minutes later, he did a circuit of the cemetery, skirted the river and walked past the old skeleton of the sugar mill. If anyone had been lurking around, they were now well and truly gone. Satisfied, he turned on his heel. His boots sank into soft dirt. Automatically, he swung the beam of his flashlight over the ground, and cold ran up and down his spine. An area had been freshly dug.

The wind rose, and an icy scattering of rain hit the back of his neck. He turned up the collar of his jacket, for a moment certain someone was watching.

"Get a grip," he muttered. So the ground was disturbed. This was the country. Someone's pig had probably gotten loose and churned up the ground. The fact that Eloise's body was gone had been a shock, but it was hardly likely to be buried practically across the cemetery fence.

Feeling faintly ridiculous, he shone the flashlight around the trees, letting light stab into all the darkest shadowy places. The rain became heavier. Shaking off the eerie feeling as paranoia and guilt for what he was about to do, he doubled back to the crypt.

Shivering as the chill of the tunnel struck deep, Jane ventured forward—stopping at the first turn. For long moments she debated whether to continue or run for help; then a muffled sound made the skin at her nape go all goosey.

With a last glance in the direction of the cellar,

she rounded the corner and continued following the glimmering trail of oil. The faint stirring of cold air told her that the tunnel must have another opening for fresh air to be channeling through. She turned another corner, then another, slowing as light glowed. Cautiously, she switched off the flashlight and halted at an intersection. To her left, the tunnel continued; to her right it opened into a small, bunker-like room.

After the pitch black of the tunnel and the narrow beam of the flashlight, it took long seconds for her brain to decipher the abrupt overload of color and movement glimpsed through the half open door. A man and a woman—both soaked in red.

At first her mind insisted that the red was paint. Somehow Emily had spilled paint on herself and Etienne—although it couldn't be Etienne, because he had left. Then Emily swung something heavy, and red sprayed from his nose. Blood.

Jane shrank back into the tunnel, huddling against the wall, her mind reeling. A flickering glow in the tunnel behind her warned her. Heart pounding, she inched forward, then flitted past the door, into the shadows ahead. Moments later, a second man strode into the room and, with a guttural sound, grappled with the first, the attack animal-like in its ferocity.

A table was overturned, glass exploded against

a wall and for a raw moment flames soared high, limning the occupants of the room and casting a flickering glow over a collection of objects, placed at precise intervals on the wall, like pictures in a gallery. Abruptly the room went dim, lit only by the beam of a single flashlight. Jane blinked to dispel the images burned into her retina—figures blended into figures, the shapes scarcely human, everything coated in red. One of the figures picked up a wooden stool, which lay on its side by the overturned table, and swung it, clubbing a second figure to the ground.

For an agonized moment Jane stared at the tableau, her mind numb, body icy with shock, then instinct kicked in.

Move back. Stay in darkness.

Huddling close to the floor, she inched deeper into the tunnel.

The man who'd used the stool turned and stared directly at her, and Jane froze, trying to remember if she'd made a sound. She was certain he couldn't see her; the flashlight beam flooded him with light, and she was in darkness.

Time seemed to stretch out and expand as he continued to stare, probing the darkness. Then he turned back to Emily, clamped a hand around her throat, lifted a knife and plunged it in.

Eight

Jane shook John awake.

His eyes popped open, uncannily alert, as if he was too on edge to sleep properly. "What is it?" he muttered.

Jane jerked back the bed sheet. "Get up. We've got to go."

John's eyes were wide as he hopped on one foot, pulling his jeans on over his pajamas. "What happened?"

Jane searched feverishly through his drawers and tossed a shirt at him. She was icily cold, and she couldn't stop shaking, but her mind was clear. "There's a bad man downstairs." She blinked, closing out the images. "A robber."

"Did you call the cops?"

His whisper was so practical and matter-of-fact,

that for a moment she couldn't think. She shook her head then wished she hadn't; her head *hurt*. "The phone's dead." She had tried every phone in the house. None of them worked.

"You sound funny."

Jane tossed his sneakers at him, then raced into her own room and grabbed her duffel.

When she returned to John's room, he was struggling with the buttons of his shirt. She noticed his pockets were bulging with Matchbox cars.

With fingers that shook, she helped him with the final button, then clamped his hand in hers, ignoring his outrage as she dragged him toward the door. They had already taken too long. They needed to move.

"Wait!" His fingers twisted and slid out of hers. He dashed back to the dresser, grabbed two objects and tried to force them into his already full pockets.

Jane snatched the candy bar and the photo from him, and shoved them in her own pockets, which were empty. "You have to come now," she said coldly. "Or I'll leave you behind."

For a moment the expression on Emily's face as the man's hand had clamped around her throat rose up, temporarily paralyzing her. Her head felt funny—thick and hot—and she was dizzy. All she wanted to do was lie down and close her eyes, but she couldn't. Emily was depending on her.

John's hand slid into hers.

"Don't cry."

"I'm not."

Tightening her grip on John's hand, she dragged him down the stairs, slipped down the back passage and out the back door. Threading through the back yard, they negotiated a fig tree, climbed over the ancient picket fence and ran.

The moon was high, but the narrow crescent didn't provide much light. Normally Jane would have been spooked by the shadows, but tonight, the darker, the better. She tripped and fell, skinning an elbow and bumping her nose. Immediately she climbed to her feet and kept moving. She could hear John beside her, his breath pumping, his sneaker-clad feet thudding on the hard ground. They entered a thicket of trees, and abruptly she was on her own. Slowing to a halt, she spun and retraced her steps, searching the gloom. She found John clutching his ankle.

"I've twisted it."

She stared at the pale flash of his face in the moonlight, and once again the stark images swam in front of her, making her heart race. For an endless moment she couldn't breathe and the dizzying ache in her head felt like a heavy weight, then oxygen whooshed into her lungs.

"Get up," she said harshly.

She had to help Emily, but she was also responsible for John, and she couldn't leave him. She
had already thought about hiding him in the trees,
but it was a known fact that the only time John
Toussaint ever stopped moving was when he fell
asleep. She couldn't trust that he would stay where
she put him.

Gripping his hand, she pulled him to his feet and
slung an arm around his waist to support him. As
they walked, misery wound through her. She lifted
a hand to her nose, which hurt, and flinched. Her
fingers came away wet. She couldn't see it in the
dark, but she could feel it and smell it; blood was
dripping all down her front.

Gritting her teeth, she kept them both moving.
By her calculations, they were now about a quarter mile from the road, and the nearest house was
probably that far again down the highway.

The wild urge to leave John and run as fast as she
could quivered through her, but she kept her panic
in check, fixing her mind instead on other possibil-
ities. They could skip the highway altogether and
go cross-country to the next house. The only problem was, she hadn't ever ventured that far, and she
didn't know exactly where the house was located.
It could be close to the road, or it might be set back,
like the Dexters' place. If she miscalculated, they
could end up taking more time instead of less.

The flash of headlights and the sound of a vehicle confirmed her decision to get onto the highway. Flagging down a passing car would be the quickest way of getting help.

The man cleaned the blood from his hands and retraced his steps, climbed the cellar stairs into the pit, then exited through the trapdoor in the barn. As he straightened, the beam of his flashlight swept the floor, picking out the oily outlines of footprints. His jaw tightened as he examined the perfect impression of a child's sneaker.

Seconds later, he was in the house. John's room was empty, and so was the girl's.

Coldly, he searched every room, every wardrobe, including the attic. When he found nothing, he started on the grounds. The faint moonlight revealed what he was looking for—a trail of footprints in the damp grass, disappearing over the fence and arrowing in a straight line toward the road.

He examined his watch. He calculated that at least fifteen minutes had passed while he had searched. There was still time.

With careful control, he climbed into his vehicle, swung around on the gravel and headed for the highway.

* * *

By the time Jane and John made it to the road, the glow of taillights was long gone.

Jane stared at the long stretch of dead straight highway, then resolutely turned south. Panic spasmed through her, the urgency choking, but her head was feeling stranger and stranger, all hot and prickly, and her nose was blocked solid.

John's fingers tightened on hers, jerking her along faster. At some point his ankle had gotten better, and now he was threatening to take charge.

"Where are we going?" he demanded.

Dazed, Jane kept her gaze glued to the road ahead, afraid that she would miss the driveway. "The neighbors."

When they got there, she would be able to use their phone and call the police—and an ambulance. Emily needed an ambulance.

She heard the car long before she saw the headlights, the sound of the engine a low vibration that hummed on the surface of the road.

The vehicle got closer, and suddenly the glare of the headlights was blinding. Jane waved, trying to attract the driver's attention, but instead of slowing, he seemed to be accelerating.

As the car got closer and closer, the roar of the engine deafening, it occurred to her that the reason it had taken so long to see the headlights was because the vehicle had turned out of the Dexters' driveway.

Shock reverberated through her, but she was so tired, she hardly registered it. The car swerved, the headlights pinning her. A shaft of pain drove through her head, and in a surge of blind panic, she shoved John away.

Nine

Tyrone Brady arrived at the scene bare seconds after the police and the ambulance crew. He'd been lucky; he'd been out at a party and was driving home when he'd caught the details of the accident on the police band. Apparently there had been a hit-and-run.

Tyrone had no affinity for death or disaster—in fact, he had a dyed-in-the-wool respect for anyone who was deceased. That respect had been roundly beaten into him by both his mother and his grandmother, but it was a fact that, ghoulish or not, from what he was overhearing, this added up to a homicide case.

Swerving in behind one of a number of police cruisers, he grabbed his camera, notebook and flashlight, his stomach hollowing out at the thought of a death. It was his first week as a reporter with the *Lassiter Daily*. He had a degree in journalism, a fascination for hard news, and he could touch type one hundred and forty words a minute, but so far he hadn't done much more than write about local sports and create the cooking page. He didn't mind the ball games, but some days he wasn't real interested in what folks wanted for their hors d'ouevres when there were plenty of people either starving or homeless beyond Lassiter.

Whether his boss's disinterest in his career was down to the color of Tyrone's skin or the fact that Marty Billaud was known to sink a gallon of homemade rum most weekends, he didn't know, but one thing was for sure, he was itching to sink his teeth into a *real* story.

Tyrone skirted the cops cordoning off the area and directing traffic, working his way as unobtrusively as possible toward the small knot of ambulance officers working on the victim. He didn't want to be forced away before he'd had a chance to at least get some pictures. Feeling definitely ghoulish, he raised his camera and, for lack of anything else, took a photo of the medics. The resulting flash lit up the night.

A small wiry man swiveled around and glared. "You! Cut that out and come and shine your light here."

Tyrone recognized Dr. Arnold Carpenter—a well-known local personality. Reluctantly stepping forward, he directed the beam of light on the victim and flinched, almost backing off a step. There was so much blood that at first he could barely make out whether Arnold was working on a human being or a small animal. Finally he realized the victim was a little girl.

Arnold's expression was calm and focused. "I need light—*there*."

Tyrone swung the beam where Arnold indicated and watched as Arnold wiped an arm, exposing clean, unbroken skin. With a swift movement, he jabbed a needle into the muscle and attached a plastic tube, which snaked into a bag of some clear solution.

Light blue eyes fixed on his. "Hold that up. It needs gravity to feed in."

Tyrone's fingers closed on the bag of fluid, and a shudder rolled through him. He stood, feeling as awkward as an oversized crane as he watched the small deft man working on the body, checking the neck brace that obscured most of its upper torso and chin, then sliding a needle into the other arm.

A second medic checked for a pulse, then relinquished her wrist. "You're wasting your time, Arnold. This one's gone. We don't know how long she's been out here. There's no radial pulse that I can find, there's no carotid pulse, and she ain't breathing. And she's cold."

"Yeah, there could be a good reason for that." Arnold exhaled hard, his breath pluming like mist on the night air. "Winter's on its way. It's a cold night."

A stretcher was dropped beside the body. Arnold and a second medic lifted and strapped her. Tyrone followed, keeping the bag of fluid elevated as they loaded up. Then Arnold took the bag of saline solution, hung it on a metal rod that clamped onto the side of the stretcher and motioned for Tyrone to move back.

"Step on it," Arnold said briefly, directing a sharp look at the driver. A split second later, the rear door was slammed closed.

"Only because it's you asking, Arnold," the driver muttered. He shook his head and shot Tyrone a frustrated look as he swung into the cab. "You want your story? It's four words—dead at the scene."

Slamming the door closed, he turned on the siren. The wheels spun, throwing out mud and gravel. The ambulance wallowed and fishtailed, then finally gained traction. Seconds later it pulled out onto the road, falling in behind one of the police cruisers, which was acting as an escort.

One of the police officers squatted down beside

the plowed-up ditch. "Shoot," he muttered. "There goes our only piece of evidence besides the body."

He pointed at the deep ruts the ambulance had cut. "This was a hit and run—we think. Hard to tell now."

The static of the radio in the nearest cruiser blared. A second officer leaned into the cab and picked up the mouthpiece.

With a curt motion, he returned the mouthpiece to its resting place and gestured at the officer squatting to examine the wheel ruts. "Yo, Crenshaw, time to go. We've just been reassigned. Someone just lit up the cemetery. Damn kids. I hate Friday nights."

Several days later, two more bodies surfaced—literally—in Detroit, the time of death estimated at approximately a week earlier. Burton Coley attended the autopsies and collected what evidence he could, but it was hard to glean anything conclusive after the victims had spent a week immersed in Lake Erie. Other than minute traces of gypsum and the signature removal of hair, he had nothing to add to the case except the new location and an even stronger resolve: one of the victims had been sixteen, the same age as Coley's sister.

Coley continued to liaise with the police departments involved, but as suddenly as the killer had shot to nationwide prominence, he dropped from sight. Twenty-three killings, and suddenly…nothing.

For a murderer who had killed so consistently and for so long, to have stopped meant one of two things: either he had become too incapacitated to perpetrate any further crimes or he had died.

It happened.

As powerful and elusive as a killer might be, he didn't possess immortality; like every other Joe on the planet, he had to die sometime. The fact that their boy had most likely passed away by means of either an accident or natural causes was both a blessing and a frustration. Lone women, and all the communities that had been affected by his crimes, could breathe a little easier, but the file remained open, the murders unsolved, and Coley, now an investigative agent with the FBI, continued to worry at the case in his spare time. The situation was a bitch. Dead or alive, Coley and a lot of other law enforcement professionals *wanted* this guy.

The Atlanta PD and the Bureau worked on the bizarre series of murders on and off for another five years, but with no further killings, and no further information, their budgets didn't justify spending any more time or money. The case was closed.

Part 3

The Harvest

Ten

Present day

The heat on the aircraft was killing. According to the stewardess, the air-conditioning, which had failed shortly after takeoff, had been fixed, but, repaired or not, so far the only discernible result was that humid air was being blown in his face instead of none at all.

After thirty minutes, his armpits were wringing wet and the smell of sweating passengers was thick enough to cut. The woman who had taken the seat next to him and, incredibly, introduced herself to almost every passenger within earshot, had complained non-stop.

Patience tested, he slid the novel he'd bought shortly before takeoff out of the pocket of the seat in front of him and began to read, sinking into the cold methodical cadences of a police procedural. Two hours later, on page 256, all the hairs at his nape lifted. Stomach tight, and oblivious to his companion's non-stop bitching about the heat, he turned the book over and stared at the publicity shot of the author—at a face that should have turned to dust twenty-five years ago.

The name "Jane" jumped out at him, when before it had blended innocuously with the dramatic cover of the book.

The author was surprisingly young; in her early thirties, with dark brown eyes, dark hair, porcelain pale skin, her cheekbones high and tight. The only aberration marring the smooth elegance of her appearance was a small crescent-shaped scar on the left side of her jaw, a scar he remembered seeing two and a half decades ago. But what *he* remembered didn't matter. It was what *she* was remembering that worried him.

He had bought the book on impulse, minutes before boarding the flight. Normally he only read non-fiction, and if he picked up a novel at all, he chose one by a male author, but this time he'd been in a hurry, and the packaging had been hard-nosed enough that he'd simply ignored his usual preference and paid for the book. The fact that he could so easily have *not* picked up this particular book and so missed what was unfolding beneath his nose made him break out in a cold sweat.

His stomach clenched as he considered the implications. Despite the fact that it was the author's first book, the novel was a bestseller, reaching number one on the *New York Times* bestseller list. According to the back cover copy, Jane Gale's rise to literary stardom had been meteoric. Both *People* and *Time* magazine had glowingly reviewed her work, along with numerous other print and Internet publications. Her sales figures were in the millions.

He turned to the front pages and checked the publication date, which was several months previously. He didn't know much about the publishing world, but he was willing to bet she'd written this book at least a year, maybe eighteen months, ago. That meant she might have another book close to completion right now. He wondered what the subject matter of her current work in progress was. Although, judging from the success of this story, she was unlikely to deviate from her chosen topic, which was murder.

The tension in his stomach tightened into something akin to panic—and just as quickly translated into anger.

The bitch. He couldn't believe it.

He had checked.

He had read the report of her death in the *Lassiter Daily*. The information had been there in black and white. She had *died*.

Yet through some trick of fate she had survived. Her biography in the book stated that she had been found, left for dead, on the side of the road after a hit-and-run accident—that she was a Jane Doe, and had no recollection of her life after surfacing from a coma some months later. At that time her age had been estimated at seven years, which, from memory, wasn't far wrong.

A long pink fingernail tapped on the cover of his novel. His head jerked up, and he found himself staring at the shiny face of the aroma in the next seat. For a moment he couldn't make sense of the sounds that issued from her mouth; then the low, bitter diatribe registered. He recalled her name: Myra Waltham.

"*Shut. Up,*" he enunciated softly.

She flinched. All the color drained from her cheeks, and for a full second her mouth gaped even wider, but for the first time since she'd taken her seat, apart from the time she'd spent stuffing food into her face, she was silent.

Satisfaction eased some of the fury and tension that locked his muscles. He knew from his intensive study of his own appearance, mannerisms and body language that his eyes were icy clear and, when he chose, almost unbearably direct. It was a fact that most people didn't hold eye contact for long unless they wanted to pick a fight or instigate sex. In almost any other situation, direct, prolonged eye contact was as deliberate and physically invasive as a blow.

Ten minutes later the flight landed. As soon as he'd gotten clear of the airport, he checked the publishing house's name, slipped his cell phone out of his pocket and placed a call.

Patiently, he waited out the receptionist and, after being politely fobbed off with a mailing address for fan letters, was put through to an editorial assistant. A cheerful voice answered, but the voice turned noticeably cooler when he asked for Jane's address.

"I'm sorry, we don't give out those kinds of personal details. If you want to write to Ms. Gale, you can do so through us or her literary agency. They accept mail and forward it on."

Armed with a new telephone number, he dialed once more. This time he hit gold: the name of her agent. With the name of someone so directly connected to Jane, he was certain it wouldn't take him long to track her down. Finally, when he reached his apartment, he sat down at his desk and began searching the Internet.

Apparently Jane was very private; she didn't even have her own Web page as many authors did, though that didn't stop the flow of information. Fans had set up Web sites for her, and they were filled with information. One fan had been avid enough to dig back into Jane's past and had found a newspaper article that had been run years ago, when she'd been recovering in hospital.

The facts leapt out at him. Jane's accident had happened twenty-five years ago, just outside Lassiter, in the state of Louisiana.

His heart slammed in his chest. If he'd had even the tiniest doubt about her real identity, it was gone. The timing, and the place, was correct.

His unease deepened as he slowly scrolled to the end of the article. A year after her accident, after efforts to locate her family had failed, Jane had been adopted by a wealthy New England couple, the Gales. But despite the new beginning—and penniless, amnesiac waif or not—she had refused to change her first name from the Jane in Jane Doe, so she had become Jane Gale.

Sitting back in his chair, he stared intently at the enlarged image of the woman on his computer screen.

The fact that she'd kept the name Jane was threatening. She had clung to what was hers with a tenacity that was alarming. She could have chosen any number of pretty names to go with her new life, like Lisa or Melanie or Annette—but no, she had stuck with the name that labeled her as a person who hadn't officially existed until she'd been found on the side of the road and the state of Louisiana had to issue her a new identity. She hadn't even bothered to add an *I* or a *Y* to the name to pretty it up. She'd stuck with plain Jane.

Aside from the unpalatable fact that he was sure it meant she had retained a part of her memory, even if only subconsciously, it demonstrated stubbornness and a singular determination to confront the fact that she'd been abandoned.

The past was important to her. It had leaked onto the pages of her book—even if she didn't consciously understand what she was writing.

As he continued to stare at that smooth, ladylike facade, he experienced a curious moment of disassociation, as if everything—his ordered life, the past he'd literally buried—had been dug up and exposed. He wondered if she was in any way aware of what she was doing, then decided it didn't matter. Her conscious mind might be locked out of her past, but somehow the writing process was taking her back to that previous life. Closer and closer to him.

Eleven

Lassiter, Louisiana

Jane parked her rental SUV at the beginning of Plaisance Street and studied the attractive cul-de-sac. The houses were large and rambling, the plantings tending to towering oaks and magnolias, gnarled drifts of wisteria and the stately, graceful arch of phoenix palms. Front yards were enclosed with wrought iron and clipped hedges, giving glimpses of smooth lawns and tubs spilling a bright assortment of geraniums and impatiens.

In the midst of Lassiter's burgeoning sprawl of houses and shopping malls, the street was an elegant backwater, built on cotton and sugar money, and reminiscent of some of the older residential streets in New Orleans—which was why she'd left it until the end of the day. With the light fading, it would be just plain stupid to go anywhere near the rougher northern end of Lassiter. Canvassing parts of it in daylight had been bad enough. She had been variously abused and pitied, mistaken for a religious nut and just plain ignored. The last house-holder had slammed the door in her face, leaving her staring at peeling green paint and a rusted fly screen, and wondering what on earth she was doing knocking on strangers' doors. She had just finished a book, and she had a month before she had to start on the next one; she could have stayed at home and put her feet up, or maybe even gone to the Bahamas.

As she pulled the key from the ignition, a cloud slid across the yellowish glow of the setting sun, darkening the already murky evening. Frowning, she checked the sky. A thunderhead hovered, heavy-bellied and threatening, and the rain that had teased all afternoon finally looked like delivering.

Ignoring the clammy heat and the stiffness that had crept up on her and threatened to send her limping back to the air-conditioned comfort of her motel room before she reached her daily target of one hundred houses, Jane climbed out of the SUV, wincing as pain shot up her left thigh and lodged like a burning coal in the small of her back.

Not for the first time, she doubted her sanity in

searching for a past that had never made any effort to find her. She had a photo of a small boy that was at least twenty-five years old and no idea who he was, or how she had come to have his photo in her possession.

When she'd woken from a coma at what the doctors guessed was age seven, partially paralyzed and alone in the world, she'd been like a newborn baby, her mind utterly blank. The accident had cracked three ribs, broken her back and hip, shattered her left femur and initiated massive internal bleeding. When she'd been located, almost bled out and with no discernible pulse, she had initially been pronounced dead, but one of the ambulance officers had continued to work on her during the trip into town, putting in large intravenous lines and pumping her full of saline solution and O negative blood. Just before she arrived at Lassiter General, a carotid pulse was located and she began to breathe.

Dr. Cuvier, the surgeon, had expected her to die on the operating table. The procedures required to stabilize her were invasive enough on an adult, let alone a fragile, small-boned child, but she hadn't died. Through some freakish chance, she had survived the initial surgery and the later procedures to repair damage to her spine, hip and leg. Cuvier's explanation had been that the trauma of the accident and the cold snap had somehow combined to induce a state of suspended animation. Her mind and her body had simply shut down, then stayed shut down for seven months.

The day she'd come out of traction had been the day she'd woken up but, unlike her body, which had slowly mended, her mind had remained stubbornly blank, wiped clean by what the experts termed traumatic amnesia.

For years the mystery of who the little boy was had pulled at her. The fact that she'd had the photo when she'd had little else meant it was important, and she'd clung to it while she'd waited for her parents to collect her. Mind blank or not, she'd been old enough to understand that someone in the Lassiter area had been feeding and clothing her. Someone should have cared enough to pick up the phone and tell their local sheriff or police department that a little seven-year-old girl was missing and they were worried.

At thirty-two, the fact that no one ever had still ticked her off.

She hadn't materialized out of thin air; she had family—somewhere—and it should have been possible for them to find her, or for the authorities to trace *them*. She allowed that twenty-five years ago things had been different—it was, after all, a whole other century—without the sophisticated communication and computer systems that were now in existence, but even so...

As she reached inside the vehicle for her handbag, a fat droplet of rain exploded on the roof.

"Great," she muttered. After a day spent perspiring in one of Louisiana's hottest summers on record, rain was all she needed.

On impulse, she grabbed her cane. An ungraceful balancing act later, she locked the car and started along the sidewalk, left leg dragging slightly. Normally she didn't limp or use the cane, but there was nothing normal about knocking on nearly five hundred doors in four different neighborhoods over as many days, and it was a fact that after four days she still hadn't adjusted to the heat. Her white blouse and tan pants hung on her like soggy sheets, making her feel clammy and irritable. Even the air felt damp and heavy, pressing in on her lungs and making every breath an effort. She had quickly learned to adopt the slow, almost lazy walk of the locals, but her body's internal thermostat had refused to alter its Maine setting, no matter how slowly she moved. The second she stepped out of the air-conditioning of either her car or her motel room, her body went haywire and every pore opened up.

She paused at the gate of the first house, which occupied the corner section. Like the land it was built on, the house was large and slightly unkempt, as if the owner didn't have either the resources or the time to bring order to the property. Massive oaks crowded together, spreading their limbs wide enough to shade most of the lawn, and what grass had managed to survive was cut ruthlessly short. The garden itself was almost nonexistent, but the bare effect was softened by an ancient rose that rambled over an equally ancient wrought iron fence, its creamy petals preternaturally bright, the scent heavy enough to make her head spin.

As she bent to read the name on the lichen-encrusted letterbox and investigate the latch of the gate, the slight twisting movement sent a shaft of pain down her back. Taking a deep breath, she straightened and for long moments hesitated, weighing up the viability of continuing on to the house versus giving in for the night. Then the feeling registered that she was being watched.

Her gaze caught the movement of a filmy white curtain, the glimpse of a shadow, as if someone had just let the curtain drop and stepped back out of view. Abruptly, something about the sneakiness of the anonymous watcher hiding behind the concealment of the curtain burned.

Jane glanced at the letterbox again—at the faded legend, *Toussaint*—lifted the latch on the gate and stepped through. If she had any sense, she would go back to the motel, take an anti-inflammatory and soak in the tub until she felt halfway human, but common sense had never been her strong suit. The entire length of her spine, from her shoulder blades to the base, burned, the pain like a slow burning fire, and the old fury that went with it surfaced as naturally as oil bubbling up through water.

Jaw clenched, she closed the gate and started up the path, ignoring the watcher, her left leg stiff, her foot already numb in patches as the damaged nerves, tangled up with scar tissue, gave up the ghost. After the day she'd had, seven o'clock on another one of Lassiter's steam bath evenings was the wrong time to piss her off.

According to her ex-neighbor, who had been sleeping with her ex-husband, she could be "difficult." According to her ex-husband, who had been sleeping with practically anything that moved, she was the original mechanized bitch from hell.

Jane had taken both insults as compliments.

In contrast to her stockbroker ex-husband, with his shifting bank accounts and sliding morals, she liked steel. It was durable, and it was honest. Whichever way she sliced it, she would rather do things her way—the direct way—than hide behind either legal fine print or the fine Southern lace Mrs. Toussaint apparently favored.

The cloud cover seemed to press even lower as she approached the front door, the humidity pressurized and intense, a last kicker of heat as the heavens finally opened and fat droplets pelted down, splashing her shoulders and back.

Her gait was uncertain and clumsy as she mounted the steps and reached for the doorbell. Pain washed through her in waves as she listened to the buzzer, the moment taking on a surreal quality as the rain thickened, blotting out the sepia-toned sunset and turning the evening gray.

Angry or not, this was going to be the last house. As physically strong as she was, she could take only so much before her back and her leg gave out.

Over the street, lights came on, glistening on the slick road, and abruptly, the rain grew torrential, the downpour muffling the distant sounds of traffic and locking her into the claustrophobic environs of the porch. Jane was on the verge of leaving when the darkened entrance flooded with light and the door swung open.

Blinking, she adjusted her gaze upward. After the curtain-twitching episode, she had expected a woman, but "Mrs. Toussaint" was most definitely male.

His gaze dropped to her cane; then he dug into his pocket, pulled out a wallet and peeled off a twenty.

Jane stared blankly at the note; then understanding hit. He thought she was collecting for charity.

A bubble of humor clogged the back of her throat. She'd spent days guarding her purse, expecting to be mugged, and now she was actually being offered money.

Suppressing the mirth, she made brief eye contact. The little boy in the snapshot would be a man in his late twenties or early thirties now, which fitted with the approximate age of the man standing in front of her, although little else did, besides the fact that he was olive-skinned, with black hair. Not for the first time, the impossibility of the task registered. It had been twenty-five years. The transition from child to adult rendered her photograph close to useless. "I don't want money."

Reaching into a flat side pocket of her handbag, she pulled out a laminated copy of the snapshot. She'd learned early on in the door-knocking business never to reach directly into her purse, because that kind of movement could be assumed to be threatening, and it also opened her up to having her wallet snatched.

After the first day of varying degrees of abuse, and unsettling interest in her jewelry and designer handbag, she'd bought a cheap handbag, dressed down and left her jewelry, along with most of her cash and credit cards, at the motel. She'd also cut down on the items she carried in the handbag to a few essentials, and kept the small amount of cash, the one credit card she needed and her cell phone in the glove compartment of the rental. As a final precaution, she made sure to carry her car keys in her pocket whenever she left the vehicle, so that if her bag was snatched, she would still have transportation.

The light caught the distinctive planes of his face as he examined the photo. Taking advantage of his momentary distraction, she studied the cut of his cheekbones, the shape of his jaw, trying to marry the angular planes with the soft, unformed bone structure of a four- or five-year-old boy. He was tall, a shade over six feet, with broad shoulders and the kind of lean, tight build that indicated he either played a sport or put in regular time at the gym. There was no way she could project the likely height or physical build of the boy in the photo; the only real guidelines she had were age and skin tone, hair and eye coloring, and Toussaint *was* old enough and dark enough.

His gaze connected with hers. "Where did you get this?"

"I've had it since I was a child." Automatically, she asked the question. "Do you recognize him? Or anything about that picture?"

"Yeah. It's me. And that's the old fairground."

Shock jolted through her. For a moment she thought her hearing was faulty. She'd heard "No," "Sorry," and four-letter renditions of "Get lost" so many times that "Yeah. It's me" took a while to sink in.

"How did you get my address?"

Blankly, she studied his face. His expression was impassive, the tone of his voice cool. "I didn't. I've been canvassing the town, looking—"

She had been about to say, "looking for you," but suddenly that seemed too intimate, bordering on intrusive, when he evidently had no idea who she was and wasn't happy that she had his photograph.

The moment was disorienting, a reality check she hadn't expected. For years she'd thought of him as family—perhaps a cousin, or even a brother—but it was clear there was no bond between them other than the one she had created.

His gaze fixed on her cane. "Are you all right? You look like you need medical attention."

And he didn't want her passing out or injuring herself on his property. "I'll be fine." But the long minutes spent standing in the chilly damp of the porch while the rain pounded down hadn't improved her condition. Her entire lower back and left thigh were in spasm, the tension in her muscles vise-like. If she walked back to her car now, she would get soaked, and the likelihood that she would fall was high. "I don't need medical care. All I need is to sit down for a minute."

And ask a few questions.

After twenty-five years of living with a mystery, she figured she was entitled to five minutes of his time.

Long seconds ticked by. He didn't want her in his house, but with the rain teeming down, he couldn't in all conscience close the door in her face. Finally he stepped aside and indicated that she should precede him.

Taking a deep breath, Jane entered the warmly lit hallway of the house, glancing around curiously as she waited for Toussaint to take the lead. The hallway runner was rich but threadbare, the walls decorated with oil paintings and framed needlework. The front parlor mirrored the faded graciousness of the hall, with dark, ornate furniture and heavily embossed wallpaper. Even from the outside, the house had a museum-like quality, like a faded remnant from another time.

The sensation of stepping into the past was intense as Toussaint bypassed a curving staircase, his gait fluid and smooth as he stepped into dense shadow, and Jane was abruptly aware of the stupidity of walking into a strange house with an even stranger man. Despite the chronic problems with her leg and back, she was normally fit and strong, and she had taken self-defense courses, but even if she were completely well, she wouldn't like to take on Toussaint.

After the museum-like quality of the rest of the house, the kitchen was unexpectedly bright and modern, with stainless steel appliances and a microwave, and some of Jane's tension dissipated. In these surroundings, it was hard to imagine Toussaint wielding an ax.

His eyebrows lifted, as if knew exactly what was going through her mind. "I drew the line at cooking on a wood range."

Toussaint pulled out a chair, and Jane sat down. "I guess I must seem like a nutcase to you."

He poured coffee into a mug and set it down in front of her. She noticed he'd already added milk, and, when she tasted it, sugar.

"I've just come off my shift. I don't get paid to think until six tomorrow."

Shift. That sounded like he had a job in a factory, although if he was paid to think, he had to do something more than assembly-line work. She studied the long line of his back as he filled his own mug, and an intense curiosity ate at her. The T-shirt was Nike and fit like a glove; the jeans were faded, his sneakers funky. His hair was short, but the cut was crisp and clean. She couldn't imagine him in a factory. Maybe he was a supervisor?

She lifted the mug and took another sip, and the hot liquid steadied her. Reaching into her bag, she extracted a bottle, shook a pill into her palm and managed to scatter several more on the kitchen table.

His hand clamped around her wrist, and, grimly, she waited him out while he read the label on the bottle.

"It's an anti-inflammatory. Sometimes the nerve damage gets away on me."

His gaze connected with hers as he scooped up the spilled pills, tipped them into the bottle and screwed the cap on. He dropped the bottle into the opening of her purse. "I had to check."

"What?" A tight smile stretched her mouth. "Did you think I was a drug addict?"

"I've worked narcotics."

So that was it, the wariness and the attitude; she should have guessed when he said he did shift work—he was a cop.

"What happened to you?"

"Good question." And if he couldn't answer it, that was another door closed in her face—approximately number seventy-six today. She pulled out another photo, one taken of her not long after the Gales had taken her home to Maine. She looked thin and sickly, and was confined to a wheelchair, but it was the closest she could get to her appearance before the accident. "That's a picture of me twenty-five years ago." Briefly she explained the history. "I'm trying to trace my family. You were my starting point."

He studied the photograph. His gaze swept her face, as if he were trying to connect the two. She could understand his dilemma. He didn't look much like *his* childhood photo, either.

He shook his head. "We're not related. My father was Chippewa. His family live in Mississippi, and the Toussaints are thin on the ground. My mother was an only child. She died when I was two. Aside from a couple of elderly cousins, there isn't anyone else."

Another door closed. After actually finding the boy in the photo, the dead end was hard to accept, but she had to. John Toussaint knew who he was, and he knew his family. If anyone had lost a child, he would have heard—especially one around his age. "How about friends?"

"I've got a good memory for people and faces, but my father and I moved around a lot. I only visited Lassiter a couple of times to stay with family over the summer. One of those visits must have been when this shot was taken. Apart from that, I never lived here. A couple of years back I inherited this house and decided to move south. About six months ago I transferred in."

"From New York?"

"You picked the accent."

"It's not hard." The short vowels, the hard-assed look that said he would bounce you off the nearest wall if you got in his way. He might have been in Lassiter six months, but he hadn't acclimatized. Compared to the slow, liquid drawl of the locals and their languid walk, he was like a coiled spring.

"What about you? New Hampshire?"

"Maine."

He grinned. "Close. Strangers in a strange land."

The moment of companionability formed a rough throb in her throat and almost undid her. It was odd to consider that, after all the searching, the years of wondering, she had finally found him, and the only thing they had in common was that, in Lassiter, they were both out-of-towners.

He asked questions, and she answered, providing him with her name, the name of the motel she was staying at, along with a short, potted history of her life—including the fact that she was divorced. When the questions stopped, she realized just how much information she'd hemorrhaged when it was information from John Toussaint she wanted.

She had needed *him* to remember for her—to

give her back the chunk of her life that had always haunted her. The fact that his memory appeared to be as blank as hers when it came to his childhood was momentarily unacceptable. "You're sure you don't remember anything?"

His features shuttered. "Sorry."

Only he wasn't. She could tell. He'd given her a few minutes of his time, allowed her to recover her composure and in the process put her through a mini-Inquisition, but her time was up.

The recognition that her search was over was bittersweet. She had the dubious pleasure of closure for this little piece of her past, at least. She just hadn't been prepared for the fact that, apart from checking her out for a criminal background, Toussaint wasn't remotely interested in her. Worse, he couldn't wait to get rid of her. He was polite, restrained, but his patience was visibly thinning.

Gripping the cane, she eased to her feet. He moved, as if to assist her, and she flinched. Abruptly, she couldn't bear for him to touch her—could hardly stand being in the same room with him. It was a childish reaction, but she figured that after all she'd gone through to locate him, she was due a five-minute tantrum. "Thank you for the coffee and your time."

Hooking the strap of her handbag over her shoulder, she limped into the hallway, keeping her stomach muscles tight to limit the jolt to her vertebrae. She kept her focus on the ornate front door, closing out the dark, faded elegance of the house and the presence of John Toussaint directly behind her.

When she reached the door, he leaned past her and opened it. "Your photographs."

She slipped the snapshot of herself into her bag and handed him the one of the small boy. "That one's yours. Keep it."

Toussaint watched as she limped down the path, negotiated the gate and climbed into a classy SUV. When she'd arrived, he had studied her from the moment she'd exited her vehicle until she'd disappeared beneath the roof of the porch; then he'd walked to the kitchen, retrieved his handgun, checked the load and answered the door.

Plaisance Street was in a good neighborhood, but he was a cop, and lately he had upset a few people—notably the Laurent brothers, who had both been indicted for drug trafficking. She didn't look like the kind of woman who would spend time with either Sonny or Beau or any other member of that unholy brood, but he hadn't wanted to take any risks.

When he'd opened the door, his first impression had been confirmed. She had been conservatively, even boringly, dressed, no make-up or jewelry, dark hair clipped back at her nape, a slim but nicely curved figure all but hidden by clothing that was a size too large. He hadn't smelled alcohol, and her eyes were clear and direct, which indicated she wasn't using. If he had seen any signs of either drug or alcohol use, he wouldn't have allowed her in the door. After ten years on the force, he had zero tolerance for addicts and drunks.

He glanced at the snapshot in his hand, perplexed. The memories he retained of his childhood were vivid. He remembered his grandparents in this house. He remembered his uncles and the old sugar plantation that had been in the Dexter family for years, and the farm, which had eventually been cut up into a subdivision. He even recalled going to the fair, although he had no recollection of this particular photo being taken.

He watched as she drove slowly down the street, negotiated the tight cul-de-sac, then drove back past his house to the intersection. The brake lights of the SUV glowed red, then winked out as she accelerated down LeFort Street toward town, presumably heading for her motel.

Frowning, he slipped the snapshot into his wallet. As plainly as she'd dressed, Jane Gale was a distinctive-looking woman, with cheekbones that made his mouth water. Even as a child, she would have been distinctive. If he'd met her, he should have remembered her.

He was a cop; by definition, he didn't like mysteries. He would look up some old records, but he hadn't wanted to promise her anything. She had been a Jane Doe, so the chances that he could unearth information the authorities had failed to find twenty-five years ago were slim. If he found anything, he would contact her. He had her details— finding her would be easy enough.

Shrugging his shoulders, he closed the door. He had a reputation for being tough on women and a propensity for choosing women who were just as difficult. Jane Gale wasn't his usual type, but despite the plain, sexless clothing and the schoolmarm hair, something about her had impressed him. Maybe it had been the steel that had underlain everything she'd done and said—she had actually knocked on who knew how many doors searching for him. Or it could be the way she'd studied him, like a cop with a sheet. There had been nothing remotely sexual, or even female, in the way she'd looked him over. She had simply checked him out, asked her questions and left.

No smile. No awareness. No emotional involvement.

Twelve

Beach Haven, Maine

Claire Pettigrew peered into the shadows cast by the large, weeping cherry that shaded Jane's back lawn, attracted by a flash of white. Her youngest son's new kitten must have slipped out a window and followed her when she'd walked next door to check on the house.

Slipping the house key back into her pocket, Claire ducked beneath the intricate web of trailing branches, stepping lightly, eyes peeled. There was nothing quiet or biddable about Cricket, and there was no point in calling or wiggling her fingers; every chance he got, the little fluffball scampered outside and got himself lost. So far she'd had to retrieve him from Ila Burns's garage, old Mr. Tomlinson's back yard and once, from the road. The one bonus was that, with his fluffy white fur, he was ridiculously easy to spot.

Another flash of white pulled her farther into the shrubbery, beneath the heavy branches of a fir. She stood for long seconds, waiting for her eyesight to adjust, her impatience mounting. The sun had just set, and the moon was rising, casting a soft, buttery glow over the landscape, but beneath the fir the darkness was close to absolute.

A movement at the periphery of her vision caught her eye, and she turned, staring intently at the brick patio that formed an alcove at the rear of Jane's house. For a pulse-pounding moment she thought someone was there, but when nothing else registered, she turned her attention back to the bushes.

The movement came again, and the shape she'd thought was a folded umbrella suddenly made sense. There was someone standing in the lee of the house near the back door, where she had stood just moments before. As she watched, he turned, studying the garden intensely. His gaze came to rest on the tree Claire was standing beneath, and the marrow in her spine froze: he was looking for her.

Just feet away, leaves rustled, and Cricket bounced out from beneath a shrub, his white fur neon-bright beneath the full moon. His back arched like a question mark when he saw the intruder, and, with a bird-like chirruping sound, he streaked in the direction of home.

The shadowy figure watched as the kitten disappeared beneath the fence. Long seconds passed as he continued to scrutinize the garden; then he turned and walked up the drive, something metallic glinting in one hand.

A short time later, the faint purr of an engine sounded, and Claire caught a glimpse of red taillights as a car slid past the driveway.

For long minutes she stood, immobile, beneath the fir. When she could finally move, her breath came in rough gasps. Clumsily, she pushed through the brush. A branch stung her cheek, and roots hooked at her feet. Shoving through an overgrown clump of lilies, she stumbled onto an exposed stretch of lawn. In the moonlight, the patio where the man had stood loomed ghostly bright.

Clenching her teeth to stop them from chattering, she backed away from the light. Hugging the shadows, she edged along a thickly planted border, pushed through a hedge of hydrangeas and scrambled across the fence to home.

Lassiter

The rain had petered out to fitful bursts chased along by a capricious wind, and the clouds were ragged enough to allow glimpses of a full moon, as Jane closed her motel door behind her. Dropping her cane and handbag on the sofa, she limped across to the kitchen counter to unload the Chinese takeout she'd bought from a drive-through.

She walked through to the bathroom, flicking on lights as she went. Gripping the vanity for support, she opened the bathroom cabinet, thumbed two painkillers from the foil packet and chased the pills down with a glass of water. Nausea welled. Grimly, she kept her jaw clamped and her throat closed.

When the painkillers kicked in, she would do a few stretching exercises to ease the tightness in her muscles. She knew from experience that if she left them, she would wake up feeling even stiffer.

As she set the glass down, she caught the flash of her reflection in the mirror. Her eyes were so dark they were almost black, her lips and skin bloodless. She looked exactly how she felt: ill, exhausted...and empty.

Toussaint had proved to be a dead end—he hadn't remembered her—but at least he *existed,* which verified her search. Even if she discovered nothing else, at least she could cross him off her list of mysteries. Tomorrow she would visit the library and read through back issues of newspapers, just in case there was some detail she'd missed; then she would take a drive out to the stretch of road where she'd been found and see if anything jogged loose in her memory.

With slow, careful movements, she made her way back to the kitchen. As hungry as she'd been, she didn't want food yet, but she had to eat, otherwise the anti-inflammatory and the codeine would make her feel even sicker.

Sitting at the dining table, she slowly forked rice and vegetables into her mouth, barely tasting the food.

Her cell phone beeped, and she tensed. Calmly, she set the fork down. For the past few months she'd been the target of an obsessed fan—just one more good reason to get out of town for a month. She didn't know the caller beyond the fact that he identified himself as a fan. Her local precinct had tried to track him down, but so far all they'd come up with were a list of people with stolen phones, and a second list of false addresses and false names.

Since he'd started calling just weeks after her book had hit the bestseller lists, she'd changed both her telephone and cell phone numbers, and installed a caller ID system at home. She'd also changed her mailing address and had all her fan mail directed through her agent's office, cutting out any direct link to her.

By the time she'd dug her cell phone out of her

purse, the caller had disconnected. Jane stared at the small screen. A message flashed, telling her she had seven new voice mail messages.

This was the first time today she'd heard the phone ring, which wasn't surprising since she'd kept it in the glove compartment of the SUV. All the calls but this one must have come in when she'd been out of the vehicle, which had been most of the day.

Her stomach clenched. The phone was new, and so was her number. She didn't know anyone in town, and she hadn't given out her number to many people. One of the messages could be from Mayet, the proprietor of the motel, or perhaps Toussaint, although nothing in Toussaint's attitude when she'd left his house had led her to believe she would ever hear from him again. But that would only account for two messages, not seven. Her parents and her agent knew where she was staying and what she was doing, but Jane didn't expect a call from either. Her mother had rung the previous evening to let her know they would be away for the weekend, staying with friends, and Ellen, her agent, was out of town at a conference. It was possible her neighbor, Claire, who was keeping an eye on her house was trying to get hold of her, but not likely unless there was an emergency.

After connecting to voice mail, she waited for

the first message to play. The mellow tones of the caller held her frozen for long seconds until, with a jerky movement, she terminated the call.

Somehow the stalker had gotten hold of her cell phone number—again. From the contents of the message, he'd also found her unlisted home number *and* found out that she wasn't there.

She turned off the phone and placed it on the table. She felt like throwing it as far as she could— but she would need it as evidence. The officer who had been dealing with her harassment case would need a record of the calls.

Jane slipped her address book from her purse, found the number of the Beach Haven police department, picked up her phone and tapped in the numbers. When the call was picked up, she asked to be put through to Detective Newman's extension and left a message.

The harassment had just escalated. So far the stalking had been confined to letters and phone calls, all innocuous in themselves, except that there were so many: thirty letters so far, and in excess of one hundred phone calls—and counting.

Newman had cautioned her that if the stalker had gone to so much effort to contact her by telephone and letter, he would probably go the extra mile and find out her street address. Jane didn't have any evidence that he had been near her home, but the thought that he had, at the very least, driven by her house, sent a shiver down her spine. Her only consolation was that, even if the stalker knew where she lived and that she was away, he couldn't know where she physically was right now.

As she snapped the phone shut, the motel phone rang.

Adrenaline pumped, then common sense reasserted itself. It was probably the front desk ringing to ask if everything was all right with the room.

Dismissing the notion that somehow the stalker *had* found her, she picked up the receiver and, out of sheer habit after months of unwelcome calls, waited for the caller to speak. The hollow sound of the connection hummed as whoever was on the other end also waited; then, with a quiet click, the call was terminated.

For long seconds she remained frozen, chills running up and down her spine; then the disconnect beep registered.

No one had spoken, but someone had been there, and if it hadn't been the front desk, then it had been someone who knew her name—because the operator had put the call through to her unit. It was possible that a mistake had been made, the wrong unit number had been dialed and, disconcerted by the silence, the caller had simply hung up. But any ordinary caller would have checked, and this person hadn't. Jane hadn't heard a thing, which was creepy in itself. There had been no background music or noise, no breathing, just silence, as if the caller had held his breath.

Or placed his hand over the phone.

Jane dropped the receiver into its cradle, then immediately picked it up and dialed the operator. "You just put a call through to me. Can you tell me who that was?"

The woman's voice was polite. "We just put the calls through, ma'am. We don't ask who's calling."

Jane took a deep breath, trying to stay calm. She'd weathered months of harassment; she refused to go to pieces over what amounted to just one more call. "Did the caller ask for me by name?"

When the receptionist replied in the affirmative, Jane's grip on the receiver tightened. "Was the person male or female?"

There was a small silence. "Are you saying you've just received a prank call, ma'am?"

"Yes."

"The caller was male. I don't know who he was. He didn't give me a name. Just a moment, please."

There was a brief silence, the muffled sound of voices, as the receptionist talked to someone, then, "Here's Mr. Mayet."

* * *

Five minutes later, Jane held on to her temper by a thread. Mayet was mid-fifties, short and stocky, and as sour as day-old milk. "What I want is simple. No calls whatsoever, and I would like to change my room."

Her present unit was too exposed. Her front door and the rental could be seen from the road. She didn't know if the call was connected with the fan who'd been stalking her, whether it was local or out-of-state, but she wasn't taking any chances.

Mayet wasn't happy. She'd interrupted his both dinner and his favorite television show, but he reluctantly agreed to change her room to one that was more private.

The new unit was a carbon copy of the one she'd just vacated, but it was tucked away at the rear of the complex next to a utility shed and had the bonus of a small carport for the SUV. Within half an hour, Jane was settled, the one suitcase she'd brought unpacked, and her small stock of breakfast food stored in the kitchenette.

Mayet had handed her the key, his gaze reserved as he made a show of checking each room and checked out her possessions at the same time. His gaze lingered on her laptop, and Jane's jaw clenched. It didn't take a brain surgeon to work out that he was suspicious. When she'd arrived she'd been well dressed, and now she was wearing dime store clothing, had a cheap vinyl bag slung over her shoulder and was receiving crank calls.

He eyed her diary where it sat on the coffee table along with the cell phone. "We don't allow working girls at the Palm Court."

Jane didn't bother to keep the incredulity out of her expression. She was the least likely example of a "working girl" she could imagine. She wouldn't say she hated sex, or even disliked it, but she wouldn't walk across a street, much less into a bar, to find it. She eyed Mayet coolly. "And how, exactly, would you define a 'working girl'?"

Before the man could answer, Jane retrieved a book from her briefcase and dropped it on the coffee table. "That's what I do for a living."

He picked the book up and turned it over in his hands. "You write books?"

Mayet made it sound as if she dug graves.

"I'm here doing research." The research wasn't for a book, but he didn't need to know that.

As soon as she closed the door behind the motel owner, Jane picked up her cell phone, rang the Lassiter PD and was put through to a Detective Miller. She needed to know more about the call to her motel, and the only way to do that was to get the police to trace it. If the call had been locally placed, then she was in trouble.

Miller was polite but noncommittal. He would check on the calls to both her cell phone and her motel, but she would have to come in and fill out a formal complaint first. Even then, he couldn't promise anything. Apparently phone crime was rife, and tracking the caller would likely be a deadend.

Jane somehow managed to keep her temper, made an appointment to see him the following afternoon and hung up.

After showering, she got ready for bed, then lay in the darkness, her mind too wired to sleep. Her stomach was churning, but at least the medication had kicked in.

A distant memory of lying immobile as a child, staring at hospital ceilings, made her tense. She'd lost count of the hospitals and the operations, but she'd never forgotten how it had felt to be trapped in a body that couldn't function normally.

On impulse, she took the phone off the hook. That was one source of tension she could do without. Mayet had agreed to hold all calls, but she couldn't be sure that one of his staff might not forget.

Thirteen

The Lassiter police station was located in the oldest part of town. It was an elegant Federal-style building that stood cheek-by-jowl with a grand Greek Revival fantasy that housed the city council and the mayor's office.

Jane lingered on the sidewalk, delaying the moment when she had to walk into the police station, taking a few moments to soak in some sun and enjoy the busy heart of Lassiter. As Southern towns went, it was supposed to be one of the prettiest. The town center had been preserved, and beautified with shady trees and paved areas. Narrow and intriguing lanes led off in several directions, and cafes and designer shops dotted the main street.

A tall dark man in a business suit walked past. His gaze swept her, paused on her breasts, then briefly locked with hers. He muttered a phrase, and then he was gone. Disconcerted, Jane turned, and found he was watching her over his shoulder. He grinned and winked, teeth white against his tanned skin, and she quickly looked away, cheeks burning.

That was the second time that had happened this morning. The first time she had thought the phrase—which had been muttered in what she took to be Cajun French—was an insult, but this one had been in English. *"Nice outfit."*

With a jolt she realized both men had been flirting with her.

With curiosity she watched a similar byplay across the street; the easy acceptance of the compliment by the woman, the languid swing to her hips as she strolled, and Jane felt the charm of Louisiana seep into her bones. If anything aside from the liquid drawl and the heat could inform her that she was in the South, this was it. Men complimented and women flirted—the byplay as intrinsic to Louisiana as good coffee and beignets.

As she waited to cross the road, the sun burned on her shoulders, reminding her that despite being on vacation, she hadn't taken the time to see any sights or even sit by the pool. In contrast to the Southern belles strolling the streets, she was as pale as a lily.

Checking the time, she crossed the road, breathing a sigh of relief when she stepped out of the sun into the reception area of the police department. The room was large, airy and cool after the heat outside, with the soothing sound of a fan circulating overhead. After introducing herself at the counter, she sat down to wait, relieved to be off her feet. She felt much better—her movement good enough that she didn't need her cane—but she was babying her leg today.

Detective Miller emerged from a side door and directed her along a corridor to an interview room.

Two officers were vacating the room as Jane paused at the open door. A uniformed female officer and Toussaint, unmistakable despite the fact that the T-shirt and jeans had been replaced by a suit.

As Toussaint held the door, recognition flashed in his gaze, along with something else that made her stomach tighten. She had a moment to register the subtle woodsy scent of cologne and the fact that he seemed even taller, his shoulders broader in the suit jacket; then they were past and Miller was ushering her toward a seat.

Toussaint lingered, chatting with Miller and holding the door for the patrol officer as she doubled back and collected a file from the table.

Jane settled herself in her seat, acutely aware of Toussaint. He was talking to Miller, but his body was turned toward *her.* She glanced up, and his gaze locked with hers—sharp and uncomplicatedly male. Awareness shivered up her spine and grabbed her belly. She blinked, abruptly aware of her femininity in a way she had never been—not even in college, when sex should have been a powerful distraction, though it had never lived up to its press.

The fact that Toussaint, of all men, had aroused that reaction in her was shocking in itself, although she should have been prepared; he was the third man who had paid her attention this morning.

Disconcerted and uncomfortably warm, Jane transferred her attention to the room, the pale green walls and high molded ceilings, and the tall bank of sash windows that looked out onto a shady courtyard.

Since she hadn't had to dress down to go knocking on doors, she'd taken extra pains with her appearance, enjoying the ritual of winding her hair in a knot, applying make-up and painting her nails. The linen suit she was wearing was plain—a sleeveless top and trousers in a cool oatmeal color—but the fabric draped nicely. Even her jewelry was understated: simple gold studs and a knotted gold chain that sat in the vee of her top.

Yet, plain or not, somehow an outfit she'd seen as cool and businesslike had transformed itself into sexy—or maybe it was simply this place. In Lassiter, the layers of polite convention she was used to simply didn't exist; the subtle intricacies of the mating game had been replaced with a disconcertingly frank appreciation of sex that permeated the air, as primitive as a drumbeat.

The door closed behind Toussaint, and Jane removed her cell phone from her bag. As she activated the phone and set it on the desk, she could still hear the rumble of the receding conversation, although not the actual words; Toussaint's voice was clipped and curt, the woman's accent softer, definitely Southern.

She registered the warmth in her cheeks and the fact that her pulse rate was still up: both definitely feminine reactions and, for her, distinctly out of character. Last night she had barely registered that Toussaint had been male; his gender hadn't mattered beyond the necessities of her search. This morning, for some reason, it did.

Detective Miller opened a notepad and started the interview, and Jane settled in, her gaze automatically running over the paraphernalia of police work: the video camera and monitor, a tape recorder, and bare, pale walls. She'd had at least seven interviews with Detective Newman in Beach Haven; she knew the drill by heart.

Miller sat back in his chair. "Did you recognize

anything at all about the call to your motel room?"

"No. Whoever it was didn't say anything."

"That's not consistent with the calls you've been getting, but it could be the same guy. Either way, I can't do much more than check with the telephone company. If he didn't speak, then he can always argue he'd made a mistake and hung up. That's hardly harassment."

"But if you trace this call to a physical location, there's a chance you can make an arrest."

"It's possible, but we'd have to confirm that he's your stalker first."

Jane clamped down on her frustration. "Whoever's been calling is a criminal, and he gets off by scaring women. He keeps changing phones and identities. He's practiced and he's smart—if you don't move on this, he'll get away."

Miller didn't so much as blink. "What about your ex-husband?"

What about him? "Paul has a girlfriend. I imagine his phone conversations are satisfying enough without bothering me."

"That doesn't mean he wouldn't call to harass you. In a lot of cases, the ex turns out to be the offender. It could be that the call to your motel, which is out of character for the stalker, was from him."

"Possible, but not likely. I've been through this

with Detective Newman. Paul is a stockbroker. He likes numbers—especially ones with dollar signs in front of them. He wouldn't do anything to jeopardize his wealth."

Miller picked up the novel she'd brought with her. "He must have wanted a piece of this action."

"He did, but legally, he can't have one. We have an agreement. I have no claim on any part of his business, and he doesn't have any claim on mine. Believe me, he's winning."

Miller made a note on the pad. "Would you like coffee?"

What she would like was a whole new life. Jane took a breath and let it out slowly, willing her pulse to slow. She was getting nowhere. Miller's logic, and the methodical way he was going about investigating this case were impeccable. She hadn't expected anything more or less—it just didn't solve her problem. She wanted this guy caught, and the fact that he had changed his pattern could mean that he had made a mistake, but the opportunity of tracing him to a physical location was rapidly slipping away. "Yes. Thank you."

While she sipped her coffee, Miller listened to the messages that had been left on her cell phone voice mail.

"There's a message from the Beach Haven P.D.,

a Detective Newman. Looks like you've had a break-in."

Jane took the phone and replayed the message. Her neighbor had seen someone leaving her house last night and called the police. A patrol had investigated and discovered that her house had been broken into.

Minutes later, Miller put through a call to Detective Newman, introduced himself, then handed the phone to Jane.

Newman was brief. An officer had checked out her house and interviewed Claire. The back door had been forced, but nothing appeared to have been touched. They'd concluded that Claire, who had been doing her nightly check of the house, had disturbed the intruder, and he'd left without taking anything.

Jane went limp with relief. Before she'd gone away, she'd left her jewelry and personal papers in a safety deposit box at her bank. All a thief could take were appliances and furniture, all of which were easily replaceable with insurance, but even so, the thought that anyone had walked into her house, let alone touched or taken anything, was upsetting.

After Jane hung up, she checked her watch. It was 10:30 Eastern time. Claire would have gotten her youngest child off to nursery school and should be back at the house. She dialed again.

Claire repeated exactly what Detective Newman had told her. She paused. "Jane, I think he had
a gun. I told the police, but—" She let out a breath.
"Maybe it's no big deal. I'm sure lots of people,
including the pizza boy, have guns, but even so...
there was something..."

"What?"

"Something creepy about him."

The back of Jane's neck tightened. Claire had
four children, half a dozen pets and a seat on the
local PTA. She managed her life and all the trau-
mas that went with motherhood with clockwork
precision and considerable humor. If she thought
something was creepy, then it was.

"If you don't want to keep an eye on the place, I
can get a security firm, or I can come ho—"

"Not on your life. You've waited years to track
down your family, and now you've got rid of that
rat, Cahill, you finally can. When I go over to
check the house, Bill can come with me. He needs
the exercise, anyway."

And no one in their right mind would challenge
Bill Pettigrew. He was six feet two and solidly
built—an ex-Navy engineer who had seen action
in the Middle East.

"And by the way," Claire added, "speaking of
Cahill, it wasn't him last night."

Jane hadn't actually considered that Paul could

be a suspect. Whoever had broken in had been careful to remain concealed and inconspicuous. It had been sheer chance that Claire had arrived at the property while the break-in was in progress. For a start, her ex-husband wasn't much of a handyman and had never bothered with tools. If anything had needed fixing, Jane had usually done it, or called in a professional. Added to that, Paul's bouts of bad temper had always coincided with a half bottle of Southern Comfort—which ruled him out of the meticulous stakes. Sober, he was pretty much incapable of taking a door off its hinges. Drunk, there was no way.

"Whoever it was—" Claire's voice wobbled, "he was taller, and he didn't have—"

"A designer suit?" Jane interjected, trying for a lighter note, because Claire sounded dangerously close to breaking down. "Hair mousse? A pinky ring?"

"—that pretty-boy swagger," Claire finished. "And Paul may have been a clothes horse, but he *never* had a pinky ring."

"He does now. Goes with the new girlfriend."

Claire made an inelegant sound. "Thank goodness you never had children. I'm sure they would have been nice, but that man shouldn't be allowed to breed."

Fourteen

He parked beneath a shady tree, locked his car and studied the imposing facade of Lassiter's library. Pulling a baseball cap down low over his forehead, he adjusted the fit of a pair of thick, horn-rimmed glasses, checked that his mustache was in place, and strolled up the broad fanning steps and into the lobby.

Inside, the building was cool and dim. A children's story hour was taking place in one corner of the room, the murmur of storytelling barely audible beneath the wail of a small baby and the noisy crowing of a chubby toddler as he pulled books from a shelf.

A harassed young mother and the librarian who had been manning the desk lunged to stop the toddler before he emptied the entire shelf, and, briefly, the toddler's screams completely drowned out the storyteller's voice.

When the librarian noticed the man waiting at the desk, she hurried over, her cheeks flushed.

He made his request, and she selected the reels of film he'd asked to view, barely glancing at him as she tried to keep an eye on the toddler, who was once again roaming.

He signed for the microfilms and walked into the room she indicated he could use for viewing: a small office located to one side of the building with a view of the car park. Settling at the desk, he inserted the first reel of film, satisfied that he had barely impinged on the woman's consciousness, and even if he had, she wouldn't remember him as anything more than a middle-aged man with glasses and a mustache.

He scrolled through the first reel, noting the newspaper dates, until he hit the day after Jane's accident and stopped to read the brief report stating that an unidentified female child had been found dead at the scene, presumably the victim of a hit-and-run accident.

He sat back, the coldness building in his chest. That was the report he'd read all those years ago—and believed. Once he'd found out that Jane was dead, he hadn't bothered searching the paper for any further details. As far as he was concerned, there were none to be reported: dead was dead.

With rigid control, he flicked to the next issue and began scanning the pages. His gaze locked on the lead story, and his jaw tightened as he reached for his pen and made a note of the people who had dealt with Jane's case.

He had already checked on the surgeon. Cuvier had died two years ago, so he was no longer a part of the equation. He didn't think it was likely anyone could throw any light on who Jane was, because it would have come out twenty-five years ago when the police and welfare agencies were actively trying to locate her family, but you never knew when some small piece of information might connect with someone.

He scrolled ahead to the next issue and found a candid interview by a junior reporter named Tyrone Brady, a lighter character piece about one of the ambulance officers who had attended Jane's accident. Apparently Arnold Carpenter, who had a reputation for pulling off miracle saves, had persevered despite the fact that Jane had had no pulse. Because of Arnold's efforts, she had started breathing just before they reached Lassiter General. Once she had arrived at the hospital, he had refused to go home, insisting on staying with her until she had gone into surgery. Arnold Carpenter had saved her life, and, in the absence of any family to look out for her, he had felt responsible.

A small photo of Carpenter accompanied the article: a wiry man with a shock of gray hair and a long, thin Gallic nose.

He frowned. He would check and see if Carpenter was still alive. By all accounts he had been on the verge of retirement when he had saved Jane. With any luck, after twenty-five years, he was also dead.

He would also check if Tyrone Brady was still in Lassiter. He'd slipped up once, and the loose end that Jane had become now promised to destroy the life he'd so carefully constructed. This time he didn't plan on leaving anything at all that could connect him to this flea-bitten slice of the South— or Jane Gale.

Carefully removing the reel of film, he took out a handkerchief and wiped it free of prints, then methodically began viewing the remaining reels. When he was finished viewing and taking notes, he double-checked that every reel was clean of prints, then, on impulse, slid the first reel back into the viewer. As he scrolled through to the story he wanted to view again, a vehicle turning into the library parking lot distracted him.

His pulse lifted a notch when he saw that it was a silver SUV, although there was no need to suppose that it belonged to Jane—that particular color and model were popular. Then, as the SUV parked, he caught a glimpse of the plates. Shoving the chair back, he stepped away from the window, just far enough that he could watch without being seen.

Jane pulled her keys out of the ignition, relieved to have a quiet, neutral place to spend the afternoon. Her complaint was registered, and the break-in at her house was being investigated; now all she could do was wait. The break-in—upsetting as it was—couldn't have happened at a better time, because it had increased the officials' urgency to catch the stalker. He had escalated from harassment to breaking and entering, and Claire had been certain he'd had a gun, which had pushed the stakes even higher. Added to that, Miller and Newman now had Claire's eyewitness testimony to back up her own.

Pausing at the front desk, she waited for the librarian, who was busy supervising the end of what looked like a children's story hour. For a few minutes the room was awash with toddlers and young mothers. Her eye was caught by a little boy who was intent on evading the reach of his mother. With a squeal, he wriggled away from her fingers and ran smack into a man's leg. A large hand reached down and steadied the boy, whose bottom lip was now wobbling, but before he could burst into tears, his mother scooped him up, laughing.

For a moment Jane was transfixed by the pretty woman and the plump little boy. As the woman cradled the toddler on one hip and pushed through the door, the baby stuck his thumb in his mouth and began sucking, his expression absorbed, and Jane experienced a sudden fierce pang of longing. The longing took her almost as much by surprise as the earlier sexual arousal had. Children had never been an issue with her and Paul. It had always seemed better to hold off on starting a family until the mortgage was paid or Paul had gotten a promotion he wanted, and, in the end, Jane had been glad. If they'd had a child, she would have been tied to Paul for years.

It seemed that today was a day of emotional highs and lows. Everywhere she went, almost everything she saw, struck a chord, as if here, in her "home" town, she was sensitive to every nuance. She had hoped that being in Lassiter would stir up the past so she could find closure; but it seemed to be having the opposite effect. The past remained locked away, as blank as ever, it was her present that was being disturbed.

The soft burr of a telephone drew her attention back to the front desk. Jane waited until an older woman with a sculpted bob and a librarian's tag hung up, then asked to view microfilm records of old newspapers dating from the week of her accident.

"There's someone using the viewer at the moment." She checked a room that opened off the main library and came back looking perplexed. "The gentleman must have finished. Funny, I didn't see him go."

With brisk movements, the librarian pulled a register from beneath the desk and opened it on the counter.

She ran her finger down the page. "That's a co-incidence. Mr. Brown requested some of the same records."

Jane went still as she watched the librarian pull out a metal drawer and begin searching through a box. Call her cynical, but she didn't trust to coincidence. Mr. Brown was about as phony as Mr. Smith.

"They're not here. I've got records for part of that year, and the year after." She searched through again and frowned "I don't believe this. The reels should have been returned to the desk. It's possible Helen misfiled them, but she isn't sloppy."

"Do you mind if I check the room? It's possible they may still be there."

Heart pounding, Jane searched the room, then sat down at the desk. The seat was still warm, and so was the viewer.

There was a reel of film still threaded into the machine.

Taking a breath, she activated the viewer. A split second later, one of the missing reels came up on the screen, and all the fine hairs at the back of her neck lifted. The screen was paused midway through the original report about her accident, the one that stated she had been pronounced dead at the scene.

For a moment Jane stared blindly at the black and white print; then, pushing her seat back, she lunged for the door, cursing when pain jolted up her leg. She realized that the fact that both the viewer and the seat were still warm meant "Mr. Brown" had just left.

Gritting her teeth, she kicked off her shoes and half limped, half ran, out of the library, halting at the top of the steps as the door swung to behind her. A car turned out of the parking area and into traffic, but the vehicle was a small hatchback with a child peering out of the side window. The young mother at the wheel didn't seem a likely candidate to be her a stalker.

Heart pounding, she shaded her eyes while she scanned the remaining cars, trying to remember what vehicles had been parked when she'd arrived, but when she'd locked the SUV, her sole focus had been on getting inside, out of the heat, not on checking car models and license plates. Besides, so many vehicles had now vacated the parking area, the idea that she could remember what had been there when she had arrived was ridiculous.

The baking heat of the stone steps registered on her bare feet. "Ouch," she muttered.

Limping back inside, she avoided the incredulous stare of the librarian, slipped on her shoes and retrieved her purse. After emptying the Ziploc bag that contained her medication, she gingerly removed the reel of film from the machine, careful to touch only the edges with her fingertips. She wound it up, then enclosed it in the plastic bag and stowed it in her purse. The box it should have slipped into was missing, which meant "Mr. Brown" had probably picked it up in error and taken it with him, along with the other films he'd stolen. The boxes and films were tagged with magnetic strips, so the fact that he had managed to get them out without an alarm sounding meant he had probably dropped them out the window, exited by the front door, then retrieved the boxes from the garden.

Whoever "Mr. Brown" was, she had taken him by surprise. He must have seen her arrive and sneaked out when she'd first walked into the library. A small shudder worked its way up her spine when she considered how close she'd come to meeting him face-to-face. Unless he had gone out the window, as well, he must have walked right by her, just steps away.

She tried to remember who she'd seen in the library. The crowded scene at the front door replayed through her mind: the small toddler cannoning into a man's leg, the hand steadying him. The chill in her spine increased. When she'd first stepped into the library, she hadn't seen any men, and she hadn't noticed any walking past her, which meant that the man she'd seen leaving had in all likelihood been the stalker. She had stared right at him and not seen him.

But he had finally made a mistake. He thought he'd taken all the films, but in his hurry, he'd forgotten the one that was still in the machine.

Grimly, Jane hooked the strap of her handbag over her shoulder and headed for the front desk. She might not have taken note of his face, but now she had an eyewitness who could describe him, and, with any luck, there would be at least two clearly discernible fingerprints on the film in her bag.

He watched as Jane exited the library and limped to her car, critically examining just how incapacitated her injuries had left her. Once he'd found out her new name, it had been incredibly easy to find out almost every detail of her life, including the intimate ones. He had looked up her hospital records and learned that she had made an almost full recovery from injuries that should have killed her. He'd also checked up on her ex-husband—just in case he was still in the picture and could prove to be a problem—and he'd found out that not only was the husband old history, there was no man in her life.

Leaning forward, he started his car and followed the SUV, relieved when the air-conditioning kicked in. Jane pulled in to her motel, and he cruised past, made a left onto LeFort Street and headed for the oldest part of town.

Minutes later, he parked, collected the items he'd bought from the back seat and locked the vehicle.

The padlock securing the shed door was still stiff, but it worked well enough since he'd sprayed it with lubricant. The door swung open on well-oiled hinges, and cobwebs stirred in the faint breeze as he stepped inside. Reaching into the shadows, he found a switch and flicked on a light, then closed the door, shooting the bolt.

With privacy ensured, he lifted the glasses off the bridge of his nose and peeled off his fake moustache. The disguise was rudimentary but effective, and, as it had turned out, he had needed it. The librarian could describe him, but all she would remember was the fact that he was middle-aged and white, and that he had glasses and a mustache. The description fitted a large percentage of Lassiter's male population, which, at this time of year, included a healthy influx of tourists.

He picked up his shopping bags and a flashlight that was stored on a shelf, and moved further into the shed.

The fact that Jane had walked in on him in the library upset him. She had practically looked straight at him, but he didn't see how he could have acted any differently. He had wanted to check if she was researching the past, and the most obvious way had been to get a look at the library's register by requesting to view records himself. Since he was requesting material, it had seemed thorough to check through what she was likely to research and make a list of any leads she might be following.

What he'd seen in one of those old newspapers had shocked him. The information wasn't obvious—years ago, he had missed it—but it was there for anyone who researched with purpose to find.

All in all, the risk had been worth it. Jane arriving at the library at the exact time he was there had just been bad luck.

He turned on his flashlight, ducked through the

trap door, descended the ladder into the storm cellar and walked along the hand-hewn tunnel. Several twists and turns later, he entered a small room.

After setting his bags on the trestle table in the center of the room, he examined his purchases, excitement tightening his chest. When his paraphernalia was set up, he began to work. An hour later, he opened an old wooden trunk positioned in one corner and began setting the scene, irritated to see that despite careful packing with layers of tissue paper and the extra insurance of moth balls, some of the pieces had been attacked by insects. Shaking off a damp sawdust-like residue and the husks of small insect bodies, he began hanging his works of art on the walls. Absorbed, he positioned the latest addition and stepped back to admire his handiwork.

Myra still had her mouth open. She was entirely recognizable.

Thirty minutes later, he emptied out the boxes of microfilm in the bottom of his shopping bag. One of the boxes bounced across the floor, and he realized it was empty.

He picked up the box, opened the flap and stared into the empty cavity. His chest went tight—his heart hammering so hard he couldn't breathe—and for a moment control deserted him.

When his vision finally cleared, he stared blankly

at the carnage. Masks had shattered, hanks of hair and chunks of wax were sprinkled amidst a tangle of uncoiling film, and the charred remnant of a piece of hair that had found its way onto the lit burner filled the room with acrid smoke.

He stared at the mess he'd made, hands twitching, caught in the familiar paralyzing aftermath of his rage, as helpless as a fish flopping on dry land.

It was too late to pull back now. He had followed his plan to the letter and performed the ritual: the kill was complete.

He had also made a monumental mistake. In his hurry to get out of the library, he had left one of the rolls of film in the viewer. He couldn't be certain Jane had discovered it, but he had to assume she had. If that was the case, the reel—complete with his fingerprints—would almost certainly be with the police by now.

Fifteen

Toussaint's pager went off before he reached the office. Pulling onto the side of the road, he thumbed in a short code and got Hazel in dispatch.

"Hey, hotshot, we've got a body, and it's a weird one. Right up your alley."

"I thought I came here to get away from all that?"

"No, sugar, you came here for the women."

Toussaint grinned. He could as good as see the good-natured smile on Hazel's face. She was in her late forties, married, with grown-up kids, and she mothered every cop in the precinct. "Then how come I'm so lonely?"

"From what I've heard, it isn't because the female population hasn't been trying."

"Hey, I date."

"Honey, when you date, the evening doesn't end at nine, if you get my drift."

"Who told you that?"

"Officer Leonard. A very disappointed Officer Leonard, I might add."

"I don't fraternize on the job—"

"Is that what they call it where you come from?"

"—and I don't kiss and tell. And I come from here…originally."

Hazel laughed. The line clicked as she put him through to the chief.

The flies were hovering. They could sniff out a body a mile and a half away, even before it started to smell, and this one had been out in the open all night and a good part of the day.

When Toussaint reached the scene, the patrol officers had secured the area and the evidence techs were ready to go. The woman was partially wrapped in the kind of standard PVC trunk liner that was available from stores across the country. Her head and her legs were visible. After pulling on shoe covers and thin latex gloves, Toussaint walked across the grass and lifted the flap that covered the woman's torso.

Gatreaux caught up and made a gagging sound. "We're gonna need masks."

"If you're going to throw up, make sure you do it away from the body."

Even after years working homicide, Toussaint couldn't be objective looking at a victim, no matter the age or the gender. In his opinion, death didn't become anyone.

Beside his shoulder, the camera clicked and whirred, and he shifted aside while Roland covered all the angles.

The woman had been stabbed several times, and the bruising pointed to a rape. The ligature marks around her neck told him that she had most likely died by strangulation but by far the most disturbing aspect of the body was that her hair had been removed, along with the scalp.

The woman was Caucasian, slim, with good muscle tone. Not young—in her early forties, probably—and tanned, as if she'd recently spent time at the beach. He noticed the white band around the fourth finger of her left hand, denoting that she was married and the ring had only recently been removed. There was also a pale band around her left wrist, where she'd worn a watch, and small piercings in her lobes for earrings. It was hard to make a judgment, given the trauma her body had been subjected to, but given the absence of needle tracks, tattoos and multiple piercings, Toussaint deduced the victim was more likely to be a middle-class woman than a prostitute.

If she was married and had a job, identification should be easier, because she would be missed. On the flip side, it could make the process more difficult, because she probably didn't have a record, so AFIS would come up blank on prints. If their victim lived alone and no one bothered to file a missing-persons report, identification was going to be difficult, with no clothing, no I.D. and no hair on her head.

Toussaint went through the process and made his notes, stepping aside while samples were taken and prints were lifted. The medical examiner arrived to satisfy the legal niceties and pronounce the victim dead. An initial examination was done to ascertain the likely time of death. No big surprises there. She had been dead at least forty-eight hours—long enough for decomposition to have started. Lividity indicated that the open field was not the scene of the homicide; she had been killed elsewhere, then transported to the field and left in easy view of anyone driving or walking along the road.

The killer had taken no particular pains to hide his victim; he had wanted the body to be found quickly.

Toussaint strolled to the point at which the owner of the farm, Alec Wade, had claimed to first see the body. There were no tire tracks flattening the grass, which meant the killer had stopped on the road, flipped open his trunk then carried the body into the field. Any chance at obtaining a clear footprint had been compromised by the fact that both Wade and his dog had walked over the same ground the killer had used. In any case, the probability that they would have been able to obtain a viable print was low, because the ground was too dry to easily indent, and the grass was long, effectively cushioning every step.

Toussaint walked over to where a patrol officer was sitting with Wade. He was shaky. He and his wife had bought the property to retire. They kept a few cows, but they didn't particularly care about making money; they just wanted somewhere peaceful where they could have their dog without neighbors complaining, and where the family could come and visit.

Toussaint let the man talk on until he was relaxed enough to start sipping his coffee, then he slid smoothly into the interview. Half an hour later, he had everything that Wade could give him, which wasn't much.

He handed the man his card. "If you think of anything you missed, give me a call. Sometimes details come back later."

Wade took the card, his fingers shaking.

Toussaint assessed the other man's body language. Wade was automatically a suspect, and they would investigate him, but Toussaint didn't think he'd done it. Whoever had killed the woman had been amoral and calculating. The scene had been carefully thought out, almost staged. Wade barely had the stomach to hold his coffee down, let alone perpetrate a rape-murder in his own backyard.

The evidence tech, Angie, stepped around Roland, a sports bag filled with her equipment in one hand, evidence bags in the other.

Toussaint lifted the crime-scene tape so she could duck under. "Anything useful?"

Angie set the sports bag down, dug in her pocket for the car keys and unlocked the trunk. "No prints. The trunk liner looks new, fresh out of the packet, but…" She held up a paper bag with a label proclaiming that it held a strand of hair. "I'm guessing this belongs to someone special."

"Have you taken a sample from Wade?"

"And the dog." She raised her brows. "He was nicer."

"Lets hope his DNA's on the register."

Angie grinned. "You have got to be joking. He's a Lab. Now, if he was a Rottweiler…"

Later on that evening, Toussaint received a positive ID on the victim's prints, courtesy of a juvenile misdemeanor.

Her name was Myra Waltham, a forty-two-year-old sales rep from Wisconsin. She had disappeared a week ago, after flying to Washington for a conference. Her husband claimed that she had simply never come home.

David Waltham was presently being held for questioning but, despite the fact that, according to his neighbors, he had any number of reasons for wanting his wife dead—one being her frequent infidelities—he wasn't currently on their list of prime suspects.

Waltham owned a shoe store in Wisconsin, and his mother-in-law had moved in for the week to look after their two school-age children. Between working and his home life, Waltham's alibi was firmly in place. Given that he had had dinner at home on the evening in question, and stayed up to watch a TV show with his mother-in-law, he couldn't possibly have been in Lassiter during the window of time in which the killing had taken place. The flight time alone was several hours, and the killing hadn't been quick. Taking into account the various stages of bruising and the partial granulation of some of the wounds, it had been a drawn-out process.

After hours of intensive investigation, they had a preliminary psychological profile, a cross-reference to a bizarre series of old, unsolved murders—

courtesy of the missing hair and the chemical traces found on the victim's face—and no prime suspect.

Toussaint's phone buzzed. He reached for the receiver, not lifting his gaze from the notes he'd made. There was something… He just couldn't make the connection.

"Hey, buddy."

Toussaint suppressed a groan. Tyrone Brady from the *Lassitor Daily*. That was all he needed. Tyrone was a black Creole with an earring in one ear, an engaging grin and the sharpest nose for a story in the business. He played it cool, but he was a barracuda when it came to getting details. "Don't you guys ever sleep?"

"We're just like you, Toussaint. Work all hours at a glamorous job, get paid a small fortune, and the public loves us."

Toussaint's mouth twitched. "Not that I last heard."

"Well, one out of four ain't bad. I heard you boys are burning the midnight oil over there. Care to tell?"

"The chief is issuing a statement in the morning."

"Hmm, let me see, that would be about a female, mid-forties, raped, murdered…and scalped?"

Toussaint let out a breath. "Where did you get that?"

"A little birdie told me."

"You mean you paid someone at the morgue a backhander."

"I'm not at liberty to expose my sources."

"And I'm not at liberty to confirm or deny any details."

"It's one hell of a scary crime for Lassiter, Detective. People are gonna need to know what's happening."

"They will. Tomorrow."

Sixteen

At 5:00 a.m. the next morning, a car slid into the small residential cul-de-sac of a nice neighborhood that backed up to the Palm Court Motel, its headlights extinguished. The door swung open and the driver emerged, a knapsack in one hand.

After opening the knapsack, he pulled on a pair of latex gloves, then slipped on a set of night-vision goggles and, as calmly as if he owned the place, walked up the drive of a brick and tile house. Skirting the pool, he eased through the heavy tangle of undergrowth that filled the back of the property. Breath hissing at the effort it took, he pulled himself up and over a tall board and batten fence, let himself down, and stood in the grounds of the Palm Court Motel.

* * *

Jane woke, eyes wide, heart pounding. The aftermath of a recurring bad dream shuddered through her, and she jackknifed, pushing the covers aside. Her feet sank into carpet as she stood, arms wrapped around her middle while she listened. She didn't know what had woken her aside from the dream—maybe the caretaker getting an early start, or simply the unfamiliar sounds of Lassiter waking up.

Her heart rate returned to something approximating normal as she stared into the smothering blackness. The dream was uncomplicated but persistent; she'd had it off and on ever since she could remember. It involved her running and—surprise, surprise—a shadowy figure chasing her. The wonder of it was that she hadn't experienced any bad dreams months ago, when the stalking had started. For it to happen now, when she had the extra stress of coping with researching her past, was an added annoyance; the one thing she could do with was a good night's sleep.

She stopped, cocking her head, aware that something had changed since her interview with Miller.

Before, everything about the stalker had been deadly serious, now it seemed...diminished. Maybe it was the fact that she had almost caught him red-handed at the library, or the description the librarian had supplied: an older man wearing a baseball cap, balding, with thick glasses and a mustache. Creepy and disturbing as it was, it was hard to feel intimidated when she was being stalked by Groucho Marx.

A rustling sound made her go still. She stepped over to the window, lifted the curtain a bare inch and stared outside, straining to see something—anything. As private and secluded as this unit was in relation to the street, one of the disadvantages was that it was overhung by heavy trees and cut off from the street lighting. The other unit she'd occupied had always had light, even on the darkest nights; this one was stygian inside and out.

A faint breeze rattled through the trees, the sound eerie enough to raise gooseflesh on her skin, and Jane dropped the curtain. If there *was* anyone out there, she would have a hard time hearing him.

The memory of the moment in the library, when the newspaper article about her accident had appeared on the screen, sent a faint shudder through her.

She'd driven straight to the police station, but most of the staff had been in a meeting, and Miller had been out on a call. She'd compromised by leaving the tape at reception for him, a note stapled to the bag. From her own research into police procedures, Jane knew that getting a fingerprint checked could take time. If it happened to belong to a local felon, Miller would have the prints on file, but if the print belonged to someone from out of state, the process could take days. There was also the possibility that there was no record of the print to check against, because the stalker had never been booked for a crime.

The wind lifted, and the rustling turned into a scratching sound as the leaves of the oleander just outside her window scraped against the glass, making her flinch, and something inside Jane snapped.

She was tired of jumping at every sound; tired of waiting for the next intrusion into her privacy; and most of all, she was tired of waiting for Newman and Miller to solve her problems.

Her mind felt clear for the first time in months. She didn't have the resources to catch the criminal who was bothering her—only the police could do that—but there *were* things *she* could do.

The first thing was to change her thinking.

The stalking was getting worse, not fading, which meant that her reaction to the stalker's tactics was satisfying enough that he had upped the stakes. He was getting off on her fear. Solution: cut fear out of the encounters. It was the anticipation that was killing her, not the actual calls. As a child, facing a long list of operations, she had learned to shift her mind away from fear and pain by simply giving herself something else to think about. It had been a while, and she didn't think a game of solitaire would do it, but she would simply apply that tactic to this fear.

The word steadied her, because that was all this involved: tactics. The guy was a shadow, a worm. He skulked, too frightened to show his face. He was probably completely inadequate when dealing directly with women.

The first thing to do was send out her own message. She was going to make it difficult, even unpleasant, for the stalker to continue harassing her. That meant buying herself some time to get organized. For today, at least, she needed to disappear.

She checked the luminous dial of her watch. It was just after five in the morning; the sun would be up soon. If she wanted to get out undetected, she had approximately fifteen minutes.

Slipping her watch onto her wrist, she left the lights off and felt her way around the bed to the chest of drawers that stood against the far wall. Her knee bumped on the corner of the dresser. Simultaneously, her arm brushed against a lamp that she'd forgotten was set on one end. The lamp wobbled and rocked before she steadied it, the sound of the brass base hitting the mahogany veneer alarmingly loud.

Heart thumping, and suppressing the insane desire to laugh, she steadied the lamp, took a deep breath and ran her hand down the drawers until she hit the third one down. Giving herself a stern talking-to, she sobered up, slid the drawer open and rummaged through by feel.

She pulled on a pair of loose cotton trousers and a tank top, and laced on a pair of sneakers. None of the clothes were black, or even particularly dark—in fact, she had no idea what color these particular ones were. Smothering a grin, she felt around until she found a covered elastic band, bumping her knee again on an open drawer, and knocking clothes to the floor. Her first priority was to get out of the motel unseen, the second to act as normal and as invisible as possible when the sun did come up. If it turned out she'd mismatched her colors, she would have to go shopping.

Scraping her hair back, she coiled it at her nape and secured it with the band; then, feeling for the edge of the bed, she sat down and tied a cotton scarf around her head to hide her hair, knotting it at her nape so it wouldn't come adrift. As disguises went, it wasn't much, but it would do until she got away from the motel.

Hooking the strap of her purse over her shoulder, she felt her way out to the lounge. On impulse, she took the time to collect her cell phone, which she'd left on the coffee table, and slipped it into her bag. The phone might be a liability in terms of the calls she'd been receiving, but it could also keep her safe.

She paused at the front door, her hand on the knob. *No. Uh-uh.*

Somebody was stalking her, and she had no idea of the hours he kept. Whether he was dangerous or not, she had to assume that he was watching this unit, and that would most likely mean the front door. If she wanted to leave undetected, she would have to do it another way.

Retracing her steps, she stopped at the bathroom and opened the cabinet over the vanity. She ran her fingers along the first shelf until they knocked against a box. She slipped the box into her bag, then repeated the action until the contents of the bottom two shelves—which contained her pain medication—were in her bag. If Groucho broke in, he wouldn't get away with her codeine.

Flattening one palm against the wall, she moved out of the bathroom, then went left at the door, in the direction of her bedroom. When she reached the open doorway, a faint grayness around the curtains told her she was out of time.

The sliding door into the lounge slid open and was just as quietly closed.

The man shrugged out of his knapsack and set it on the carpet. With efficient movements, he removed a pistol, checked to be sure the clip was securely in place and slipped the gun into a black shoulder holster that was invisible against the black of his sweatshirt. The unit was darker than he'd expected, so he left the night vision gear in place. Sliding a knife from the pack, he straightened, the blade held at his side.

A faint sound jerked his head around. Moving slowly in the confined quarters, his peripheral vision impaired by the night vision gear, he padded toward the hallway that led to the bedroom.

Jane ignored the bedroom's sliding door, which opened onto the front deck, and stepped across to the window. Because this particular unit had been built near the utility area, where the space was too confined to build two units back-to-back, the window opened onto a dense wall of shrubbery. She zipped her bag closed and pulled the strap over her head so that the bag hung, satchel-like, beneath one arm.

Slipping behind the curtain, she gently opened the window and pushed the sash wide. Gripping the ledge, she lifted first one leg over, then pivoted and lifted the other over, grimacing as damp oleander leaves brushed her arms. She held herself suspended for a beat, avoiding the temptation to simply drop onto the ground and risk making a noise, then lowered herself slowly, the motion smooth.

The room was empty.

He glided to the bed and stopped. In the greenish light of the goggles, the contents of the room were clear: a double bed, a chest of drawers, a dressing table.

He placed his hand on the rumpled bed. It was still warm.

Wary now, he moved across to the closet. When he ascertained that was empty, he checked beneath the bed, then systematically began searching the unit.

He returned to the bedroom and surveyed the unmade bed and a drawer that hung open, tilted at a slight angle, and frowned at the sloppiness. He couldn't believe it. She had escaped.

It was possible she had gone for an early morning walk. Her medical reports had indicated that, because of the severity of her injuries, she kept up a high level of physical activity. She had needed to push herself to rehabilitate her body and to keep it at a level where she could function normally. But the last report had been made ten years ago, when Jane had been in her early twenties and had undergone an operation to free up nerves caught in scar tissue. He hadn't been able to isolate any details about her medical history since, and he had assumed that for the past ten years she had settled into a fairly sedentary lifestyle.

It was possible she was still a fitness nut, but not likely. He'd watched her at the library and at the motel unit the previous evening. Both times she had been limping, and last night she'd relied heavily on her cane. If she was out walking, it would be a short one.

Sliding the knife back into its sheath, he checked the bathroom and noticed the medicine cabinet door left ajar.

Abruptly, the untidiness irritated him.

Somehow the disarray didn't seem characteristic. The book Jane had written had had more emotion than he liked, but she hadn't minced words, and she hadn't wasted any, either; she had been precise about the details. He had automatically assumed that in her personal life she would be just as neat and tidy; it was unsettling to discover he was wrong.

That element of the unknown was one of the things he disliked about this situation. As much as he'd studied her over the past few days, Jane was still an enigma.

Moving back out into the living area, he stared at the pristine neatness of the lounge. The kitchen was also tidy. He surveyed the order with a sense of satisfaction: a place for everything, and everything in its place.

He checked the cupboards and the dishwasher. She hadn't had breakfast yet, which could account for the fact that she hadn't made a mess and would also mean she should be back soon.

He stood at the sliding glass door in the lounge, surveying the area out in front of the unit through a small gap in the curtains. Her SUV was still parked in the carport. Satisfied that she couldn't be too far away, he returned to the bedroom.

He was in now. He could wait.

Jane inched through the unkempt garden at the rear of her unit, and into the denser belt of trees and palms that ran along the fence line at the rear of the property. Her unit was directly behind her, the carport off to the left. If she veered right, she would walk into the side of the adjacent unit, which stuck out at an angle. Finding the fence—and her escape route—should be a cinch, but it was still so dark beneath the thick cluster of trees that she could barely see her hands held out in front of her.

Brushing the fleshy leaf of a shrub aside, she ducked her head, trying to avoid the inevitable shower of moisture. Water dripped off every leaf and literally poured off some; already her scarf and shoulders were drenched. Her palms hit solid wood, and she halted her forward movement and felt upward. The fence was wooden, not masonry, which should make it easier to climb, but it was higher than she'd bargained on. Clearly Mayet had a thing about privacy.

She paced a few steps to the right, then to left. There was more light right next to the fence, where the bushes had been chopped back and cleared away, probably to protect the fence itself, but the clean-up had stripped the trees of their lower branches and left her without a foothold.

With one dicey leg, she needed a boost up. Once she could get leverage, with the strength in her arms—put there by years of levering herself in and out of wheelchairs, then by regular swimming—getting over the top wouldn't be a problem.

It occurred to her that Mayet would have at least one ladder in the tool shed next to where the SUV was parked, but she instantly dismissed even attempting to gain access to the shed. He would certainly have it locked and probably alarmed.

Pushing back a vine, she inched through a thick wall of shrubs and stood at the edge of the motel drive. A faint mist wreathed the unit she'd just bailed out of and left condensation on the windows.

Now that she was actually outside, the scare she'd had seemed faintly ridiculous. If she was at home and Claire caught her sneaking around like a commando in the early dawn, she would never live it down.

She shifted position slightly, easing the load on her weak leg. A cold shower of droplets splashed down from the overhanging branches, further wetting the bare skin of her shoulders and making her shiver. As ridiculous as skulking in the motel garden at five in the morning might seem, her reality was that her home wasn't safe, either. Her house had been broken into, and Claire had had the fright of her life.

The description of the anonymous figure walking away with something that had looked like a gun at his side sent a rivulet of cold down her spine. He didn't sound like the same man in the library, but then it had been dark, and Claire had been justifiably upset. Ridiculous or not, she had to be cautious.

Edging along a few more feet, she came within inches of the carport and the SUV. She unzipped her bag and felt around for the keys. It was tempting to simply walk the few steps it would take, climb into the vehicle and drive away.

A faint rustling made her stiffen. She stepped back further into the shelter of the trees and onto something that moved.

A yowl erupted from beneath her foot.

A dark shape rocketed through the undergrowth and across the drive, now clearly visible in the early morning light. It was a big tortoiseshell cat, the size of a small dog—and it looked like it would bite. Mayet's cat had been creeping up on her in the dark.

When her heart stopped pounding, Jane let go of her keys and adjusted the strap of her bag on her shoulder. The sun was up. If she walked across to the carport she would be clearly visible. Turning on her heel, she returned to the fence.

From memory, the fence extended across the entire back of the motel complex, enclosing the pool area and the car park out front. The whole place was hemmed in like a concentration camp.

Gritting her teeth, she jumped. Pain jolted along her spine as she hooked her arms over the top, and her bag smacked against the wood making a loud slapping sound. *So much for a covert operation.*

She twisted and managed to get one leg over, then the other. Taking a deep breath, she lowered herself to the other side and began negotiating the backyard she'd ended up in. With her luck, there would be another monster cat.

A low-pitched growl told her it wasn't a cat this time.

As she emerged from beneath a row of fruit trees, she saw the neat shape of a back yard with planted borders, a manicured lawn, two gnomes poised with fishing rods over a limpid pond—and a large pen that contained what looked like a big, muscular black lion.

"Hey, boy," she whispered as she limped past. She was good with dogs. They loved her.

The rottweiler threw itself at the enclosure. The clash of chain link was drowned out by a deep throaty roar, and a line of slobber arced through the air, glistening like quicksilver as it wrapped around a small decorative shrub.

Jane limped faster.

The blurred image of a face appeared at the window of the house. In the split-second glimpse she had it resembled nothing so much as a mirror image of Mayet—this time in curlers.

Busted by someone who looked like she could be Mayet's sister.

Jane groaned and made a beeline for the road.

Seventeen

The sun slid over the jagged montage of city buildings and the distant line of masts that marked the snaking contours of the Lassiter River as Jane walked into a twenty-four-hour service station. Fifteen minutes later, she'd freshened up, established that she was color coordinated in a hot pink tank, and navy pants and scarf, bought coffee and a stale sandwich, and found a phone booth that still had a directory in it. While she ate and sipped the coffee, she checked through the listings of rental car agencies. When she had finished her breakfast, she tossed the crumpled cup and wrapper in a nearby bin, and strolled up the sidewalk, looking for a taxi.

It was 7:30 in the morning. She had at least an hour to kill before any of the rental agencies opened. On impulse, she walked into the park. A jogger ran past, and then another. An elderly woman strolled by with a big, friendly golden retriever ambling at her side. Further along, on a grassy bluff above the river, an early morning aerobics class was in session.

She unwound the scarf from her hair, spread it out on a flat area and sat down. Automatically, she began to run through a series of stretching exercises, working her muscles until the stiffness in her lower back and thighs began to ease; then she moved on to more precise sets of exercises, working individual muscle groups until her skin was flushed with heat. It had been days since she'd worked out properly, and she couldn't do her normal routine here. For that she needed weights, a gym and a pool, but in the meantime she could enjoy the morning and reflect on the fact that, finally, she had applied her intellect to the stalker problem.

Just after nine, she climbed out of a taxi and paused on the sidewalk in front of a rental agency. Sliding her phone out of her bag, she called the rental company she'd hired the SUV from and asked them to collect the vehicle from the motel. She hadn't left anything in it, and it was clean. They would charge her for the pick-up, but if she wanted to remain incognito for the day, it would be worth it.

As she slipped the phone back in her bag and stepped inside the agency, it rang. She checked the "Private Caller" message flashing on the screen. Her stomach did a familiar somersault, then knotted up, making her feel sick. Gritting her teeth, she reminded herself that this was Groucho she was dealing with, not Carlos, "The Jackal," picked up the call and lifted the phone to her ear. "Piss off."

She thumbed the disconnect button and shoved the phone back in her bag, satisfaction easing her tension. That should fix his male fantasy.

An attendant cleared his throat.

Jane lifted her head, still glaring. "I want to rent a vehicle."

"Yes, *ma'am*."

He ducked down and pulled a book from beneath the counter, and Jane hid a grin. If that was what it took to get some respect, maybe she would do it more often.

He opened the book and spun it so she could see the list of vehicles and prices. "Did you have anything particular in mind, ma'am?"

She was tempted to say, "A truck—four-wheel-drive," just to keep the respect flowing, but the jump required to get in the driver's seat was more than she could manage. She looked down the list. Her reality was comfortable seating and plenty of legroom—nothing too low-slung or too high. And she needed anonymity. "I'll take the Ford sedan. Four door."

He looked vaguely disappointed, but what the heck. She wasn't responsible for *his* fantasies, either.

After leaving a message for Miller to see if he'd come up with anything on the microfilm, Jane went for a drive to examine the stretch of road where her accident had happened.

Sugar Hill Road was no longer the narrow, deserted country lane it had once been. Over two decades of expansion had seen Lassiter sprawl out into its hinterland, and now the road no longer traversed an empty stretch of farmland but a conglomeration of suburbs and small farms, most of them comprising just an acre or two, and an industrial area clustered around the old sugar plant itself.

Jane drove slowly, eyeing the houses and front yards, looking for one that was old enough to have been around when she was a child. This section of road was arrow straight and, according to local legend, a speed trap and an accident hazard, because people always drove too fast.

The police report noted that while the notorious straight had been a contributing factor in her accident, it had also probably saved her life, because if the road had been winding, the chances were no one would have seen her after she was hit.

But as connected as this stretch of highway was with her past, her mind stubbornly failed to see anything even remotely familiar in the landscape. It was a possibility that she had been hit elsewhere, then dropped on this stretch of road and left, but not likely. *She had had her duffel bag with her—*

Jane braked; the car rocked to a halt. A truck cruised up behind her, honked and blew past, almost catching the front bumper of the Ford, and she realized she'd stopped in the middle of the road. With clumsy movements, she turned the wheel and depressed the accelerator. The vehicle jumped ahead, tires crunching on gravel, rear end fishtailing as she hit the softer surface of the shoulder, plowed through a clump of weeds and came to rest on a thick cushion of roadside grass.

Moving on automatic pilot, she killed the motor, pushed the door open and climbed out, desperate to recapture the moment that had spawned that breakthrough and find her way back to the tiny chink that had opened up in her mind.

The wind was hot on her face, the scent of burning rubber pervasive, but she felt curiously disconnected from the physical details. Her mind was focused on what was happening inside her.

She had had her bag with her.

A burning pressure started behind her eyes; her chest felt crushed by emotion. For a split second she had connected with the child she'd been. She didn't think she had experienced an actual memory; what had happened had been less direct, more a tapping into the knowledge that child had had.

That child.

Jane found herself sitting on the ground, arms wrapped around her knees, legs folded up close to her chest, rocking. She felt as if she were staring down a tunnel, staring back in time, her head on fire, her skin icy.

Always before she had managed to distance herself from that little girl, hide behind the myriad facts and details of the investigation and the newspaper reports, but that child had been *her,* and something had happened. Something bad.

She had been running away; she was certain of it. Why else would a child—would *she*—have been alone on the road at night?

She had been running from something, and then the accident had happened.

Before, she'd concentrated on why she'd had so little with her—a candy bar and a photograph tucked in her pocket—rather than on *why* she'd been on the road that night. The mystery of the photograph, a tantalizing link to the past, and the family that had never shown up to claim her had consumed her. Now the fact that she had been only seven years old and alone hit her like a belly punch.

She had studied the police report countless times, and she knew she was practically sitting on the spot where the accident had happened. She stared at the road, eyes blind, still focused inward. Chills shuddered through her, as if the fragile imprint of the past was still here, shimmering around her, filtering into her skin. She could almost feel, almost reach through and touch...

"Are you all right? Do you want me to call an ambulance?"

Jane's head jerked up. The voice was cracked and raspy with age, and belonged to a woman who was eighty-plus if she was a day.

The old lady indicated her cane. "I'd make it across that rough patch, but I'd probably break a leg, and then I wouldn't be any use to you at all."

"It's all right." Dazed, Jane pushed herself to her feet to prove she was fine. She hadn't heard the woman's car, but it was there, a small dusty Subaru parked in the entrance to a driveway.

The old lady eyed the Ford doubtfully. "If you need a lift...?"

"The car's okay, I just had a little scare—and a tangle with a truck."

"Carl Reding passed me in his truck further down the road, almost put me in the ditch. Twenty years ago, his daddy did the same thing. Same family, different truck," she said dryly. Shaking her head, she began the slow progress back to her car. "This piece of road is a killer."

The mention of the amount of time that had passed between near-accidents galvanized Jane. "Wait." Reaching inside the driver's side door, she retrieved her handbag and pulled out the photo of herself when she was small. If the woman had been living in Lassiter when she'd been hurt, she might recall something. Briefly she recounted the facts of the accident.

The woman rummaged in her bag, fitted a pair of spectacles to her nose and studied the photograph. She lifted her head and peered at Jane over the top of the lenses. "You're *that* little girl?"

Hope flared. "You remember me?"

"I remember the night you got hit." She gestured into the distance. "My name's Fay Collins, and that's my place over there, behind that subdivision. When the accident happened, none of those houses were there, just trees. I remember seeing the lights…." She focused back on Jane. "That was a long time ago. My husband, Eric, was alive then."

"Twenty-five years."

She frowned. "I was sure you died. I remember thinking how awful it was that a child had been killed."

"I was pronounced dead at the scene, but one of

the ambulance officers kept working on me when everyone else had given up."

Fay handed the photo back. "That would be Arnold Carpenter. He was an ambulance officer for years. Arnold hated to lose anyone. I remember when he pulled old Herb Reding out of the river. Herb was usually drunk as a skunk, and that day was no different, except that he'd died. Somehow Arnold managed to bring him back, but he was reeling by the time he finished. He swore black and blue Herb's lungs were full of whiskey and not river water."

Jane slipped the photo back in her bag, heart pounding, fingers shaking. Meeting Fay Collins was a breakthrough. Fay had remembered her— even if it had only been *after* the accident had taken place—and now she had another name: Arnold Carpenter. He was a local and had been tied in with the ambulance service for years. It was possible that he might know something about her that everyone else had missed.

"Is Arnold still alive?"

Fay tossed her cane into the back seat of her car, then levered herself into the driver's seat. She chuckled. "He's alive, all right. Arnold's no fonder of giving up his own life than anyone else's. Last count, he was eighty and still going strong. It's a standing joke that Arnold Carpenter won't be shuffling off this mortal coil until he's good and ready."

* * *

Jane parked the Ford out on Landry Street, half a block from the motel, collected her purse and locked the sedan. She had already dropped off the keys for the SUV at the rental company office and ascertained that they had collected the vehicle. Now all she had to do was pack and leave, attracting as little notice as possible. Given that it was full daylight, the hope that she could leave undetected was faint, but she was no longer as apprehensive of the stalker. The fact that he had broken into her house was frightening, but giving him his marching orders over the phone had slammed the door on her fear. He wasn't infallible—just persistent— and he had already made a mistake in leaving that microfiche at the library. Sooner or later he would be caught.

She started toward the motel unit, sticking to the shaded areas and adopting the slow, leisurely pace that worked so well in the sultry afternoon heat. She could hear children splashing in the pool and the distant bark of a dog. A fat bumblebee weaved in front of her, its hum almost ridiculously loud as it zeroed in on a colorful hibiscus flower. Somewhere a lawnmower started. The noises were innocuous and everyday, and redolent of summer. As she stepped out from beneath the sheltered overhang of the motel, she automatically pushed her dark glasses more firmly onto the bridge of her nose. Heat sank into her skin, and the tension generated by her roadside encounter drained away. For the first time in months, the threat of the stalker didn't feel overwhelming. For the first time in months, she felt she could breathe.

As she rounded the corner, a cooling breeze provided relief from the heavy heat, and the empty carport came into view. She reached into her handbag and extracted her door key. As she settled the strap of her handbag more comfortably on her shoulder, a faint movement caught her eye.

She slowed, fingers tightening on the key. The movement came again. The curtain in the lounge had moved.

Frowning, she stepped sideways, taking cover beneath the feathery shade of a clump of palm trees. The breeze gusted more strongly, and another movement drew her eye, this time to the left of the curtain. The front door was open.

Automatically, her mind flipped through options, searching for a legitimate reason for the door to be open. Housekeeping could be extra busy and working late, or maybe this unit at the back was last on the list. The breeze gusted again, and this time the front door blew open all the way, giving her a view of the living area, although she couldn't make out much because all the curtains were pulled and the sun was on the opposite side of the building.

Gaze fixed on the darkened opening, every muscle on alert, she moved forward. As she mounted the steps to the small deck, it became obvious that whoever had been inside, it hadn't been housekeeping. The couch had been overturned, the cushions slit. Shreds of fabric and stuffing trailed over the floor, and glass littered the carpet where a vase had been smashed into the television screen.

Backing away from the door, she fumbled for her cell phone, turned it on, and searched for the number of the Lassiter PD.

Her phone beeped while she selected the number, and she registered that she had three new messages.

She put the call through and waited for reception to pick up. Detective Miller wasn't in, but they could put her through to someone else.

Seconds later the phone rang on an extension and a dark, masculine voice answered. John Toussaint.

Jane swallowed, for a moment utterly blank. Her chest felt tight, her throat locked closed, and with a choking, gasping sound, she hung up.

Eighteen

Toussaint punched the number that connected him back to the front desk. "Who did you just put through?"

"A woman. She wanted Miller."

"Figures." Thoughtfully, Toussaint hung up.

The small choking sound replayed in his mind. He frowned, and pushed his chair back from his desk and the series of memos that had been generated more than two decades ago. Maybe it was because of the material he had been reading through, but it passed through his mind that the caller could be Jane Gale.

The phone rang. It was Hazel again.

"There's been a break-in at the Palm Court motel down on Landry Street. Someone needs to get down there right away, before the motel owner, Alfred Mayet, has a coronary."

"What about Miller?"

"Miller's just called in. His kid's home sick from school. And before you ask, Burrell's working late shift today, Charpentier and Gautreaux are already out on a call, Smith's off sick, and Wade and Boulet are down in the interview room with a suspect. You're it, honey."

Toussaint reached for his jacket, reluctant to leave the Waltham case, but he had wanted hands on and he had wanted a small town. Looked like he had both. "I'm on my way."

Hazel gave him the address. "And, by the way, just so you know, the motel unit that got broken into belongs to the same woman Miller's been dealing with over a harassment case. A Ms. Jane Gale."

Toussaint's attention sharpened, his interest more than piqued.

He found the file on Miller's desk and took a few minutes to read through the notes. Apparently Jane Gale had hit the bestseller lists, and all the weirdos had come out of the cracks. One of them had turned out to be her ex-husband. He hadn't understood the word "no" on two occasions, and both times he'd been talking with his fists.

He had thought the woman who had just called

and made that small sound could have been Jane; now he was certain of it.

Minutes later, he was in traffic, negotiating the mini-rush hour that clogged Lassiter's streets when school was out, his mind still on Jane.

When she'd walked into the station yesterday in that classy pant suit, her hair piled on top of her head, she'd looked good enough to stop traffic. Miller had been dazzled; he had been dazzled. She was clipped and cool, as pale as a magnolia, with a northern bite he guessed he'd gotten addicted to.

But whether he was intrigued or not, he would have to keep it on ice. Mixing business and pleasure was never a good idea, and especially not in a town the size of Lassiter. The situation was volatile enough as it was. One way or another, both times Ms. Gale had hit Lassiter, she had managed to place herself at the center of a crime wave.

Jane positioned herself in front of the open front door of her unit, her jaw set. Ever since she had informed Mayet that the unit had been broken into, he had spent his time alternately trying to barrel his way past her to inspect the damage, and beating a path between his office and her unit, barking into a phone, haranguing both the police and the firm that had supplied the locks.

Everyone within a one-yard radius—plus a chunk of downtown Lassiter—knew by now that Mayet wasn't happy. Someone was messing with his phones and smashing up his motel, and a mat that had sat in the center of the living area had been stolen. The patrol car that had pulled into the parking space right out in front of reception wasn't a good advertisement for business, and now, just to tick him off, the press had arrived.

The reporter who stepped around Mayet as the motel owner waylaid the uniformed officers paused at the bottom of the steps, camera in hand, and introduced himself as Tyrone Brady. He cocked his head to one side. "Don't I know you?"

"No." Jane, used to cameras, and avoiding the press, simply sat down on one of the two small chairs situated to one side of her front door and turned her back on Brady, making it difficult for him to photograph her. He would have to walk through the garden and crouch down to achieve any kind of publishable angle.

He surprised her by taking the other seat. "Yeah, I do know you. You're the lady author from out of town: Lassiter's very own Jane Doe. Heard you've had a few problems." He craned around to look inside the door, lifted his camera and clicked the shutter. "From the look of your unit, more than just a few."

Jane reached into her bag and took out her diary. "No comment."

Brady was at the top of her list of people to interview. Along with Arnold Carpenter, he had attended her accident; he was the reporter who had filed the story stating she had died. But not now. Not today. If Brady wanted to persist, he would, but at the moment, intruding on her privacy would be downright rude. With relief, she saw that the two officers had finally reached the scene of the crime, naturally with Mayet in tow.

"Okay," Brady said, frustrated, "so where's my story?"

Mayet took the bait like a hungry shark. The diatribe was lengthy and detailed; Brady's eyes glazed over after the first sentence. This was a difficult town, and Mayet wasn't a wealthy man. He relied on regular business clientele to make a buck and not the fickle tourist trade—of which Jane was a part. The last thing he needed was to look like some two-bit pimp caught with his pants down, or, worse, some kind of clearing house for weirdos which, Jane construed, also applied to her.

Two more officers arrived—a woman and a man. Then a dark voice cut Mayet off in midstream. "Where is she?"

Jane's stomach clenched. She stood and turned, using the back of the chair for support. Toussaint's gaze touched on hers, and for a moment she felt ridiculously connected to him.

"You covering this, Toussaint?" Brady sounded like a cat that had gotten the cream. "That's like sending in a cannon to shoot down a bird with a broken wing. Where's the fire?"

"Stow it, Brady. What you see is what you get."

"Now *that* I seriously doubt." Brady shoved his notebook in his pocket and slipped the cap back on his lens. He glanced at the trashed unit and lifted his shoulders. "This time, maybe. But, Toussaint? Call me when something does happen, huh?"

Toussaint surveyed the destruction. "You've pissed off someone."

Jane winced at the wording. Her moment of triumph had rebounded on her with a vengeance. "A fan who doesn't like taking 'no' for an answer. He called my cell phone today. I told him where to go."

"Looks like he's no good at following orders."

The female officer, Angie, appeared at the open door with a baseball bat held gingerly in one gloved hand. "He used this. And a knife. Although we can't find anything sharper than a bread knife, so either he took it with him or used one of his own."

Toussaint jerked his head toward his car, offering her a comfortable seat while he and his partner worked through the process, then moved to the devastation of the motel unit.

Jane sat down, relieved to be off her feet and insulated from the proceedings. She watched as he worked the scene: calm and collected, a wink for the fingerprint tech, a conversation in some kind of male code about a football game for the photographer. And all the time, Mayet paced the fringes like an enraged Chihuahua.

Toussaint came and sat down beside her, and passed her a paper cup. "Coffee. Sorry, it's a bit cold now, but it's got plenty of sugar in it."

Jane sipped and watched while he made notes. With his attention directed away from her, he was easier to study. When he was finished, he sat back, his gaze unreadable.

Jane stared into her cup. She noticed he took his coffee black, so he had gotten this specifically for her. Very smooth. She lifted a brow. "Now for the interview."

"You've been through a few. I've read the notes Miller made."

Jane finished the coffee and felt her heart rate kick up a few beats as the caffeine flooded her bloodstream—or it could be Toussaint. As men went, even in a suit—*most especially in a suit*— he was an adrenaline rush.

She filled him in on the state of play with the

stalker. She toyed with the empty cup and finally slotted it into the drink holder. "I think it's the same guy who's been calling me, although one of the calls was…different." She stared at a flowering hibiscus and tried not to shudder. "He didn't speak."

"And he usually does?"

"He likes the sound of his own voice."

"Anything else different about that particular call?"

She drew a measured breath. "He knew exactly where I was. He didn't call my cell phone, he called the *motel* and asked for me by name. Only a handful of people knew where I was staying. My mother, my neighbor, my agent—and you."

"And your stalker. Or one of them."

"No. Yes." She shrugged, confused. The thought that there could be two different stalkers made her stomach churn. "Someone knows." She rubbed her brow and wondered if her headache was going to turn into a migraine. "It's got to be the same guy. Detective Newman said he would escalate, that he would start following me physically. Looks like he was right."

Toussaint flipped his notebook closed. "Miller checked on the phone records to see where the call originated from, but the number was blocked, so it's going to be tough, if not impossible, to trace him. If it's the same guy, he's not averse to getting up close and personal, and he's also experienced at breaking and entering, which broadens his profile."

Mayet tapped on the window.

Toussaint's gaze connected with hers. "Will you be okay here?"

"Sure." Better than out there with Mayet.

"I'll see what I can salvage, but it looks like he didn't leave much. Have you contacted your insurance company?"

Insurance. That mundane detail, on the heels of the shock she'd just had, was abruptly too much. "My favorite thing to do."

He picked up his cold coffee and drank, his throat working steadily. "No matter what happens, there's always paperwork."

Mayet tapped again, and Toussaint set the empty cup in the drink holder, pushed the door open and stepped outside.

Toussaint took Mayet up onto the deck, so he could keep an eye on progress inside the unit while he conducted the interview. From what he'd seen since he'd been in Lassiter, the evidence team was thorough. Angie was famous for taking her time. In true Louisiana style, her voice and movements were slow and graceful, but that outward appearance of indolence was deceptive. If Angie missed something, it didn't exist.

Roland was the opposite of Angie in appearance: tall, thin and restless, with a wicked sense of humor that covered up a good mind. As casual as they both seemed, Angie and Roland were a good team. They had attitude, which, in Toussaint's opinion, was a sign that they cared.

Mayet jerked his head in the direction of Toussaint's car. "Maybe *she* trashed the room."

"Ms. Gale called it in to begin with."

"Doesn't mean anything."

Toussaint turned his head. Jane was still in his car, her passenger window open to let in the faint breeze. She could hear every word. "Jane, hold up your hands."

They were slim, elegant. "It's not her." He held up a plastic bag containing the thumbprint they'd lifted off the baseball bat that had been left in the bedroom. "Whoever used the baseball bat was large, male and too dumb to wear gloves."

"I don't care if she didn't do it." Mayet crossed his arms over his chest. "She can find somewhere else to stay."

Toussaint's gaze strayed around the room and came to rest on the lighter patch of carpet where the mat under the coffee table had been. The sun struck in at an acute angle and picked out a dull spot. He stepped into the room and went down on his haunches. "Angie, there's blood beside the coffee table."

There wasn't much—just enough to darken a few fibers—but enough to get a conviction. Angie waited for Roland to finish with his camera, then opened a small paper envelope and pulled a pair of scissors from her kit.

Mayet stepped in the door.

Angie's dark eyes snapped. "*Out,* or I'll have you restrained."

Toussaint straightened, and Mayet reverted to muttered Cajun. Angie calmly snipped the fibers she needed, picked them up with tweezers, and transferred them to the envelope and labeled it. "Maybe our boy cut himself while he was having his little party?"

"And maybe pigs can fly." It was always possible that the blood belonged to the vandal, but with the knife *and* the mat missing, Toussaint didn't think so.

Half an hour later, with the evidence team gone, Mayet finally distracted by a tour bus and an APB out on the maid who'd been scheduled to clear the unit, Toussaint walked Jane into the vandalized living room.

He didn't think the maid was involved with the

crime; it was more likely that she had looked at the mess, thought about the problem she was going to have dealing with Mayet, and walked, but he was interested in anything she might have seen. Especially in light on the fact that he had found signs of a forced entry in not one place, but two.

Mayet had sworn that the doors had been in perfect condition before Jane moved in, and Toussaint was inclined to believe him. The motel owner was irritating, but he was particular, and both sets of marks had been fresh. But it did leave him with an interesting situation. One break-in was believable. Two, on the same day, wasn't.

Pausing just inside the front door, Jane surveyed the destruction. She was still a little shaky, but now that she'd recovered from the first shock, she was able to take in a detail that normally she would never have missed. "My laptop's gone. It was sitting on the dining table."

Toussaint flipped out a small notebook and made a note. "Do you have details?"

"Not on me. The details were in the case and—"

"—naturally, he took the case. Anything else?"

The faint humor in Toussaint's voice penetrated. He could have left this part to a patrol officer, but from the first moment he'd arrived, he had been keeping an eye on her and had created a barrier Mayet hadn't been able to get past. After the way they'd met and the blank finality of leaving his house the night before last, Toussaint had to be the most unlikely dragon slayer she'd ever met. "Just my sanity. I was practically wired into that laptop."

She skirted the dining table, gingerly stepping over a dollop of boysenberry yogurt that had soaked into the carpet. The kitchen was awash in cereal, and in the bathroom, cosmetics and toiletries had been emptied onto the floor, and her shampoo and conditioner had been squirted onto the tiled walls like ketchup.

In her bedroom, every piece of clothing had been slashed, along with her suitcase. Jane picked up as she went, using the suitcase as a trash can. Mayet would get professional cleaners in, but still, she didn't like the idea of anyone else handling personal articles like her clothing.

Toussaint fitted an empty drawer back into its place in the dresser, then began helping her clean up. He tossed a handful of scraps of lace into the gutted suitcase. "Looks like he left no stone unturned."

Jane felt her cheeks warm. That lace had once been underwear.

Toussaint's phone beeped, and he straightened, walking from the room as he answered the call. She could hear the low register of his voice as he talked out in the living room. As she piled ripped bedding in a corner, a part of her stayed attuned to him. She hadn't thought about it in a long time, but there was a certain bedrock comfort in having a man around. Toussaint, by his mere presence, had somehow neutralized the shock of the vandalism, reducing its impact so that, one step at a time, she had coped with it.

Half an hour later the worst of the mess was dealt with and Jane had isolated the only other item that was missing: a small pouch of jewelry containing earrings, a diamond pendant she'd received as a twenty-first birthday gift from her adoptive parents, and a charm bracelet. The jewelry was technically replaceable, and every piece was covered by insurance, but the pendant and the charm bracelet were an emotional loss.

The bracelet was delicately made and engraved with her name. Catherine Gale had given it to her on the day the adoption had been approved, the day that had become her official birthday. Every year she had received a new charm, and it had become as much a highlight for Catherine as it had been for Jane to unwrap each new addition.

Tossing the cloth she'd used to wipe down the bathroom in the laundry basket, Jane returned to the living room, feeling distinctly shaky. The day had started on a discordant note with her early morning escapade, and it hadn't improved. The charm bracelet had meant a great deal to her. Each piece had been carefully selected and given with love: a teddy bear for her seventh birthday, a butterfly when she'd turned eight, a tiny ballet dancer the year she'd finally gotten out of the wheelchair and walked. There had been fourteen charms in all, the last one given on her twentieth birthday, and each one was a treasure trove of memories.

Toussaint pocketed his cell phone, his gaze sharp. "What's happened?"

"My jewelry's gone."

He didn't ask if her insurance would cover it. Something on her face must have told him that no amount of money would cover this loss.

Toussaint made her sit down out on the deck while he made a hot drink. Relieved to be out of the unit, breathing fresh air, Jane sat, then obediently sipped her second cup of hot, sugary coffee while Toussaint noted down a description of the missing pieces and periodically answered his phone, which seemed to ring every few minutes.

The sugar and the warm breeze—the sheer normality of Toussaint's voice as he answered calls—steadied her. The only positive to the day was that since she was no longer door knocking, she had taken all of her cash and credit cards with her, so the thief hadn't managed to get his hands on those. But now, other than what was in her handbag, she effectively had nothing but the clothes she was wearing.

Emptying her cup with a grimace for the concentrated sweetness, she carried it to the kitchen along with Toussaint's, then rinsed and stacked them in the dishwasher, before walking to the office to settle her bill. Toussaint slipped his phone in his pocket and fell into step with her, and not for the first time, it occurred to Jane that he was too high-powered for this. Brady had made the comment that Toussaint covering this crime had been like sending in a cannon to shoot down a bird with a broken wing.

She glanced at Toussaint's profile. "You don't have to baby me. I can cope with Mayet."

"All part of the service."

Toussaint held the door of the motel office, and Jane stepped into the claustrophobic room, inordinately glad for his presence while she paid her bill. While the receptionist was swiping her card, Mayet popped his head around the corner from the small lounge he seemed to live in, took one look at Toussaint and went back to his program.

When she stepped outside, Toussaint escorted her back to her car, studying the new rental with a frown. "Follow me. I'll find you another place to stay."

The "motel" was a bed and breakfast with a separate guesthouse, run by a couple from New

England who had recently settled in Lassiter. Toussaint had stayed in the guesthouse when he'd first moved, while he'd debated whether to buy an apartment in town or move into the house in Plaisance Street.

At this time of year the Kyles usually kept the guesthouse free for any family who wanted to come and stay, but it was presently empty, and she could have it for the next week if she wanted it.

She wanted it.

The guesthouse itself was a small, modern, fully contained cottage with its own private courtyard, set on the grounds of the Kyles' house. She was welcome to use the pool, and there was a park just over the back fence if she wanted to go for a stroll.

Mary Kyle showed her through the cottage, while Toussaint disappeared into the garage, where Bill was busy dismantling a truck.

The cottage was bright and airy, furnished with antiques and decorated in restful creams, which provided an ideal backdrop for Mary's hobby, which was painting.

Thirty minutes later, Jane wrote a check for a week's rent in advance. Then, after using the small bathroom in the cottage to freshen up and comb out her hair, which had gradually worked loose from its knot, she walked out to the Ford, admiring the gardens on the way. The contrast of the

Kyles' neatly manicured estate to her trashed motel unit was absolute. The Kyles were as different from Mayet as East Coast lobster from crawfish, and the relief of moving away not only from Mayet but from the vandalism was huge.

She still felt disoriented and a little shaky, an aftermath of shock and the fact that she hadn't eaten since before lunch. She needed food, and she needed somewhere quiet to regroup, but before she could have either, she had to go shopping. As pretty and welcoming as the cottage was, it contained no food.

When she walked to her car, Toussaint stepped out of the garage, his sleeves rolled up, his jacket over one arm. His gaze moved critically over her. "No cane today?"

"I took drugs instead."

Her leg was still aching, but it was bearable; two lazy days and the stretching exercises had done wonders.

"If you're up for it, I'll take you shopping."

When she lifted her eyebrows, he opened the passenger door of his car. "The department stopped paying me at five."

Checking her watch, Jane saw with a mild sense of amazement that it was a quarter to seven. She settled into the seat, relieved not to have to cope with Lassiter's traffic, and feeling even hotter and stickier than usual, but there was no point in thinking about a shower until she had fresh clothes.

Toussaint reached across to the back seat. A faint whiff of cologne teased her nostrils. Despite the heat, she couldn't help noticing he'd somehow managed to stay cool and fresh.

He handed her a granola bar, still chilled from the small cooler in the back seat, and unwrapped one for himself.

Jane's mouth watered as she removed the foil wrapping and the enticing smell of peanuts and chocolate hit her olfactory senses. "Are you a mind reader?"

"Just a Boy Scout. Always prepared."

The sideways glance that went with the last part of his comment was laced with an unexpected humor, and Jane's stomach tightened with the kind of tension she hadn't felt in years. She could be wrong, but for a second she'd been certain Toussaint was flirting with her.

Nineteen

Toussaint drove north toward the center of town. He stopped for a light and checked out his passenger. She'd closed her eyes, resting her head against the passenger side door. The setting sun angled in, glancing over spare cheekbones and a defined jaw.

She was a strange mixture. The first time he'd seen her, he'd thought she was either blind or a cripple; the second time the limp had almost disappeared, and she'd looked cool and elegant. Now, with her hair loose and her tank top exposing surprisingly broad shoulders and well-muscled biceps, she looked more like Linda Hamilton in *The Terminator*.

The light changed, and he signaled right, taking an underground ramp into the parking garage of a large mall. When he parked, she straightened and unsnapped her seatbelt.

"I won't be long."

"I'm coming with you."

Her gaze was wary.

He pulled his key from the ignition and pushed his door open. "I've got to pick up a couple of things myself."

It was true that he needed to shop, but he was more interested in keeping an eye on Jane.

Since she'd knocked on his door two nights ago, he'd done some checking, and, from a professional point of view, he was more than interested. She'd survived a hit-and-run as a child, weathered a messy divorce, and was presently being stalked by a nut claiming to be a fan. Her house had recently been burglarized, and now her motel unit had been trashed.

Jane Gale was either the unluckiest woman on the planet or something very strange was going on.

Aside from his purely professional interest, he was concerned on another level: she was a woman on her own, and vulnerable.

Toussaint had worked a lot of years in law enforcement, and he guessed he was hardened, but it never ceased to tick him off when women and children were victimized. She'd held up through the ordeal when most women, and some men, would have been in tears. It hadn't been until she'd found out that her jewelry was missing that the shock had really kicked in. He'd seen that kind of delayed reaction before. When a crime happened, for a while the effort required to get through the law enforcement process distracted people, then reaction set in.

Everyone had their triggers. It was usually the small things, the personal objects that had been taken or destroyed, that hit home. Jane had weathered the loss of her clothing and computer, but when she'd discovered her jewelry was missing, her face had gone paper-white.

She hooked her handbag over one shoulder and lifted both arms to twist her hair into a knot. The sleek tank top she was wearing stretched even tighter across her breasts, and he looked away.

Who was he trying to kid? His motives weren't all altruistic: he was male, and he was breathing.

Jane was uncomfortably aware of Toussaint beside her as they walked into the mall. His offer to take her shopping had been as unexpected as his presence beside her was now. Through the afternoon, he'd been solid and steadying and *there*. That description made him sound like an old sock, worn and comfortable, and that was the last label she would ever attach to him.

He was the kind of man who would always attract feminine glances—not cheesecake handsome, more chiseled and aloof, with a smooth, muscular way of walking that had turned more than a few heads.

He had challenge written all over him, which made it all the more surprising to Jane that he seemed to want to spend time with her. She wasn't particularly gorgeous, and she was no extrovert. She preferred to spend her time in quiet pursuits like reading or walking. Toussaint looked like he would be as at home gliding through the serpentine back alleys of Lassiter as he was strolling through the mall, but, dangerous or not, he was definitely interested in her. She had seen the sleepy, male way he'd looked at her breasts.

The memory of that look sent a second shock of awareness through her, the jolt almost as powerful as the first, making her belly feel achy, her breasts tight and sensitive. She felt as if an alien, but definitely female part of herself had just been kicked into life and the sensations were completely out of her control. Toussaint was attracted to her, and, against all odds, she liked it.

When they reached a familiar chain women's clothing shop, Jane almost sighed with relief. The man/woman stuff had always been excruciating for her, but shopping was close to being her best talent. She might not understand men, but she had bonded at an early age with dresses and shoes. "I'll be half an hour."

As Toussaint disappeared in the direction of a music shop, Jane turned her attention to the task and made a mental list. She needed underwear and at least three changes of clothing, plus shoes, toiletries and cosmetics, and that was only a start.

Perusing the racks, she picked out several things in her size and found a changing room. As she peeled out of her clothes, she took stock for the first time in weeks. She knew she'd lost weight. Her clothes had gradually become looser and looser, but now, faced with a full-length mirror, the extent of her weight loss was impossible to avoid.

She had dropped more than a few pounds. Over the past few months the constant stress had eaten at her nerves and killed her appetite. Her bra no longer fitted, her belly was flat, and the gentle flare of her hips was gone. She stared at the hollows at the base of her neck and the sharp contour of her jaw line.

She couldn't afford to lose any more weight.

She had to start eating and paying serious attention to her physical condition. Part of the reason she was so exhausted and shaky was because her body had become so depleted. If she wasn't careful, she would get sick.

After the years spent building up damaged muscle and bone, the neglect hit hard. She'd had it drummed into her since she was a child how careful she had to be.

It was no wonder her back and leg were giving her so much pain. The joint and nerve damage she'd sustained meant she had to keep her diet rich in certain nutrients. If she neglected to eat or forgot to take her supplements, the cartilage cushioning her joints thinned and in some instances disappeared, and the area became inflamed and painful. Exercise, as much as it helped her mobility, only added to the wear and tear, and for the past few days she had been constantly on the move, climbing in and out of the SUV and stressing the most vulnerable parts of her body.

She changed into her own clothes again, grimacing at their limpness, took the clothes back to the salesperson, and chose items that were one and two sizes smaller. On impulse, she grabbed a hot pink stretch lace bra and panty set, seduced by the color and the sheer prettiness of it.

Twenty minutes later, avoiding any bright colors or eye-catching styles, she had gathered a basic wardrobe and had swapped her old clothes for a pair of beige linen pants and a soft white T-shirt. The clothes were cool, refreshing and low key, no zany prints or wild splashes of color. The last thing she needed was to attract the eye of whoever was stalking her.

She moved on to a shoe store, and added sneakers and a pair of low-heeled sandals to her growing wardrobe, then walked to the cosmetics counter of one of the major department stores. Choosing makeup, at least, was easy, since the store carried her brand, although having to hurry grated. Buying makeup and perfume was a feminine ritual that required its own time.

Minutes later, she strolled to the supermarket and bought a new toothbrush and toothpaste, and filled her basket with the toiletries and basic foods she needed.

Glancing at her wristwatch, she saw that almost an hour had passed, instead of the half hour she'd said she would need, and she quickened her step. When she stopped at the checkout, she turned to find Toussaint behind her.

He indicated the basket he was carrying. "I needed a few things."

But it was no coincidence that he was lining up directly behind her. "You've been following me."

"I was keeping an eye out. What did you expect? That I'd sit down on some bench and wait?"

His disgust was so plain, his voice so New York, that Jane had to grin. Sitting would be difficult for him, let alone waiting for a woman to shop.

She finished emptying her cart, her cheeks warming at the thought of Toussaint watching her pick out lingerie, although his focus wouldn't have been directly on her or what she was buying. He would have been watching the people around her—watching her back.

The fact that he had looked out for her momentarily made her chest go tight. She risked brief eye contact. "Thanks."

"No problem."

She emptied the last item in her cart onto the counter. Tampons. Great.

She caught the edge of Toussaint's grin and concentrated on paying. Oh yeah, he had seen them—*and* the lingerie. The man didn't miss a thing.

When they were through the check out, Toussaint took the bags from her and carried them to his car. "Now dinner."

"You don't need to—"

"I've got to eat, too, and besides, it's on the way."

He stopped at a modest family-style restaurant that specialized in Cajun food but also boasted the best biscuits and steaks in Lassiter.

Toussaint settled for a sirloin, and so did Jane. She'd been in town for several days and hadn't really sampled the local cuisine, but for now, fuelling her body was more important than experimenting.

She was aware of him watching her as they ate, not in an intrusive way, but in a checking-up way. "Good?"

She chewed and swallowed, and started on her side salad. "Very."

"You've lost weight."

"A few pounds."

He lifted a brow. "Judging from the way your clothes were fitting, I'd say more than a few."

"This year hasn't been easy." The fact that he'd noticed so much about her was as unsettling as the fact that she was reacting to him at all.

She had been married to Paul for six years and divorced for one. In that time, she had been aware of other men in a peripheral way but had never allowed that awareness to progress. Somehow, despite her focus on tracing her past—or maybe because of it—Toussaint had slipped past her defenses.

She chewed and swallowed, doggedly clearing her plate, then considered ordering dessert, but as much as she liked ice cream, she didn't want it; her stomach was full.

Toussaint ordered iced tea for them both. Jane sipped, enjoying the icy coolness.

He sat back in his chair. "Have you made any progress looking for your family?"

She set her glass down, momentarily disturbed

to realize that, as singular as the experience had been, she had almost forgotten the wisp of memory that had surfaced when she'd been sitting on the side of the highway—and her luck in meeting Fay Collins.

For a moment she considered telling him that she had remembered something, but she instinctively pulled back. The recollection had been ephemeral, the emotions it had engendered intensely private—and *hers*. After twenty-five years of blankness, she finally owned a tiny piece of her missing past. She needed to tell Toussaint, but not yet. First she wanted to sit quietly and examine what she had remembered and see if the chink that had opened up would open any wider. She had been running away, but she didn't yet know from what, or whom. With the trail years old, Toussaint wouldn't have anything more to go on than what was already noted in her file. A seven-year-old child out on the road at night with no family member to protect her, or claim her once she was injured and in Lassiter General, was by definition at risk.

That he would be interested in the information, she didn't doubt, and not just because he was a cop. The thought intensified the awareness that had set her on edge all evening. That was the second reason she didn't want to surrender anything more to Toussaint right now. Where he was concerned, she was already too vulnerable.

She lifted her shoulders. "I've got a lead." Between slow sips of iced tea, she told him about meeting Fay. "One of the first things I did was check with the hospital. Most of the medical staff who treated me have since died or moved away, but apparently one of the EMTs who was on duty that night is still alive and living in Lassiter. Maybe he'll remember something useful."

Arnold Carpenter had been one of the first people at the scene. According to Fay Collins, he had been responsible for saving her life. It was possible, although not likely, that he had seen something everyone else had missed. It was a slim chance, but Jane wasn't about to dismiss it. Her strongest lead—finding Toussaint—had turned out to be a dead end, so maybe the opposite could be true. Arnold Carpenter had lived in Lassiter all his life, he would know a lot about the people in this town. If his memory was unimpaired, he could provide the break she was looking for.

Toussaint called for the check and sat back in his chair. "I read the file on your case."

Her gaze jerked to his and clung. To say he had caught her by surprise was an understatement. "And?"

"What exactly are you hoping to find?"

"My family."

"What happens when you find them?"

The idea that she would actually find a family— a mother and father, brothers, sisters, maybe even uncles and aunts—was something she didn't often let herself dwell on.

What would she do? Knock on the door and say, "Hi, it's me, the one that got left on the side of the road, the child you forgot you had"?

She had already accepted that if she found anyone at all, the chance that she could connect with that person in any kind of satisfying way wasn't likely, but that didn't seem to matter.

The fact was, she was driven. She didn't like it, but she couldn't change. She didn't just *want* to know what had happened to her, and why, she *needed* to know. The near-death experience had affected every part of her life. Every day she dealt with the physical, mental and emotional fallout from that one event. She had worked to improve her body, bringing it to a point that was as close to normal as she was ever likely to get, but mentally and emotionally, a piece of her was still crippled.

She guessed it came down to the type of person she was. Gray areas annoyed her; black and white suited her just fine. Maybe she was just plain stubborn, but she needed to complete the picture. Loved or not—abandoned or not—she wanted closure.

She picked up her tea and stared into the cloudy liquid. Her parents had both tried to understand this trip. Catherine hadn't approved. Marcus was more understanding, but he hadn't been comfortable with her going it alone. They would both have been horrified if they'd found out that Jane had pushed her research beyond the normal avenues and resorted to knocking on doors.

The need for closure aside, Jane couldn't explain what had compelled her to such an extreme. The need to search was just there, a part of her, as powerful as a homing beacon. She could no more turn it off than stop breathing.

The liquid swirled, the damp glass reflecting the flame of the candle in the center of the table and for a moment she experienced a disorienting sense of déjà vu, as if she were viewing something she had seen before in another place, another time. Emotion expanded in her chest, fear, panic and a paralyzing urgency that gripped her as tight as a fist.

Ice clinked as she set the glass down, and, as abruptly as it had opened, the small window in her mind slammed shut, but the sense of urgency remained, transmitted down the years, an unbreakable thread that still tugged at her.

She hadn't just been running away, she had been running for help.

Someone had needed her, but she had never made it back.

Toussaint leaned forward and took the drink out of her hand as if she were a child. "The probability that you'll find anyone now is low."

"I know all about the statistics." She mopped at the spill with her napkin, glad for the distraction. He thought she was upset at being rejected. Jane didn't know how to break it to him, but she had gotten over that one. These days, thanks to the invaluable assistance of her ex-husband, rejection didn't bother her a whole lot.

She and Claire had even laughed about it over lunch. Jane had bet a hundred bucks on the fact that Paul Cahill believed not only that she had been rejected, but rejected by the best. Last month, following an encounter at their local appliance store, where she'd gone to complain about a television set she'd bought she had been proved right.

"I know it's not likely I'll locate my birth family, but what I can't dismiss is the possibility that I wasn't abandoned. It's possible I was lost. A lot of children disappear every year. If they survive the abduction, they don't stop growing—and they have to go somewhere."

Twenty

When Jane and Toussaint stepped out of the restaurant it was dark, and the street was alive with neon lighting, bustling cafés and people strolling, enjoying the balmy evening.

A shoulder caromed into hers, throwing her off balance.

"Hey, Toussaint, who's the pretty lady?"

An arm snaked around her waist, pulling her against a hard, muscled body. Her nostrils filled with the sharp scent of fresh sweat and something else, a sweetish, cloying scent that made her stomach churn. She had a fleeting glimpse of slicked-back dark hair and the glitter of an earring; then she was free, and Toussaint had the man shoved face-first into the shadowy alcove of a florist shop, an arm held high behind his back.

The man jerked against his hold. "Hey, man, I jus' wanted to meet her."

"If you want company that badly, Travis, I can arrange it. I'm willing to bet Sonny and Beau will give you up without a struggle. As it stands, we've almost got enough for a warrant." He lifted the man's arm a fraction higher. "Where's the knife?"

Fear flashed in Travis's eyes.

Toussaint repeated his question, his gaze calm and cold.

Sweat beaded on Travis's upper lip, and he spat something in guttural Cajun. Toussaint tightened his grip and, with a slick movement, extracted the knife—a short, thin blade that had been shoved into a false side pocket in Travis's trousers. With a flickering movement, Toussaint threw the knife so that the tip of the blade bit into the wood frame of the door. In a second fluid movement, he drew his own blade from an ankle sheath and held the tip to Travis's throat. "Still want to play?"

Travis arched away from the razor-sharp tip, his teeth bared in a grimace. "You're a cop. You're not gonna cut me."

"Don't bank on it."

Travis bucked against his hold, spitting abuse. The tip of the knife bit into his skin, and a trickle of blood ran down his throat. Abruptly, he went still. "All right, all right…you win."

With a practiced movement, Toussaint withdrew the knife, stepped back and let Travis go. His arm came around her, pulling her against his side, the movement masculine and possessive. Travis edged toward his knife where it still protruded from the doorway.

Toussaint tracked the movement and murmured something low and cold in a language that revealed that while his attitude and accent might be New York, his roots were set firmly in the bayou. "Don't."

Travis's gaze burned, a tic pulsed in his jaw. He spat something harsh, then turned and loped into the now curious crowd.

Toussaint slid his knife back into his ankle sheath. His gaze caught hers, fierce and cold, and with a fluid movement he pulled her into the alcove. A split second before it happened, Jane knew he was going to kiss her. His hands gripped her waist, and his mouth came down on hers, the kiss white hot and edgy. The shock of his tongue thrusting into her mouth made heat explode in her belly, and her breasts lift and tighten. With a raw shiver, she wound her arms around his neck, tilted her head back at a more comfortable angle and rode out the kiss.

As ruthlessly as he'd dealt with Travis, Toussaint took advantage of her change in posture, backing her against the wall, his thigh sliding between hers, the weight of his body pressing heavily against hers. She could feel every hard muscle, the bulge of his arousal where it pressed into her hip, and a hunger she'd thought she would never feel again flared into life. She didn't care that they were being watched, didn't care that Toussaint was probably kissing her to deflect attention from the tussle with Travis. She wanted more.

Jane felt as if she had been walking around blindfolded and now the fabric had been ripped away. She was overheated, her skin flushed. Her whole body was on fire.

She realized she was actually contemplating sleeping with him, and the leap took her by surprise. Just days ago she had been completely disinterested in men and sex; somehow, in the space of a few days, that had changed. If she was honest, all it had taken was that one direct look from Toussaint in the police interview room and she had been gone.

Sleeping with Toussaint was the equivalent of throwing herself out of the frying pan into the fire. She'd played it safe with her husband and gotten burned, but Toussaint was a lot more dangerous than her tame ex-husband had ever been.

Somebody howled like a wolf; another passer-by whistled, and Toussaint lifted his mouth, his expression intense. This time the kiss was gentler and very thorough. Restlessly, she rose up on her toes and stretched against him, and his hands slid beneath her T-shirt against her skin, the contact electric.

When he finally lifted his head, his lids were heavy, his face taut. "Time to stop."

With a final snatched kiss, he took her hand and stepped out of the alcove. "Show's over."

There was a small smattering of applause, and within seconds the knot of onlookers dispersed, the volatile situation diffused.

Keeping his fingers linked with hers, Toussaint collected Travis's knife and slipped it into his pocket. "Travis is one of the Laurent gang. The two brothers who ran it were put away last week on drug charges. He's somewhere at the bottom of that particular food chain. They think that just because I'm not from around here, I don't know the rules. If I let him walk all over me, I'd have to leave town." He glanced at her. "And so would you."

When Toussaint pulled into the Kyles' drive, he insisted on seeing her to her door. His manner was low key, but Jane just bet that would change in an instant if anything dared materialize from the shrubbery. She could almost wish that her stalker would appear.

One way or another, he had stayed close ever since he'd arrived at the motel. He'd beaten off Mayet and the other hidden demons, found her a new place to stay, taken her shopping and to dinner. Toussaint had guided her through the process, calmly and coolly, as if helping damsels in distress was an everyday occurrence, but at some point he had stepped beyond duty and friendship into relationship territory. He had made no bones about the fact that he was attracted to her.

Jane put her shopping bags down as she fitted the key in the lock. The evening had felt a little weird and displaced, but Toussaint hadn't had a problem with it. He'd been as at home in the women's wear store as he had been dealing with Mayet and her trashed motel unit.

She flicked on the hall light and turned to say goodnight. Toussaint beat her to the punch.

His hands slid around her waist, pulling her close, and if she'd had any doubts about his motives for kissing her, they were gone.

The kiss was deep and restless and flagrantly hungry, and not enough. With a muffled sound, he eased her back a half step. Jane felt the solid coolness of the doorframe against her spine, the heat of his palms against her bare flesh as he dragged her T-shirt up over her breasts.

His head dipped. His mouth fastened over one

nipple through the fabric of her bra, then the other, and the night turned molten.

Long seconds later, Toussaint lifted his head, his expression fierce as he pulled her T-shirt back into place. "I'm not coming in. If I get you on a couch or a bed, that'll be it, and I think we both need some time. Besides, I don't have any condoms, and I bet you don't, either."

Toussaint reached into his pocket, pulled out a business card and scribbled on the back of it. "That's my private number and my cell phone. If anyone bothers you, or you just get anxious, call me—day or night." His gaze caught hers, hot and edgy. He muttered something succinct beneath his breath and leaned forward for a hard kiss. "Call me anyway."

Jane stared at the two numbers he'd given her and started to thank him, but he was already on his way down the path. She heard the sound of his car engine and the crunch of gravel as he negotiated the drive.

Shakily, she carried her shopping inside, then closed the door and locked it, putting on the chain.

Her breasts felt painfully tight where they pushed against the damp fabric of her bra, and there was a heavy ache deep in her belly. Closing her eyes, she sucked in a breath. Kissing Toussaint had been like being caught up in a maelstrom. Her head was still spinning, her whole body throbbing.

She waited until the sound of his car had receded, then sat in one of the easy chairs in the living room, staring out at her small courtyard. She hugged her arms around her knees, feeling as euphoric and vulnerable as a teenager and, quite frankly, nervous. Aside from the uncomplicated desire to crawl into bed with Toussaint, her feelings for him were embryonic and so fragile she was afraid to even label them.

Toussaint locked the side entrance to the house and walked upstairs, past the formal paintings of long-dead Toussaints and his grandmother's framed needlework.

As far as art went, unlike his stepfather, he didn't have an artistic bone in his body. His one addition to the gallery had been an oil painting Etienne had had in the attic of his house, a restful study of trees and sky that did little to lighten the stairwell.

He grimaced as his footsteps echoed. He'd kept the house partly out of a sense of family obligation and partly because he'd decided that if he was going to have a real break away from city life, then he needed to do the whole lawn and garden thing. He didn't mind the outside stuff—in fact he liked it—but he couldn't get used to the echoing.

When he was a child, he and his father had always lived in small houses; then, later on, when he'd left home it had been apartment living all the way.

Fifteen minutes later, after showering, he padded downstairs in a pair of jeans, too restless to sleep. He collected his briefcase from the car, poured himself a glass of iced water from the fridge and sat down at the kitchen table. Idly, he began sifting through the notes he'd made on the Waltham case; then, on impulse, he picked up a copy of Jane's file and began to read.

Jane Gale was an odd mixture. At first glance she was attractive but a little on the quiet side, but there was an inner toughness he could relate to. She was a survivor.

She hadn't flirted. On the contrary, she'd been wary, but when she'd had something to say, she had made her point and taken no prisoners.

It had been a long time since he had been on more than a casual date. After his marriage had ended a few years back, courtesy of his career, it hadn't made sense to him to commit to anything that would tie him down like that again. But somehow he had ended up with candlelight, soft music and a pretty woman.

Twenty-One

"Got a rental firm on the line," Hazel said. "They've got a weird situation."

Gatreaux sat back in his chair and gave up on trying to get a glimpse of Angie as she leaned over her light table, peering at prints. "How come I get the weird calls as opposed to the exciting ones?"

"Honey, Toussaint's officially in charge of exciting. You're in charge of weird."

The weird situation turned out to be a perfectly ordinary sedan, filled with cell phones.

The manager of the rental agency unlocked the vehicle. "We got a call from a resident of Melville Street. Apparently the car had been sitting outside their house most of the previous day and all night." He indicated a man dressed in a coverall. "Joe here drove it back to the garage, but other than that, it hasn't been touched. As soon as I saw all the cell phones in the trunk, I called you. Since they all look used, I figured Butler, the guy who was renting it, was stealing them."

Gatreaux studied the rental agreement, his pulse lifting. "Where did you say you picked the vehicle up from?"

"Melville. It's a side road just off Landry."

"Uh-huh. Do you mind if I get a copy of the paperwork?"

While he was running off copies, Gatreaux slid his phone out of his pocket and made a call. This case had just gone from weird to exciting.

Ten minutes later, Toussaint and Miller walked into the garage.

Miller stared at the pile of cell phones in the trunk. Gatreaux had already counted. There were over forty.

Miller scratched his jaw. "What was he doing? Waiting for a call?"

"Or making them." Toussaint pulled on latex gloves. Gingerly, using his pen, he switched on one of the phones and brought up the listed numbers. He frowned. He was certain one of them was Jane's home number. If he didn't miss his guess, it was no coincidence that the vehicle had been parked near her motel. The rental belonged to the "fan" who was stalking her.

Gatreaux produced a copy of the rental agreement. "Looks like he's staying at the Plantation Motel down on River Drive."

The Plantation was an old converted house with a row of cheap units built out the back, one of which had been rented to Butler for a week. The manager, an aging Lassiter legend named Armand Curole who, according to local myth, had already preserved himself for all eternity with a steady drip feed of cheap rum, hadn't seen Butler for a couple of days and could care less. As far as he was concerned, Butler could drink himself blind or rot in some ditch, as long as he paid his bill, which he had—in advance.

Butler's room was closed up, all the curtains pulled, and the privacy sign was out.

Grumbling at the heat and the flies, Curole unlocked the door and pushed it wide.

Toussaint and Gatreaux stepped inside the dark airless room and began opening curtains, careful not to touch any smooth surfaces. Toussaint took the front room, Gatreaux the bedroom.

Gatreaux walked back out front a few minutes later. "He's not here, but a whole lot of other stuff is."

Two hours later, the evidence team vacated the premises with two boxes full of material. As evidence hauls went, it had been an impressive day.

They had Butler's rental car, his motel room and the paraphernalia associated with his obsession with Jane: copies of her books, along with photographs and newspaper clippings.

Toussaint closed the door to the motel unit. "Still no sign of Jane's jewelry or the laptop."

Angie waited while Roland popped the trunk of her car. "If Butler stole the jewelry, it should have been here."

Gatreaux stepped forward, ready to take the box from Angie and stow it. "Unless he's wearing it."

Angie wrinkled her nose. "Ew. Don't be gross." She pushed the box at his chest.

Gatreaux blushed, and Toussaint tried not to look interested.

Miller dipped his head, hiding a grin as he flipped his notebook closed and slipped it into his jacket pocket. "Hate to spoil the fantasy, but maybe he Fed-Exed the jewelry back to whatever rock he crawled out from under."

Toussaint jerked his head at Gatreaux, who was looking lovesick and devastated. He didn't think he'd ever been that desperate—yet. "We can check, but I'm guessing he didn't have time."

The situation for Gerry Butler didn't look good. He wasn't in his motel room, and he wasn't in his car. Toussaint didn't think he was anyplace where any of them could reach him now.

Butler had a history of alcohol and drug abuse, convictions for petty theft and indecent exposure, and he had done time for attempting to rob a pharmacy.

They had his fingerprints and DNA, a standard mug-shot photo, and a detailed psychiatric report. Gerry had lived life in the breakdown lane. He'd been dysfunctional and inept, making his living as an appliance salesman and failing at almost everything, including the crimes he committed.

Someone had the jewelry and the laptop, but Toussaint was willing to bet it wasn't Gerald Butler.

The Charpentier Home For the Aged was situated in one of the oldest, wealthiest areas of Lassiter. The house itself was a grand old lady, three-storied and brick, built to endure, and the grounds that sheltered the building were park-like.

Jane walked into the lobby and asked to see Arnold Carpenter. She was directed outside to the gardens, where Arnold was engaged in his self-appointed task of deadheading every rose he could reach from his wheelchair.

He gave her a shrewd look out of the clear, intense blue eyes of a child, leaned forward and snipped another deadhead. "You're Jane Gale, the little girl no one could identify. Wondered if you'd be along."

Arnold cut her off before she could ask the question. "Tyrone filled me in—Tyrone Brady, the reporter. He visits me most weeks. Said you had some trouble over at your motel. The Palm Court." He shook his head. "If Mayet has anything to do with it, you can guarantee trouble. The man's a foreigner, from Mississippi way—married into Lassiter."

Arnold made it sound as if Mayet wouldn't have been allowed across the state line if he hadn't married a local.

He gestured at the formal beds of roses. "Looks a bit like a funeral home, if you ask me, but it's pretty. As soon as my hip mends, I'm out of here. My sister's looking after the garden, but, between you and me, Violet doesn't have a clue."

A nurse came out of a side door with a tray and called Arnold's name.

"Time for my medication. They try and make it look like a snack, but…" He shrugged, gave up on the roses and gestured Jane to join him.

When he was settled with a glass of iced-tea, Arnold got straight to the point. "You want to know about your accident." He took a sip, wiped his mouth and set the glass down. "I've done a lot of thinking about that over the years. The fact that no one turned up to look for you made me angry. The only thing I could come up with was that you might have had your accident here, but you don't come from around here."

He shook his head. "When you finally came out of that coma, I came to see you. You probably don't remember, because there were so many people coming and going, and you kept drifting off, but I can remember hearing you speak as clear as day. You might have lost your memory, but you could still talk well enough, and you didn't have a Southern accent. I talked to the cops about it, and they tried to follow up, with no success. My guess was you were from out of state, maybe from Virginia or Ohio, and had somehow come adrift from your parents."

Half an hour later, Jane left Arnold to his roses. As she walked to her car, she was disappointed, but philosophical. She was aware that statewide searches had already been done and nothing had ever turned up. And no parents or relatives had ever put in a request with any of the agencies to have her found.

With the afternoon stretching ahead, she decided to go shopping. The items she had bought yesterday had been stopgap only. In this heat, she needed several more outfits before she would feel even remotely comfortable, not to mention other items that she hadn't thought about at the time, like a new hairbrush and make-up bag, and a swimsuit.

As she unlocked the car, the memory of Toussaint kissing her made her freeze in place, her whole body electrified. She was practically melting down just thinking about it. What she really needed to buy were condoms. It was a blunt fact that if Toussaint got her alone again, she would end up naked and on her back.

Swallowing, she slid into the driver's seat, put the Ford in gear and concentrated on getting out of the Charpentier Home's driveway without taking out one of the elegant stone posts.

Jane's first stop was in Lassiter's central business district, at a small boutique that specialized in elegant evening- and daywear. After perusing the racks, she decided on a floaty pink and black skirt and top that could be worn separately. Together, the outfit was sensational, clinging where it touched, the soft layers tantalizing. The halter top hid the hollows around her neck but scooped low enough to be sexy. She added a set of lingerie and a pair of classic black silk pants to the pile.

When she admired the shop assistant's nails, the woman was more than happy to give her the name and address of the hairdresser-manicurist she used.

"Ella-Marie doesn't take appointments," she warned, "so you might have to wait, but it's worth it."

Jane strolled down an interesting line of designer shops and bought strappy shoes, earrings and an exquisite enameled necklace that had been made locally, and which matched the pink outfit perfectly. Checking the time, she strolled in the direction of Bettencourt Street.

The salon was at the end of a dark, cavernous tunnel that branched off into a bar on one side and a restaurant on the other, but had the unexpected bonus of opening onto a sunny, enclosed courtyard. The premises themselves were tiny but pristine, with soothing music playing in the background.

Ella-Marie, who insisted on being called Ella, was a small effervescent woman with chic, razor-cut hair and the most elegant hands Jane had ever seen.

There was a client in the chair, and one waiting, so Jane took a seat and flicked through a magazine. Within an hour, she was having her hair washed and set.

While the rollers were in, Ella started on her nails. "Hot date?"

"Maybe." Although no arrangement had been made, and Toussaint hadn't called her since. There had just been that mind-numbing kissing.

"Well, don't waste it, honey." She winked as she got up from the chair and switched over the music tape. "If you let me do your make-up, I can guarantee you'll get laid."

Jane felt herself getting warm. There was no guarantee required. It was a certainty.

The decision to have sex with Toussaint was stamped on every purchase she'd made. He hadn't pushed last night, but if he'd had condoms on him, they would have ended up in bed together.

"That way, huh?" Ella-Marie grinned and reached for the bottle of pink nail polish she was applying. "Don't let him get it too easy. Make him work."

She stroked on the final coat of polish, then, before Jane could protest, rolled a make-up table over to the station.

"Just sit there while those nails dry and let me play. Those cheekbones… You're low-key and subtle, which is sweet, but with a little more color, you'll pack a wallop."

When she was finished, Ella blow-dried her hair, then stood back to admire the effect in the mirror.

Jane stared at herself. She enjoyed using make-up and having her hair done, but she had never looked like this. Ella had put the makeup on with a heavier hand than Jane usually used, and the effect was striking. For the first time in her life, Jane felt not just beautiful, but gorgeous.

"What are you wearing? Please don't say it's white or cream."

"Pink. A dark, rich pink."

"You could also consider red. With your hair and that skin, you'd be a knockout."

Ella grinned as Jane counted out cash. "Go get him, but look after yourself. Just remember, men are different. They don't think like us. If you can, make him wait."

Jane's cell phone rang as she walked in the door of the cottage. When she examined the screen, she recognized Claire's number.

Setting her purchases down in the hall, she answered the call as she walked through to the living room.

After dispensing with the usual pleasantries, Claire began questioning her about the stalking case. "So what about this Toussaint guy? Has he been any use?"

Just the mention of Toussaint scattered Jane's concentration. She opened up the French doors to let in some air. "You could say that."

"There must be something wrong with this line. You sound weird."

Jane caught a glimpse of herself in the large mirror over the fireplace. "I feel weird."

"Cahill's not down there, is he?"

The mention of her ex-husband's name barely registered. That relationship felt so distant and insignificant that it could have happened in another life. "This isn't about Paul."

"You mean there's someone else?"

"Well…not exactly."

"What does *that* mean?"

"I've been seeing Toussaint."

Jane held the phone back from her ear, but she still heard the outraged shriek. *"You might be sleeping with your brother."*

Jane shoved the phone back against her ear. "He's *not* my brother."

"How do you know? Have you had blood tests?"

"We don't need tests. I may not know who my family are, but he knows his—and I'm definitely not included. He's half Chippewa."

"What if he's lying?"

"He's a cop, Claire."

"And that means precisely what? He's a man."

Jane sat down on the edge of one of the comfortable armchairs, but she was too uptight to relax. "You're married to a man. You tell me."

"I'm sorry, it's just you haven't even been in town a week." Claire paused for breath. "Damn, this is scary. You haven't slept with anyone since Cahill, and I don't know if that counts."

"Which would practically make me a virgin."

"Exactly. I'm coming down there."

"Claire, you've got kids to look after?"

"I know. It was an empty threat."

Jane breathed a sigh of relief.

Twenty-Two

Lassiter's second body in two days turned up just before sunset.

Twenty minutes later, Toussaint was studying the bloated body of Gerry Butler, which had been dumped in a ravine.

"Looks like our man." Gatreaux kept his distance. "No mystery to the way he died."

Toussaint studied the area around the body. The hole in Butler's chest told him how he had died, and the unnatural way he was lying suggested he hadn't died here. Toussaint was more interested in how the body had been transported. There were no tire tracks or drag marks. Whoever had dropped the body here had had to carry him from the road. Butler wasn't overweight, but he was solidly built; it would have taken a strong man to carry him, which in theory should rule out Jane—almost.

There was always the remote possibility that she had an accomplice, but Toussaint didn't think so. Jane didn't strike him as the kind of woman who needed a man. "Only when. Looks like he was out here all night."

Gatreaux lifted a brow, and Toussaint knew what he was thinking. Only four days after Myra Waltham was killed. One killing in Lassiter was news. Two was an epidemic.

Toussaint studied the bullet wound in the man's chest. One shot through the heart, and judging from the lack of bleeding, instant death. "Professional."

"A hit man?"

Toussaint shrugged. "Just clean and quick. Whoever pulled the trigger knew what he was doing."

"Do you think it's connected with Myra Waltham?"

Toussaint straightened. "Maybe. It's a different M.O."

Whoever had killed Myra had taken his time; this guy had been clinical.

"But we have a suspect."

"Yeah." Jane Gale.

The knowledge didn't make Toussaint happy. He had followed up the lead on the maid without much hope. She claimed that when she saw the unit had been trashed, that was the excuse she'd been looking for to quit, so she'd left without handing in her notice. Mayet already made her life hell. As far as she was concerned, losing a day's pay was better than the prospect of spending hours listening to him bellyache about the damage—which brought Toussaint back to Jane. "She changed her rental vehicle yesterday. Call up the firm and impound the SUV she had. With any luck they haven't cleaned it yet."

"Do you think she did it?"

Toussaint picked up his jacket. "What I think doesn't count. I'm just doing my job."

"Uh-huh."

Toussaint gave him a look.

Gatreaux tried for an innocent expression. "I just heard you two were 'seen' in town last night, that's all."

Toussaint shook his head and unlocked the car. "Small towns."

"Hey, what's with the 'small'? We're not the Big Apple, but we're getting there."

"Two murders in one week?" Toussaint tossed the paperwork on the back seat. "You're going to have to try harder than that."

Toussaint merged into traffic, fingers tapping impatiently as he waited at a set of lights. They would have to check the blood samples, but he was willing to bet they would come up with a match with the blood on the carpet fibers from Jane's former motel unit. Mayet had complained that a mat was missing, which would work with the theory that Butler had actually been killed there. Toussaint was even prepared to bet that the killer had made Butler lie down on Mayet's missing mat before he had shot him, thereby keeping the mess to a minimum. The one tiny droplet of blood that had missed the mat looked likely to provide a major break in the case.

An hour later, the blood samples a confirmed match, he was in his office drinking hot, bitter coffee and waiting on a search warrant. At 7:30 Judge Bristow signed off on the paperwork and they were good to go.

Miller adjusted the fit of his shoulder holster and shrugged into his jacket. "Who's driving?"

Jane had just finished clearing her dinner dishes when there was a knock at the door. Her heart pounded in her chest, and the glass she was filling with iced water from the fridge almost slipped from her fingers.

Setting the glass down, she checked the time on her watch, then padded, barefoot, to the door. It was almost eight—too late for casual callers.

Toussaint was clearly visible in the glow of the security light, but when she opened the door there was nothing intimate or personal in his expression. His gaze flickered over the silky halter top and pants she had changed into when she had gotten back from town, but the glance was brief and emotionless. He was brief and to the point. They had found her stalker—dead—and they needed to ask her a few questions.

"Here?"

"The station would be better."

He waited outside while she slipped on a pair of light sandals and collected her handbag. When she was ready, she walked along the prettily bricked path to the drive. The sun was an hour shy of setting, and the Kyles' tropical garden was still alive with birds and fragrance. Somewhere off to her left she could hear a fountain tinkling. Yesterday Jane had taken pleasure in the beauty of the garden—it had been like an oasis—but now she was working on automatic pilot.

Toussaint lifted a hand to Bill Kyle, who was looking at her with open curiosity. She guessed it wasn't every day that one of their guests got taken in for questioning.

Jane swallowed, suddenly nervous. She'd been dealing with the police for months now, but always as a complainant. Now, if she hadn't misread the cues, she had just turned into a murder suspect. "Am I under arrest?"

"No, but we'd like to search the cottage."

She noticed a second car parked behind Toussaint's. Miller and a woman with dark curly hair emerged. She recognized the woman as the evidence technician who had worked on the motel unit. "What for? More bodies?"

Toussaint's glance was impersonal. "It's a matter of procedure. We need to eliminate you from the investigation, and this is the only way to do it."

Jane shrugged. "Go ahead. There's not much to search." She knew how the police worked; she had studied their methods for her books. Toussaint wasn't following procedure; he was handling her with kid gloves. He would have a warrant; her permission was a courtesy only.

Her stomach cold and tight, she rummaged in her bag, withdrew a set of keys and handed them over. As the couple disappeared in the direction of her cottage, Toussaint held the passenger door for her. He was polite, even solicitous, but the easy warmth and charm of the previous evening was gone.

When she stepped forward to get in the car, his jacket flipped open in the breeze and she saw the butt of a gun. Toussaint suddenly fell into context. For years he'd been a frustrating, missing link to her past. Now he was larger than life, more male and difficult than she'd bargained for—and a cop.

As she fastened her seatbelt, the sense of inner cold she'd felt when she saw the gun increased. Her fingers tightened on the strap of her bag, which was perched on her lap.

She felt Toussaint's gaze touch on her as he drove. He flicked on a heater, and warm air flowed over her legs, but as warm as the interior of the car grew, it couldn't penetrate inward.

Toussaint took her through to the same interview room she'd sat in when she'd talked with Miller.

"Coffee?"

"No. Thank you."

He handed her a mug anyway. She wound her fingers around it, drawing comfort from the heat. When she sipped, she noticed that, just as on previous occasions, he had added plenty of sugar.

An older, heavier man joined them, and was introduced as Vernon Boulet, the chief of police. Toussaint's voice was mild as he asked the questions, his manner relaxed, but his gaze was remote. There was no mistaking that he was a cop first.

When he filled her in on the bare details of the crime, Jane was glad she was sitting down. "You mean someone *else* was in my motel unit?"

"Butler was shot there. It's possible the killing isn't connected to you."

"But not likely." She caught a shift in Toussaint's expression. "What else?"

"A Mrs. Baker from one of the properties that back onto the Palm Court said she woke up early because her dog was barking. She saw a woman walking through her property."

Jane could feel herself growing colder inside. Everything she had done pointed the finger at her. Her early morning escapade looked suspicious, and she had no alibi other than the few minutes she'd spent in the rental agencies and talking to Fay Collins on the side of the road. No one had seen her leave the motel room, and she had spent the day mostly on her own. To make matters worse, she had changed her rental vehicle and also changed the rental firm she used, which made her look even guiltier.

Even her explanation sounded weak.

She shook her head. "Maybe it was dumb, but it all seemed like a good idea at the time."

Boulet leaned forward. "Why didn't you use the front door?"

"I thought someone was watching me. And before you ask, no, I don't have any actual proof of that, just my own paranoia."

"What difference would getting out unseen have made?"

She shrugged, feeling both helpless and stupid. "Something woke me. I got frightened, then angry. I wanted out of the whole situation, even if it was only for a few hours."

Toussaint consulted his notes. "What woke you?"

Frustration welled. "I don't know."

There was a small silence. Toussaint's expression didn't change. Boulet looked like he was carved from stone.

Toussaint held her gaze. "Why did you change your rental?"

Jane's stomach plunged. What had seemed empowering then looked criminal now. "I wanted to evade the stalker. When I went back to the motel, I was going to pack and move. The only fly in the ointment was that I couldn't figure out how to get packed and out of the motel without being seen. I had no option but to go back."

Boulet crossed his arms over his chest. "What time—exactly—did you return?"

Jane gave him a direct look. She had already answered that question at least twice. "My jewelry and my laptop are gone," she said flatly, "and so are the notes for my latest book. That's no joke to a writer. It's my living. The insurance will cover the loss, but I *need* my computer. If you want to investigate something about me, then investigate that."

Boulet looked uncomfortable. "The laptop is replaceable, and the book is in your head. You could easily formulate your notes again."

Jane rose to her feet. The word "asshole" hung in the air, and she wasn't sure if she'd uttered it or not. "If you want to continue this interview, you'll have to formally arrest me, and while we're on the subject of unsolved cases, you might try a little harder with *this* one."

She lifted her T-shirt a few inches and pulled down the waistband of her pants far enough to reveal the series of scars that tracked around her midriff. She indicated the scar on her hip. "The hood of a car did that one." She pointed to a network of fine lines across her stomach. "Apparently the windshield did those—along with breaking my back—but that's not the clincher. Most of my injuries are consistent with the impact pattern of a child being hit by a car, but somehow I ended up with broken ribs.

"Do you know how hard it is to break a kid's ribs? There were no sharp impact marks, just tire tracks. After he hit me, he ran over me. In order to do that, he had to back up, locate my body in the dark and aim his vehicle. Your report calls what happened twenty-five years ago a hit-and-run. I call it attempted murder."

Miller opened the door of the interview room,

a sheet of paper in his hand, breaking the moment and drawing everyone's attention.

Toussaint stepped outside and skimmed the report Miller handed him, pausing on the only detail that concerned him right now. The time of death was ten o'clock the previous morning, about the same time that Jane had been talking to Fay Collins out on Sugar Hill Road. Given that she had appeared on the rental agency's security tape between nine and a quarter past, then driven out to Sugar Hill, she couldn't possibly have killed Butler.

Jane breathed a sigh of relief when Boulet broke the uncomfortable silence and followed Toussaint, who beckoned from the doorway, terminating the interview, at least for now.

What she'd said had been melodramatic, but she'd been angry. There was always the possibility that she had been hit by one car and run over by another, but suddenly, at that moment, she had been sure that second option hadn't happened.

She stared at the window, surprised to see it was dark. When she checked her watch, she was shocked to discover it was after ten.

Toussaint stepped back inside the room. "That's it. You can go home."

She stared at her hands, folded in her lap. After

her outburst, she felt curiously disconnected. "You're not arresting me?"

"The evidence was only circumstantial."

She stared at the lapel of Toussaint's jacket. "There must have been someone else in the unit."

The implications sank in, chilling her to the bone. Someone must have broken into the unit and waited for her to return, but, in an unexpected twist, Butler had broken into the unit instead.

Two stalkers. Even to her, it sounded improbable. The only glimmer of hope was that, after that eerie silent phone call, the possibility was already on record.

Toussaint sat down and placed a file on the table. "There is evidence of two separate break-ins. Do you know of anyone besides Gerald Butler who is likely to want to harm you?"

Jane lifted her head and stared at him.

She should be relieved that she had escaped a murder charge, but, instead, all she could think about was that Toussaint had kept her dangling on a string when he already *knew*... She unclenched her jaw. "Is this part of the interview?"

"Jane..."

She pushed back her chair and rose, then hooked her handbag over one shoulder. "If you want a list of suspects, I can get my agent to compile one for you. I don't know what the ratio of fan mail to hate mail is, but I imagine there's a percentage. Of course, we can discount Butler, because he's dead. Then there's my ex-husband, but even if Paul knew which end of a gun was the business end, he'd probably still get it wrong and shoot himself."

Toussaint muttered something beneath his breath.

Jane stared at the window. "Maybe the killer just wanted to get Butler and it had nothing whatsoever to do with me."

"That's not likely."

"No," she said flatly. "That would be too easy." And it would solve all her problems. "The only thing I've ever done that's attracted attention has been to write a book."

"Do you have a copy on you?"

A grim wisp of humor lightened her mood. Her mouth twitched. "No. If you want a copy, Toussaint, you're going to have to buy one."

Toussaint didn't try to touch her as he strolled beside her to her car, for which she was thankful.

Just to cap off a perfect day, she registered the tall outline of Tyrone Brady. A camera flashed.

Toussaint put his arm around her, shielding her as he opened the passenger door of his car.

He slid into his seat and turned the key in the ignition, but he didn't put the car in gear. "I knew you hadn't done that killing," he said bluntly. "It was too professional, and you don't have the physical strength it took to place that body in the ravine. Added to that, it doesn't make sense that you would go through all the legal channels to stop Butler, then resort to that kind of cold-blooded murder."

"It's all right. You don't have to explain."

He shot her a frustrated look. "Yes. I do. I'm trying not to mix business with my personal life, but I also needed to cut you out of the investigation as quickly as possible."

Jane went hot, then cold. She tried to retain her fury. Today she had gotten her hair and nails done, she had bought clothes and sexy lingerie. She had spent the day anticipating the hottest date of her life. Instead, she had gotten an interview by Lassiter's finest because Toussaint had decided he couldn't sleep with her until she was proved innocent.

Twenty-Three

The lab report on the white powder on Myra Waltham's face had come back.

The substance was hydrated calcium sulphate, otherwise known as gypsum.

"Gypsum?" Miller shrugged. "What is that? Fertilizer? I guess that makes sense. She was found on a farm."

Toussaint set the file down on his desk. "Not in these quantities. I checked with Wade, and he hasn't fertilized this year, and neither did his neighbor over the road, which means it came from somewhere else."

"Maybe the perp had fertilizer in his car?"

"It's possible, but the trunk liner itself was clean, except for traces that had flaked off the body. Myra had the substance on her face before she was loaded into the trunk."

"So what are we looking for? A fertilizer factory—"

"Or a farm shed," Gautreaux cut in.

Toussaint perched on the corner of his desk.

"Or a sculptor's workshop."

Gautreaux looked queasy. "Shit."

Toussaint handed out printed-off leaflets. "Here's your after-hours reading. We're looking at a copycat of a series of killings that happened over twenty-five years ago, and the DNA is male."

The time period niggled at him. Twenty-five years ago Jane Gale had had her accident the same week as the last recorded murders. Now she happened to be back in town—right when the murders started again.

As soon as his shift was finished, Toussaint picked up a copy of Jane's book from a local bookseller, took it home and began to read.

At two o'clock in the morning, he woke up Miller, then called the chief. It was possible Jane had researched the material that had been documented about the killings, but some of the details had never been released to the public. It was also possible the details in the book were an eerie coincidence, but not likely.

At six he walked into his office, collected a file from Miller's desk, and studied the report of the break-in at Jane's house and the statement made by a neighbor, Claire Pettigrew, that Jane's ex-husband had also visited her house. According to Ms. Pettigrew, he hadn't gained access, just knocked at the front door.

Toussaint made a note and picked up the phone. Ten minutes later, a file appeared in his email box.

As he read, his jaw tightened. Jane had been reticent about Paul Cahill, and Toussaint hadn't pressed her for details. Her ex was her private business—but not anymore. Cahill had hit her on more than one occasion, at least once after Jane had left him. She hadn't pressed charges, but she'd taken out a restraining order when she left. Cahill shouldn't have been within a mile of her house.

He would check on Cahill's movements, although from the descriptions he'd heard, he didn't think the man was a likely killer.

That left him back at square one, trying to find a copycat killer basing his M.O. on some of the most bizarre murders ever committed.

At seven a.m. Jane opened the door and stood aside so Toussaint could come in. He looked tired and rumpled, with dark circles under his eyes, as if he hadn't slept.

He set her book down on the coffee table, along with a copy of the *Lassiter Daily*. "Have you been reading the paper?"

"Not since I've been here."

Picking up the paper, she sat down and read the front page report on Lassiter's two latest murders, and all the hairs at her nape lifted.

Jane's voice was flat. "When I wrote the book, it just came out. I don't know where the idea or the details came from, or why, and I didn't like what I was writing—but that was the story, so I wrote it."

The problem was, the murders seemed eerily connected to her, and right now, apart from a set of old files, she was their only lead.

Toussaint paced to the French doors and stared out at the garden. "It's possible someone read your book and committed the first murder to gain your attention."

"And used my book as a guideline." The thought made her shudder.

His gaze swung back to hers. "With Butler's death, and a second stalker in the picture, we have to consider the worst-case scenario."

They would go through her life with a fine-tooth comb. Jane had no problem with that. It was even possible they might turn up something she had missed and so help locate her family.

She was aware that that hadn't let her off the

hook completely. She was still, loosely, a suspect, but now they had a male suspect who fitted the profile more exactly.

"There's just one more thing. The old murders stopped about the time you had your accident. It could be a coincidence, but…"

The man pressed the buzzer at the front door of the Charpentier Home and waited, hands clasped behind his back as he surveyed the grounds, although the thick lenses of his glasses made the garden less than interesting.

Eventually the door was opened by a young woman dressed in a light blue uniform. He made his request then followed as she led him through a series of dim passages that eventually led out into a sunny conservatory.

She shook an older man on the shoulder, rousing him from his after-lunch nap.

Arnold Carpenter woke with a start, which only happened when he was deeply asleep. He blinked and peered at the young girl still shaking his shoulder. Bernice. "It's not time for my pills, is it?"

"You've got a visitor. Your nephew."

Arnold lifted a hand to shade his eyes, feeling punchy and irritable. He was rumpled, he needed to go to the bathroom, and the sun was pouring in, hot enough to fry eggs. It was a wonder he hadn't keeled over from dehydration. He reached for the sipper bottle on the table beside him as Bernice ushered his visitor into a chair. He surveyed the man with interest. "I don't remember a nephew," he muttered grumpily. "I don't *have* a nephew." But the door had already closed behind Bernice.

"Who are you?" he demanded. He might be old, his back and hips shot from too much heavy lifting, but there was nothing wrong with his mind. He would swear he'd never seen the cold-eyed specimen sitting beside him before. "Someone's made a mistake. You're visiting the wrong person."

"I'm your sister Cherry's son."

Arnold's gaze narrowed. "Cherry didn't have any boys. Neither did Violet." He was the only one in his family who had ever had a boy child, and then just the one. The dearth of sons had become a family joke. Old as he was, he was hardly likely to forget *that*.

The man reached into his jacket pocket and pulled out a small book. "I guess I'm more a friend of the family than a blood relative," he said easily, handing the book to Arnold.

Arnold turned the book over, eyeing it suspiciously. When he saw it was the Bible, he relaxed. Now that was Cherry to a T, forever trying to get him to read the Good Book. Not that he objected, but—

A sharp prick in his arm made him jerk. "What the—"

A large hand clamped over his mouth, cutting off his protest. The stringy muscle of his bicep twitched as the needle that had been plunged in was withdrawn.

He clawed at the hand covering his mouth. Whatever had just been pumped into his body was already making his heart race hard enough that he couldn't catch his breath. The room spun, then began to recede, but Arnold hung on fiercely. He could just see old Charlie Villiers asleep in the corner, his mouth hanging open. If only he could attract Charlie's attention, he could ring the buzzer and get help. The grip on his mouth tightened, forcing his head back into his easy chair and pinching off his nostrils. Vaguely, Arnold heard the thud of the Bible hitting the floor.

Tyrone Brady pulled into the parking lot of the Charpentier Home. Whistling beneath his breath, he collected two icy cans of beer, slipped them in his pants pockets and arranged his jacket so the bulges weren't so visible. Not that he didn't think the nurses hadn't seen right through his little subterfuge—they knew he and Arnold were having a cold one on the sly—but the charade was necessary. Like Arnold always said, rules were rules.

He folded a copy of the weekly sports digest under his arm. The home had a subscription to the paper, but those old guys fought tooth and nail for it; and once the paper disappeared underneath Charlie Villiers' mattress, Arnold went all stiff-lipped and declared that, as a matter of principle and hygiene, he wasn't touching it.

Bernice let him in and waved him through to the day room with a wink. Tyrone suppressed a grin. Oh yeah, she knew.

As he stepped through the door a faint odor made his nostrils flare. Charlie was settled in the corner, which would probably account for it. He should call Bernice to come and clean the old guy up, but if he did that, staff would be in and out, collecting Charlie and spraying the room with air freshener, and Arnold wouldn't get his beer.

As Tyrone approached Arnold's chair, he realized Arnold was asleep, too. Tyrone frowned, abruptly worried that he had gotten sick. Usually Arnold had a nap after lunch, but it was after three. He should have been up and around by now. Even though his mobility was slow in coming back after his last hip operation, he liked to move around as much as possible. The problems he'd had aside, Arnold was usually as fit as a fiddle.

Tyrone extracted the cans from his pockets,

placed them on the coffee table and sat down in the easy chair adjacent to Arnold's. His frown deepened. The smell was thick enough to cut, and there was no doubt that it came from Arnold.

Tyrone debated what to do. If he woke Arnold up, he would know that Tyrone knew he'd soiled himself, and the last thing Tyrone wanted was to embarrass his friend. He decided to wake Arnold anyway. They went back too far to let a little embarrassment get in the way of friendship.

He touched Arnold's shoulder. Beneath the covering of his shirt, Arnold's flesh felt cool. Apprehension tightened in his stomach as Tyrone gripped his friend's shoulder and gently shook him. The old man's head lolled to the side, and Tyrone's hand jerked back. He'd seen that look before. Arnold was dead.

Tyrone followed the coroner to her car. "He shouldn't be dead."

Andrea Burrell set her medical case down on the loose gravel as she rummaged in her purse for her keys. "No one lives forever, Mr. Brady."

"Arnold should have come close. He saved enough lives."

"If that was the criteria, then everyone in the medical profession would live to a ripe old age, and we know that doesn't happen."

Tyrone gave up on trying to suppress his frustration. "Arnold was *special.*"

"I heard he had a certain touch."

"You may have heard it, but I've *seen* it—and more than once. When Arnold was on a job, *no one* died—not even the ones we thought were already gone."

She slipped the medical case onto the back seat and opened the driver's door. "He was over eighty. You had to expect he would die soon."

Tyrone stared at the neatly trimmed gardens. The weight of the cans in his pockets reminded him of exactly how he and Arnold should have spent the last hour. "He wasn't sick."

"The indications are that his heart gave out."

Tyrone's jaw clamped. "Arnold didn't have a heart condition."

"Not one that was diagnosed."

"Diagnosed, my ass. He was checked and double-checked. Arnold's heart was good. What about those marks on his face?"

Burrell's expression grew cool. Tyrone could see her mind ticking over the mine field of media subject matter Arnold's death threw up: allegations of brutality to old people, followed by a timely piece on medical cover-ups. But for once he wasn't after the story, he just wanted the truth.

"He could have bruised himself any number of

ways. When he fell forward in the chair, for example."

"The marks were on his face *before* I shook him."

"Mr. Brady, his family have accepted it."

And *he* wasn't family, just a friend. That was the implication.

"I don't care," he said softly. "I want it checked out."

Something wasn't right. His grandmother would say he was going "spooky," letting his reporter's nose get away on him, but Tyrone wasn't about to budge. His gut told him something was wrong. Maybe he *was* overreacting and being too pushy. According to his wife, he regularly got up a lot of people's noses—but he couldn't not be the way he was. Arnold had always encouraged him to step forward and do what was right, to tell the truth, no matter what. If it wasn't for Arnold he would have given up on journalism years ago, and he certainly would never have applied for the job of head reporter, which he currently held. He owed that old man a debt.

Despite the fact that he was over eighty, Arnold had been too full of life to die. Tyrone was determined to find out exactly what had gone wrong.

Burrell climbed into the driver's seat and closed her door. The window slid down with a faint whine. "I don't think you've got a case for an autopsy but, because it's Arnold…like you said, he saved a lot of people."

"Who's doing the autopsy?"

"It depends who's on. Reding or Burns."

"I want Reding."

Burrell shook her head and started the car. "It's not up to you."

"Then *you* make it happen."

Twenty-Four

Angie shouldered into the reception area, juggling two lattes, her handbag and a box of pastries. Using the lid of one of the lattes, she pushed her sunglasses onto the top of her head, then groaned as they slid back onto the bridge of her nose. The sudden gloom after the blinding sunlight made the room seem cave-like. "Gee, it's dark in here."

Hazel obligingly shifted the receiver from one ear to the other, reached over and pushed Angie's sunglasses up onto her head, and offloaded one of the lattes. She finished her conversation, slapped down the receiver and swiveled in her chair to look at the destinations board. "It's nine o'clock, first shift. Miller isn't out on a call, he's not in with Boulet or taking a 'personal' break, which means he should be—"

Hazel pushed back from her seat and marched through to the field room. She crossed her arms over her chest and stared at Miller's empty desk. "Sitting right there."

Angie breezed through the door behind Hazel, dumped her bag and the pastries on her own desk, kept her coffee and dropped into Miller's chair. "He's not here. His kid's sick again."

"No kidding—excuse the pun."

"His kid's got asthma. It's the time of year."

"I know what his kid's got, and I know what time of year it is. What I want to know is why can't Miller's wife take a turn?"

Angie sipped her coffee, took a second to bliss out, then refocused on Hazel. "Because she's got a real job."

"Doing nails at some salon out the back of French Street."

"What did I tell you? Worthy." Angie examined her own nails. They were painted an interesting shade of pink, but tinged with darker smudges of graphite. Hmm… That was the problem with her job. Even if she started the day looking a million dollars, she always ended up resembling a coal miner by lunch.

Hazel muttered beneath her breath. "Miller needs his ass kicked for not writing it up on the board, and as far as I'm concerned, his wife can polish *my*—"

Angie choked on a mouthful of coffee and looked for a change of subject. Hiding a grin, she surveyed the desk, or what was assumed to be a desk. There was so much piled on it, it could be an alien spacecraft or a nuclear device, and no one would ever know. "Someone ought to tidy up."

"Yeah," Hazel muttered, refusing to be distracted, "I'd like to see Miller's wife in here with a duster—"

The switchboard buzzed. Hazel turned on her heel and headed for the door. "—because it isn't going to be me."

Angie finished her coffee and dropped the paper cup in the bin beside Miller's desk. On impulse, she began to tidy. She liked order, liked everything in neat stacks, pens and pencils lined up, which was probably why she'd gravitated to law enforcement in the first place. She liked the process of breaking down all the uncertainty that went with a crime and coming out with the kind of rock-solid evidence that a case could be built on. She liked justice. According to her mother, in another life she would have been a vigilante, but Angie didn't agree. She was passionate about the cause, and that, combined with her fussy neatness, made her damn good at collecting evidence. She shifted a file, and dust plumed up, making her sneeze. "Oh, gross."

"Talking to yourself again, Angie." Gatreaux strolled past, grabbed his jacket from the back of his desk chair and headed for the door.

"Some days it's the only way I get a conversation around here."

Vaguely, she registered Gatreaux's reply, but her attention was centered on a note that was floating loose with about a hundred others.

She'd heard Miller discussing Jane Gale's case. According to the note, she had almost walked in on the guy stalking her and found a microfilm he'd been using left in the viewer. She wanted the film checked out for prints. Another search of the desk and she located the sealed package that went with the note, and an attendant file.

Shaking her head at how lax Miller had become, not even taking the time to log in the evidence, she carried the whole file back to her desk, sat down, grabbed a Danish and began to read. Twenty minutes later, her blood boiling, she walked through to the lab, pulled on latex gloves and began searching for prints.

Using her finest, softest brush, she dusted the film, holding her breath as fine black powder floated in the air. Shaking off the excess graphite, she examined the patterns that were left. The cellulose was wide, the surface shiny, which made it almost as good as glass for retaining a print. Using a strip of clear book-binding tape slightly wider than the film, she carefully applied it, peeled it back, then affixed the tape to a sheet of plastic, thereby preserving the print.

Carefully, so as not to smudge any of the prints, she carried the film to a clear spot of counter and, using the tips of her fingers and handling only the edges, she turned it over and repeated the process on the reverse side.

When she was finished, she examined the prints. Surprisingly, there were only four. She would have expected that with an item in public use there would be many more, which meant the suspect could well have wiped the film down at some point for clearer viewing, then, because he'd left it in the viewer by mistake, hadn't had the opportunity to wipe his own prints off.

After stripping off her gloves, she labeled the prints, then moved to the scanner. From the notes on the file, the profile of the perp indicated that he would almost certainly have a record of some kind. She was positive she would get a hit once she'd entered his prints into the system.

Two hours later, Angie sat back in her seat. She'd searched AFIS and all her physical files, and come up blank. It was possible the prints would be on an FBI file she didn't have access to, but not probable. All she could do was send away the search request and see what came back.

Toussaint placed the receiver in its cradle just as Tyrone slid into the seat adjacent to his desk.

"I'm not looking for a story," Brady said quietly. "I want you to investigate something." He placed Jane's book on the desk. "A man died today. He was old, but he didn't die naturally. According to my calculations, that's the third death centered around Ms. Gale, after that stalker and the woman who got killed just like the victims in this book."

Briefly, Tyrone related the facts surrounding Arnold Carpenter's death. "He was bruised. It looked like someone held their hand over his mouth and nose. The time of death is pretty accurately pinned down. The nurse brought him a visitor around two."

"Who?"

"He claimed to be a nephew, but Arnold doesn't have a nephew." Tyrone shook his head. "It's a standing joke—or was. In Arnold's family, he was the only one who produced a boy." He paused. "You might not know this, but Arnold saved Jane Gale's life when she was a child. She was dead, and Arnold brought her back. I should remember. That was my first week on the job and my first real story, and I got it wrong. I published a death notice and the next day had to write a retraction. That mistake nearly lost me my job. Looks like you got another murder on your hands. The third one connected with Jane Gale."

Angie sidled past Brady as he strode out of the field room; then she perched on the end of Toussaint's desk. It took a lot to shake her, but the report she'd just received via e-mail had managed it.

She dropped the report on his desk. "The DNA report on the Waltham case just came back. A sample was already registered on CODIS." She took a breath and let it out slowly. "It's a perfect match. We're not dealing with a copycat. Myra Waltham was killed by the original killer."

Angie laid the bagged microfilm with Jane's note stapled to it on his desk beside the report. "You might want to check that out, too. Miller had it on his desk. Jane Gale and the librarian *saw* the guy who was stalking her, and she brought this in to be fingerprinted. He was an older guy with a moustache and glasses. Gerry Butler was thirty-five and clean-shaven. I think they saw our serial killer."

Toussaint studied the microfilm on the old viewer in Angie's lab. The fact that it covered the newspaper reports on Jane's accident and the character piece on Arnold couldn't be a coincidence.

Toussaint tried to work the logic back and put himself in the place of the man who had almost killed Jane. If he had tried to murder her, it was possible that he had checked the newspaper to ascertain the kill, then left. Years later, when Jane's book came out, enough copies were distributed that it must have been like putting out an advertisement that she was still alive. The killer had picked up her book and discovered that the only witness to his crimes had survived.

He sat back in his chair, the skin at the back of his neck tightening. He had read Jane's book; the details were eerily correct. Crazy as it seemed, it was possible that they had an almost unheard of commodity: an eyewitness to one of the most bizarre serial killers of all time. There was just one small problem: she couldn't remember what she'd witnessed.

If the killer was the original, then the motivation for killing both Butler and Arnold Carpenter fit. Arnold Carpenter was a link to Jane's past—and he had saved her. If it hadn't been for him, Jane would have died. Butler's obsession with Jane had simply put him in the way.

The reason Jane had left her unit early in the morning was because something had spooked her. It was possible she had heard the killer and gotten out just before he made his entrance. Later on that morning, she had told Butler to piss off over the phone. Enraged, he had gone to her unit and smashed it up. Unfortunately, he had run into the killer, who was waiting for Jane.

With careful movements, Toussaint unthreaded the film and sealed it back in its labeled bag, before handing it to Angie to store. As evidence, it was crucial. They had DNA on the Waltham case, but no fingerprints. On the Butler case, they had nothing—the killing had been professional and clean. With Arnold Carpenter, they were hampered by the fact that so many people had handled the body, but a preliminary autopsy had revealed a needle mark in his right arm. Now they were waiting on a toxicology report.

The ramifications piled up. Something kicked in his chest. If they really were dealing with the original killer, then Jane was his ultimate target.

At 10:30 that night, Toussaint knocked on Jane's door. When she opened it, she lifted a brow. His jacket was off, and so was his tie. For him, that practically amounted to dereliction. "Another body?" The question was flippant, but the dread that went with it wasn't.

"As a matter of fact, Arnold Carpenter died today, but that's not why I'm here. I checked out that microfilm you brought in the other day. I'll need you to come in and give a statement, and work on a description, but that can wait until the morning. We got the DNA report on Myra Waltham's killer. It's the original guy. You need protection, and I'm it."

Jane's jaw set, clamping down on the shock that Arnold had died. Even though she had spent only a little over half an hour with Arnold, she had *liked* him. "You can't just walk in here—"

Toussaint shouldered past her. "Who're you going to call? The police? Boulet just might join me. He's pretty embarrassed."

"You're not sleeping with me."

He walked into the living room and sat down, and not for the first time she noticed the dark smudges beneath his eyes. "I'll take the couch. Right now, I'm so tired even the floor looks good."

Within five minutes, he was asleep. Jane grabbed a spare duvet from the linen cupboard and draped it over him, then sat in the adjacent armchair, sipping a cup of tea.

Despite everything that had happened, the chemistry between them still existed. She was female, and he was male, and something in her psyche clicked into place every time she saw him.

On a practical level, she knew he'd had his job to do. She could even understand his reasoning for the way he'd acted. He had wanted to dispense with the law enforcement issue of her involvement in Butler's death before getting in any deeper with her, and he hadn't flinched from doing the job himself. He had escorted her to the station and taken her through the process, refraining from an arrest and the unpleasantness that would have caused. She hadn't been fingerprinted and searched, and she hadn't been locked in a cell; she had simply had to undergo the interview.

What burned was his aloofness. She didn't trust easily, but she had trusted Toussaint on an emotional level, and he had detached himself as easily as if she'd been a casual date.

She remembered what the manicurist, Ella-Marie, had said. Something to the effect that men didn't think like women. Toussaint was logical and direct, a man with his own code, honed from years of coping with violent criminals. When he made a decision, he carried it out. He had dealt with Travis one-to-one in a way that had ensured there would be no reprisals for either Toussaint or herself, and he had dealt with their "relationship" in the same way.

His methods were direct and somewhat ruthless, but at least she could trust in that. If he was here because he thought she needed protection, then she needed protection.

She had studied recent events until the facts had

jumbled in her mind, always aware that she was seeing them from her point of view. For Toussaint to arrive at the same theory—that she was connected to the killer, and in danger—was alarming.

Twenty-Five

Jane spent the morning giving a statement about the episode in the library and working with the police artist, a man named Roland, who was also their photographer, although there wasn't much she could contribute. The librarian had already offered her description, but the final picture was nondescript, the most distinctive features a baseball cap, glasses and a heavy moustache.

She was also brought up to speed with all three murders. The theories were still sketchy, the strongest being that twenty-five years ago she had been a witness to murder. Crazy as that seemed, it was the only explanation that fitted with all the killings.

She frowned when she saw a mug shot of Gerry Butler. His face was vaguely familiar. She remembered a piece of news Claire had given her after news of Butler's death had reached home. "I know who he is. He's the T.V. repairman. He used to work at the appliance shop in Beach Haven."

Among other things, the shop had sold and serviced phones. Jane had to wonder how many people had never gotten their phones back.

In the afternoon, Toussaint collected Jane and took her to the fairground.

"The annual summer fair is on. I don't know if it'll mean much, but it could jog something loose."

At present, owing to the fact that school was out, the fairground was packed with children and teenagers, and most of the rides had lines.

They stopped at one of the games. Jane stared at the clowns' masks, and a wave of revulsion rolled over her. They were cheerfully painted, but the fixed expressions were too reminiscent of the death masks she'd researched and written about.

Toussaint's hand landed in the small of her back, propelling her forward. "Anything?"

She stiffened slightly at his touch, aware that he wasn't letting up on the pressure, both professionally and emotionally. With an effort of will, she relaxed. A part of her had accepted his presence, and she was female enough that she couldn't suppress the hum of excitement she felt every time he was near, but the sense of betrayal she'd felt when he had taken her in for questioning was enough to make her wary.

She transferred her attention away from the clowns to the ranks of cute and cuddly stuffed animals, suppressing a shudder. The novel she'd written had been about a sick and twisted psychopath. When she'd sat down to write, she had intended to write a fast-paced suspense novel with a dash of humor, but *that* had come out instead.

She had wondered, as she was writing it and the story had flowed, cold and dark and electrifying, if she was awake or dreaming. Sometimes hours had slipped by while she'd typed, and when she'd looked up from her computer it had been dark. Not for the first time it occurred to her that the mechanism of writing somehow loosened up her mind, allowing the past to seep through.

Lately, when she wrote, she was experiencing the phenomenon more and more, and the sensation wasn't comfortable: a disturbing sense of déjà vu, followed by frustration as almost-grasped memories shifted just beyond her reach. One day she had been certain she was on the verge of remembering her mother. There had been nothing concrete, no physical details or a name, more an emotional tug, then the fragile wisp of memory had dissolved.

Toussaint glanced at Jane's face as they threaded through the crowds. He had purposely put her in front of the clowns' masks because he'd wanted to jog a response, but now he was sorry he'd done it. If the supposition that she was an eye-witness was correct, it was likely she'd seen a murder in progress at the age of seven.

Abruptly, he didn't want her to remember. In his job, he routinely saw death and violence, but he had never seen a murder as horrific as Myra Waltham's. No child should have to witness a crime like that.

The crowd thickened as they walked. He took the opportunity to curve his hand around her waist and pull her against his side. It was sly, and it was male, but he didn't care; he wanted her close. He felt protective and possessive and on edge. He wanted Jane, and the investigation had pushed him into an untenable position.

A little while later, as they headed for the car, he caught a glimpse of a man as he threaded his way between the booths, and his gaze sharpened. There was something familiar about the way the man moved, the tilt of his head.

He caught another glimpse as they walked onto the street. Unlocking the car, he handed the key to Jane. "Just a minute."

He loped down a side alley and came out on another street, this one lined with old warehouses that were constructed cheek-by-jowl, terrace fashion. Instead of walking to a parked vehicle, the man continued to walk, his stride easier, and Toussaint hesitated. He was getting further and further away from Jane, into one of the older industrial areas.

At two o'clock on a Saturday afternoon, it was as busy as the main street of town, with handymen and couples doing their shopping. He caught a flash of movement down a side alley. Whoever the man was, he was abruptly certain that he had realized he was being followed.

Keeping to the shadows, Toussaint walked between the two warehouses, stepping quietly until the alleyway ended in a brick wall—the back end of the old sugar mill.

Retracing his footsteps, he checked out the buildings on both sides. One warehouse had a heavy roller door; the other had a loading bay enclosed by a tall chain link fence. Both were industrial loading bays only, and everything was securely padlocked. If anyone had tried to open either the roller door or scale the chain link, the noise would have been distinct, and Toussaint hadn't heard a thing.

He checked the street without much hope. Either the man had evaded Toussaint in the milling crowd, or he had disappeared into thin air.

The following morning, after arranging for a patrol officer to protect Jane, Toussaint left for Quantico and a meeting with the violent-crime unit.

VICAP routinely liaised regarding all serial killer cases. To date he only had one bona fide local victim, but given the past history of the killer, the Waltham case qualified.

Toussaint met with the agent assigned to the case.

Rita Holworth was forty-something, plump and cheerful, and terrifyingly efficient. Before she had become an agent, she had been a trauma nurse working in Baltimore, doing triage. Shifting to law enforcement work had just been a change of battleground. Rita checked the computer system for the file.

"It's not here." She frowned. "I don't understand. According to the numbering system, it *should* be. The way we record the information has been reformatted a couple of times, but basically, the files can't be deleted."

"What about the hard copy?"

Rita reached for a set of keys. "The chances that the actual paperwork has survived are dicey, but the microfilm should be there unless there's been a fire or water damage."

Half an hour later, Rita gave up on the microfilm and led the way back to her office. "I don't believe it. The film was listed as being there." She shook her head. "I've known files to go missing, but this is ridiculous."

Toussaint paced to the window, too restless to

sit. "We could check the various police departments to see if they're still holding evidence, but that would take time." And his gut told him time was up. Whoever was killing, he was actively committing crimes *now*. They had a sample of DNA and a psychological profile. What he needed was a fingerprint

Rita leaned closer to the computer screen, scrolled down a page and smiled. "I know someone who might be able to help." She indicated the name of one of the investigating detectives who had been with the Atlanta PD. "Burton Coley. Something's finally going right today."

Burton Coley was in his early fifties and had hung up his investigative hat. These days he was teaching recruits at Quantico.

Toussaint shook hands with Coley and stepped into his office. The older man was neatly dressed, with thinning gray hair, the brown eyes behind his bifocals sharp.

Coley laid a box on the desk. "The evidence kept disappearing. Some got lost in transit, another lot went in a fire." He shrugged. "By then the killings had stopped and the case was closed, cold, so no one was crying over it. It wasn't legal, but I took home what I'd been working with. I figured that way I could ensure that if the killer ever surfaced, there would be something left."

Coley's gaze was somber and a little distant as he regarded the box. "Twenty-five years." He shook his head. "I'd like to buy back those years. That was one case I wanted to solve."

Coley opened his office door to show him out. Toussaint picked up the box and registered that Coley wanted to know if he was staying over.

"No, I'm flying out in an hour."

The sooner he got home the better.

Jane stepped out of the shower, her hair damp, a towel wrapped around herself, and studied her clothes.

Before meeting Toussaint, making a choice had been easy. To exercise, she wore sweats. To work, she wore more sweats. To date… Usually she didn't date.

Her stomach churned, and she frowned. For years she'd lived a disciplined, focused life; she'd known what was important and gone after it one hundred and ten percent. When she set a goal, she achieved it. That was one of the qualities her ex-husband hadn't appreciated. According to Paul, she was too cold, too focused, and he'd had to go outside their marriage to find the "affection" he needed.

She studied the make-up on her dresser. Now she couldn't even decide what color lipstick to wear, and that vulnerability was terrifying.

She stared at her reflection in the mirror and frowned at the naked terror in her eyes. "Okay, Jane, stop being a wimp."

Pulling open a drawer, she selected the hot pink underwear and slipped it on. Next she pulled on the filmy pink and black skirt but decided against the halter top that went with it. On its own, the skirt could be worn casually, but combined with the top, it was definitely dressy, and she didn't want Toussaint to think she'd gone to too much effort. Besides, he'd had his chance at the halter top and blown it. Instead she selected a sleeveless pink top that buttoned down the front.

Next she dried and styled her hair, applied make-up and perfume, then walked barefoot out to the living room. Peering out the window, she saw the patrol car parked outside the entrance to the cottage. Dropping the curtain, she paced back to the lounge. She felt restless and edgy. It was almost seven. Toussaint was due home any minute.

An hour later, she was almost frantic, when she opened the door and Toussaint stepped in. He dropped his briefcase and jacket on the floor, and kicked the door closed behind him. Jane didn't hesitate. She walked straight into his arms. Three people had died violently, and all of them had been linked to her. Toussaint was concerned for her safety, but he was involved with her on both a professional and a personal level, which had to put *him* at risk.

His mouth came down on hers, and she wound her arms around his neck.

Long minutes later, he lifted his head. "If you want me to talk to you in French, you're out of luck."

"I wasn't planning on a long conversation."

"And I wasn't planning on giving you one." His gaze was intense. "Are you wearing that bra?"

"Which one?"

"Don't be a tease."

"I wore it yesterday. It's in the wash."

His fingers dropped to her blouse. One button went, then another. Her throat locked up, and her mouth went dry.

One long tanned finger stroked between her breasts. "Liar," he said softly.

He bent and kissed her neck, and she almost fainted. "What took you so long?"

"The flight was delayed. Engine trouble."

She found one of his buttons, and worked it loose. Obligingly, he pulled his shirt from the waistband of his pants, and she slid her palms against the firm muscles of his belly.

He tensed. With an abrupt movement, he shrugged out of the shirt and let it drop to the floor. In the dim hallway, with the fading light gleaming on his shoulders, he was uncompromisingly male. Minus the shirt, he was more muscular than she'd thought, his pecs and abs clearly defined. "You work out."

He slid her blouse off her arms and unhooked her bra. "It passes the time."

She would bet a lot of women would like to help him pass that time. But the fact that he spent his leisure time in such a solitary way was typical. He didn't play a sport or belong to any clubs. Toussaint was a loner.

His hands spanned her waist. Then his mouth closed over one breast, and she gasped. When he lifted his head, he moved her hand downward. Her fingers slid beneath the waistband of his pants and closed around his erection.

He tensed, the muscles of his neck cording. "Now."

Gathering her skirt, he pushed the filmy fabric to her waist and peeled her panties down. She felt him prodding her belly. There was a brief surreal moment while he fitted a condom; then his hands fitted around her buttocks, lifting her, and he drove inside her.

For a fractured instant they were frozen; then

his mouth locked over hers and he began to thrust. Seconds later they both collapsed against the wall.

The fact that they had managed a condom was a miracle.

One hand stroked her hair and tilted her head back. His mouth settled on hers, the kiss slow and sensual. She could feel him hardening against her again.

"No." She was abruptly self-conscious. The front door was partly glassed, and from some angles, the hallway was visible from the lounge window. Because the sun hadn't set, she hadn't pulled the curtains. It was dim, true, and there were no lights on, but if the Kyles took a stroll in their garden, they would see more than they expected. Her fingers closed on his as she pulled him toward the bedroom. "In here."

When they were settled in bed, Toussaint fitted another condom, propped himself up on one elbow and ran a fingertip over one of the scars on her midriff, sending a shiver through her.

"When I find him, I'm going to kill him."

"Don't think about that now." Framing his face with her hands, Jane pulled his mouth to hers, then shivered with delight when he settled on top of her and almost instantly slid inside her. It was primitive and utterly female, but she needed this.

Long minutes later, he rolled on his back and

settled her against his side. Sleepily, Jane rubbed a hand over his belly. "I don't think I told you, but I'm the jealous type."

"Good. So am I."

"You know those people who talk about being happy with a glass that's half full? I'm not one of them."

"I didn't think you would be."

"We'll fight." She could feel him grinning in the dark.

"I like a good fight—as long as we can have sex afterward."

"I'm trying to give you a message, Toussaint. I'm...difficult."

"You'll get over it. And the name's John." He pulled her close in a hug that, despite his erection, was oddly asexual, more for comfort and fun than making love.

Surrounded by brawny arms and muscle, Jane felt something shift in her mind. In the space of a split second, something fundamental had changed. She wanted him when she hadn't wanted anyone in a very long time. Now she *liked* him, as well. She'd felt attraction and liking for a number of men but, somehow, indefinably, Toussaint was different.

Maybe it was the link they shared, and the intensity that arose from her drive to find her past.

Then again, maybe it was simply Toussaint. She'd never met anyone quite like him. If she was focused, he was like a laser.

"Don't analyze it. Just…" He lifted her thigh, draped her leg over his hip and slid inside her. "Relax."

Amazingly, she did. Her ex-husband had never made her feel like this, and the mistake she'd made in marrying him loomed even larger, the reason he had slipped beneath her defenses suddenly laid bare.

The man was all packaging and no substance. Unfortunately, she'd been too green to know the difference.

Toussaint's hand cupped the small of her back and slid slowly up her spine. He began to play with her hair. "You're starting to trust me."

"Maybe. But don't expect to get everything your own way, Toussaint."

Jane woke to moonlight shining directly through the window and washing across the bed.

Toussaint's arm slid from her waist. "Stay here."

The bed creaked slightly as he shifted. With a fluid movement, he straightened and fastened his pants. Moonlight glinted on something metallic, and she heard the distinctive sound of a round being chambered as he melted into the shadows.

She stared at the window. Something had moved

out there. She didn't know if it was an animal, Toussaint, or an intruder, and suddenly she didn't care. Despite the screen of shrubbery that gave privacy to the bedroom, with the curtains open, she felt exposed. Dragging the sheet up around her chin, she leaned down and snagged the puddle of white fabric on the floor—Toussaint's shirt—and slipped it on. Once she was decent, she climbed out of bed, found her track pants and pulled those on, too. The window, which during the day framed a picturesque view, loomed overlarge in the room— black and dominated by the flattened disk of the waning moon. With jerky movements, she closed the curtains, then walked through to the living room. She didn't want to be in the bedroom. If someone was out there, watching, then it was the bedroom he would be focusing on.

Toussaint ghosted into the living room. "I caught a glimpse of him. He's got night vision." He gestured for her to get down on the floor behind the couch. "Stay down, and don't move until I say."

Jane stayed down, her cheek pressed to the carpet, ears straining.

Toussaint slipped back outside and stared into the night. Someone was out there. Playing games. He did a circuit of the cottage, but he didn't want to stray too far from Jane. When he came up with nothing, he strode back inside. "Pack your things," he said curtly. "You're coming with me."

He slid down from the branch of a gnarled oak, landing lightly on his feet.

She was sleeping with the boy.

The coincidence that she had hooked up with *him,* of all people, was too much. She knew.

If he'd had any doubts, they were gone. She had remembered, and he was out of time. He couldn't afford to wait any longer.

He would have to try another way. And fast.

Twenty-Six

Toussaint slipped the microfilm into Lassiter Library's viewing machine and once again began to scroll through the photographed pages of the *Lassiter Daily*. An hour later, after skimming several editions, he went back to the page Jane had said was left on in the library's viewer.

He sat back in his chair and rubbed his eyes.

When he looked back at the screen, a name jumped out at him: Dexter.

The piece was virtually the size of a postage stamp and held about as much information. Charles Dexter had been admitted to Lassiter General with him, the same night that Jane had been taken in, suffering head injuries sustained in a car crash.

Sometimes one tiny, seemingly incongruous detail could break a case wide open. He could see why it had been overlooked in the investigation of Jane's hit-and-run, not to mention the serial killings. It was the kind of detail that didn't mean a thing to anyone but him.

His chest tightened. It could be a coincidence, but he didn't think so. Sometimes crimes remained unsolved, and sometimes there came a turning point in an investigation when information that had been elusive, or just didn't fit, fell into place. It brought to mind his White Moon grandmother's saying that if anyone ever did anything wrong, the truth would come out. All you had to do was wait.

Toussaint shook his head, disoriented. He'd thought the past was a certain way, but it wasn't.

He could only vaguely remember his mother, and Etienne's grief and anger when she'd walked out on them, and his stepfather didn't often talk about the Dexter family. Etienne's twin, Charles, had been some kind of computer expert, and Etienne's half brother, Stephen, had been a cop, but neither of them had ever kept in touch. To Toussaint's certain knowledge, aside from those two brothers, there were no other surviving Dexters, and his own family were even thinner on the ground. His father, John White Moon, an Army Ranger, had been killed in action in the Middle East before he was born. He saw his paternal grandmother and a few cousins occasionally, mostly when somebody died. On the Toussaint side, now that both of his grandparents were dead, the connection was even more tenuous. He had a couple of cousins that he knew of, one in Baton Rouge, the other in Shreveport.

He studied the report on Charles Dexter again. Now that he'd gotten over the initial shock of finding such an unexpected link, the connection seemed glaring. He couldn't believe that the local police had missed it.

He didn't like it that Etienne's family were now involved in the investigation, but he wasn't about to flinch from it.

Jane watched as Toussaint paced his kitchen, as restless as a caged animal, stopping every few minutes to stare out at his rambling backyard as if he could wrench the answers to his internal questions from the huge scarlet dinner-plate dahlias growing in clumps against the sagging fence.

The previous night they had packed all her belongings and she had moved in with him. This morning she had rung the Kyles and explained the situation as best she could, trying not to alarm them. The fact that they'd had someone prowling around on their land hadn't sat easily with either

Mary or Bill, and they hadn't wasted any time in calling in a security firm. They had offered the cottage to her for a further week if she wanted it, but Jane had declined. With her involvement in the murder enquiry, she needed to stay in Lassiter, but she wouldn't willingly endanger anyone else.

She felt Toussaint's gaze settle on her as she placed washed lettuce leaves in a colander to drain, and a delicate shiver crept up her spine.

She felt his intention a split second before his arms came around her waist, pulling her back against him. His jaw rubbed against her exposed nape, and the shiver turned into a wave of raw heat.

Sleeping in Toussaint's house and his bed for what was left of the night had been an intimate experience. He had been possessive, never letting her out of his sight for a second, and keeping her close in bed. For a man who, she'd found out courtesy of the Lassiter PD grapevine, had a reputation for being singularly aloof, the way he'd babied her had been distinctly out of character and oddly sweet.

"What *do* you know about your past?"

Jane paused in the act of slicing up tomatoes for the salad they were having with the chicken and potato casserole bubbling in the oven. Strictly, the casserole was winter comfort food, and it pushed the temperature in the kitchen up an uncomfortable couple of degrees, but with the necessity of staying inside the house under police guard all day, the simple ritual of preparing food had been exactly what she'd needed.

She shrugged. She'd long since stopped trying to force information out of her mind. "Twenty-five years ago I had a photograph and a chocolate bar in my pocket." She arranged the tomatoes decoratively in a bowl full of salad greens and scattered thin slices of red onion on top. As she reached for the olive oil, the wisp of memory she'd had while sitting on the side of Sugar Hill Road surfaced. "I also had a bag with a lot of other stuff in it, but that was never found."

Toussaint's arms slid from her waist. He propped himself on the counter beside her. "You didn't tell me that."

"I've only just remembered." With everything else that had happened, as significant as it had been for her, the memory had gotten pushed to the back of her mind.

Jane stared at a painting she'd found in the stairwell that didn't seem to match anything else in the house. The light caught it, making it glow. The colors were soft and dreamy, the subject matter restful—an avenue of shade trees, a rambling rose adding a splash of brightness. Every time she'd walked past it, she'd been drawn to it. Finally she'd moved it into the kitchen.

And like the other times, the memory took her by surprise.

The photograph hadn't belonged to her. It had been John's, along with the candy bar. When she had come to get him, he had been asleep, and she'd had to wake him up and dress him. He'd been five years old, and sleepy. Getting him to pull jeans and a shirt over his pajamas, then lace up a pair of sneakers in the dark, had been almost more than she was able to manage.

"The photo was yours," she said flatly. "And so was the chocolate bar."

Toussaint's attention was wholly centered on Jane's face; her skin had gone very pale, her gaze slightly unfocused, as if she were looking inward. That meant they had been linked at the crucial time, the time when her accident happened. "Twenty-five years ago my uncle Charles and I were also in a car accident. I checked with Lassiter General, and he was admitted for head wounds. I was treated as an outpatient. I had a concussion, which could explain why I don't remember anything. At about the same time the killings stopped."

Toussaint stared out at the sunny evening. He had studied everything he could get his hands on about the killings, including Coley's own notes. "Not 'about' the same time. *Exactly*. The last recorded linked homicide—until now—had happened just two days before, in Detroit."

Toussaint's cell phone beeped. He checked the screen and stepped outside. When he terminated the call, he walked inside and searched through the phone directory for Brady's home number.

This morning he had submitted a sample of his stepfather's DNA for testing, obtained from a hair Angie had extracted from an old sweater Etienne had lent him the last time he was home. The reasoning was inescapable. The Dexter family were linked to Jane. Etienne and his brothers were the right age to have committed the murders that ended twenty-five years ago. And whoever had committed those murders had also committed the current ones.

Unpalatable as it was, he had been proven right.

He picked up the receiver and made the call. If anyone had the information he needed, it was Brady. He had been in Lassiter when both Jane and Charles Dexter had had their "accidents." Not only had he written the newspaper reports, he had a long memory and a mind for detail. If anyone knew what had happened to Charles, it would be Brady.

Paterson, New York

Etienne Dexter opened the front door of his house.

Rita Holworth flipped open her badge. "FBI, Mr. Dexter. I need to talk to you about the murder of Myra Waltham."

Etienne's heart pounded, and his Adam's apple took a painful trip up and down his throat. He'd been waiting half a lifetime for this knock on his door, but... He frowned.

"Who?"

Rita Holworth slipped the badge in her purse, her smile brisk. "It's all right, Mr. Dexter. We know you didn't do it. John's already established that you were consulting on a bridge repair in Boston when the murder happened. It's your twin brother we're interested in."

Shortly after the APB went out, Charles Dexter was picked up in Atlanta. His print matched the lone print that had been found in Burton Coley's box of evidence. One of the most bizarre and dangerous killers in history was finally caught. He had been found occupying a park bench.

Now Toussaint sat in an interview room and looked into the vacant eyes of his stepfather's twin. They were genetically identical, although they no longer looked that way. Etienne was upright and lean; Charles had shrunken in on himself, the dent on his forehead visible evidence of his incapacity.

After the head injury he'd received in the accident twenty-five years ago, he was barely functioning.

Toussaint pushed a mug of coffee toward Charles and watched as his uncle took it with shaking hands. "Why don't you go home, Charles?"

For a moment Toussaint didn't think he had comprehended the question, then Charles frowned, staring into the mug as if he could pull the answer out of his coffee like a rabbit out of a magician's hat. "C-can't," he stuttered. "Not al-lowed."

He lifted his head, cocked it to one side as if he was listening. "Locked in." He shook his head, his gaze puzzled. "Now…l-locked out."

Toussaint opened his briefcase and brought out a notepad and pen. "Hey, Charles. This time we're going to draw. I'll draw my house. How about you draw yours?"

Toussaint drew a rudimentary rendition of a house, complete with smoke coming out of the chimney, but Charles's drawing didn't have anything to do with rooms or chimneys.

Toussaint pointed at the seemingly random scribble. "What's that?"

When there was no reply, Toussaint positioned his house drawing next to Charles's page, pointed to his own picture and repeated his question.

Charles frowned. "House," he muttered, and picked up his coffee.

Toussaint pointed to Charles's page. "So what's this?"

Charles looked at him with contempt. "Barn."

Toussaint left the interview room, picked up a phone and dialed Gatreaux's mobile. For a few seconds the vagueness in Charles Dexter's eyes had disappeared, and he'd been lucid, looking back into the past.

They had already searched the old Dexter homestead and come up with zip. There was a garage on the property, but it was reasonably modern. It was more than likely that the barn Charles had been locked in as a boy had been demolished, but there was also the possibility that it was located on a piece of land that had been subdivided off and sold separately from the house—and was still in existence.

Seconds later, he was put through to Gatreaux's voice mail and left a message. Disconnecting the call, he picked up his briefcase and left for the airport.

There was still a lot of legwork to be done, but if his theory was correct, Charles had been committing the murders in the same cities where his twin, Etienne, had worked—an extra kick for one of the most bizarre killers in recent history. With the patchy information he had managed to obtain so far, the pattern had initially made Etienne look guilty, but once Toussaint had begun logging Charles's movements, as well, what was happening had become clear. Charles had been clever, but not clever enough. A couple of times Etienne had been called away, but the murders had occurred anyway. Myra Waltham's murder added another twist. Despite the DNA evidence obtained from the strand of hair on her body, neither Etienne nor Charles could have committed that murder.

Stephen Dexter studied the house next door to Toussaint's property on Plaisance Street, then eased his vehicle up the narrow driveway. The Samuels had both left for work before nine this morning, taking their small toddler to daycare. No one was home.

Settling the ball cap on his head, he picked up one of the fist-sized decorative rocks in the garden to reveal the spare key, then walked to the back door.

Minutes later he had set up his laser equipment in the master bedroom and aimed the device at one of Toussaint's kitchen windows. In broad daylight it was unlikely anyone would see, let alone register, what the tiny dot of color was.

An hour later, the call he'd been waiting for came. If there was one thing he knew, it was cops.

Nothing was more boring than a protection detail, and when cops got bored, like everyone else, they liked to eat.

Jane handed the patrol officer his phone after she'd ordered the pizza.

Toussaint had organized two officers to guard her. Marc was inside, and there was a second officer, Lewis, staking out the garden. Both men were armed and in constant radio contact, with frequent check-ins. In theory, all the bases were covered.

Three-quarters of an hour later, the food arrived. The pizza was congealed, the coffee bitter and lukewarm, not hot, but Jane scarcely cared. She was eating to fuel her body and pass the time until John came home.

John. She stared at the mausoleum of the Toussaint house, experiencing the surprise that crept up on her every time she considered how radically her life had changed. It seemed strange to think of Toussaint in such an intimate way.

Fifteen minutes later, Jane curled up in a small armchair set to one side of the coffee table and flipped through a magazine. She yawned, barely able to keep her eyes open.

Marc was already asleep.

Panic surged through her, but it was too little,

too late. She stumbled to her feet, gripping the table, and the room spun. Her fingers brushed the cell phone she'd left there. It skidded away, slid off the side of the table and bounced on the floor.

Jane clung to the table. Her vision was impaired; she felt dizzy and faintly sick. With an effort of will, she shuffled toward the phone.

This time she managed to pick it up. Staggering back to the chair, she sat, using the table for a support. Keeping her gaze doggedly fastened on the small screen, she brought the menu up, then selected her saved numbers. Grimly, she scrolled down the directory. The phone beeped, and her stomach lurched as the screen flicked back to the menu. Somehow her thumb had slipped, canceling the directory.

Taking a deep breath, she tried again, but her lids kept sliding closed, and it was getting harder and harder to direct her fingers. She brought up the directory again, but something was wrong with her hand-eye coordination, because she dialed the wrong number.

She heard the call picked up, the cheery voice asking if she had an order. She had gotten a local Beach Haven restaurant that did take-out. Abruptly, the call was terminated. Seconds later, it buzzed with an incoming call.

Jane stared at the phone, her mind blank, then the phone slipped from her fingers.

* * *

Stephen Dexter hung up, satisfied. He slid the cell phone he'd taken from Butler—and which had so conveniently been preprogrammed with Jane's number—into his pocket.

Turning the key in the ignition, he put the pizza delivery van in motion and headed for Plaisance Street. Two minutes later, he turned into Toussaint's driveway and stepped from the van.

The front door was locked, but then, he hadn't expected anyone to open it for him. He slid a Browning from his shoulder holster, then used the butt to tap sharply on the glass. The old dimpled pane resisted but finally gave, breaking like brittle toffee. Reaching inside, he unlocked and opened the door. "Simple."

He walked down the hallway, into the living room. Ignoring the man slumped in a nearby chair, he boosted Jane up and over his shoulder, and walked out the door.

Like taking candy from a baby.

Twenty-Seven

Toussaint boarded the flight to New Orleans. When he was seated, he took out Jane's book and began to re-read it.

"Oh, I've read that one. It's good."

Toussaint acknowledged the woman in the seat beside him with a faint smile. She had her own book out and had already returned to it—another murder mystery.

Toussaint stared at the dark, moody cover and the obvious enjoyment on the face of his seating companion, and all the fine hairs at his nape stood on end. The connection with Myra Waltham suddenly clicked into place. According to the information on the back cover, Jane's book, now in its tenth printing, had sold more than two million copies so far. Toussaint was willing to bet that a lot of them had been sold at airports to customers just like the lady he was sitting next to, people who were chained to a flight for several hours and wanted relief from boredom. It finally made sense of a victim that had seemed to have no other connection to Jane than the way she had died.

Myra Waltham had flown to Washington for a conference and had never made the return flight home. With serial killers, there was method in the selection of victims. A serial killer was by definition a successful criminal who had refined his methods to a very high degree. Few victims were impulse or opportunist killings, because the element of risk was too high. Above all else, the serial killer needed to empower himself by fulfilling his fantasy.

Toussaint was willing to bet the killer had been on Myra's initial flight, probably seated close to her.

That didn't explain everything. One fact stood out. There hadn't been any fresh bodies for twenty-five years. The theory that the killer had somehow gone dormant due to death, capture on other grounds, or some kind of incapacity or medication didn't hold water after spending just thirty seconds in Charles's company. Even if Charles hadn't been mentally disabled, Toussaint didn't think that theory would ever fly. Charles didn't have the ability to plan or carry out a murder now, though before his accident, Charles Dexter had been seriously mentally ill. His reality hadn't borne any resemblance to anyone else's—except the killer who was copying him now.

And that killer had not only figured out that Charles was the original "killer," he had gotten hold of Charles Dexter's DNA and left it on Myra Waltham's body.

Gatreaux walked into the evidence lab with a package he'd managed to lift off the Fed Ex guy before he made himself at home in Angie's office.

Angie swiveled in her chair and gave him a cold look over the top of her glasses. It wasn't the look he'd been hoping for.

Gatreaux handed over the package. "Hey? What did I do?"

"I heard you guys arrested John's father. Didn't anyone ever teach you the Golden Rule? We don't take down each other's moms and dads."

"He's wasn't arrested, just questioned, and *I* didn't make the decision. That was Toussaint's call."

Angie sniffed.

Gatreaux slunk back to his desk and the mountain of paperwork that waited for him.

Angie slipped the packaged evidence, returned by the Shreveport PD, who were also running a case against the Laurent brothers, to one side and turned back to her email. A message with an attachment had just arrived in her inbox.

Clicking on the icon, she opened the message and then the attachment. Goose bumps spread down her arms as she studied the result.

She'd been waiting for a reply to her query on the prints on the microfilm for days; it had been unusually slow in coming.

Her heart kicked when she saw the name listed.

Etienne Dexter had a mentally disabled twin named Charles. Both men had a half-brother, Stephen. And it was Stephen's name on her screen now.

The reason she hadn't gotten the result on the print in a timely fashion was because it had had to come from the FBI archives.

Stephen Dexter was an FBI agent.

Picking up the phone, she placed a call, then set the receiver down, frustrated. Toussaint's phone was turned off. She checked her watch. It was possible he was on a flight. She would try again later.

Logging off the computer, she collected the evidence on the Laurent case and carried it down to the evidence room to sign back in. Digging in her pocket, she located the key.

As she strolled down the corridor to the rear of the library, she smelled smoke. A split second later, the source of the fire was clear. Smoke was billowing out of the open door of the evidence room.

Placing the package on the floor, she covered the few steps to the open door, slammed it closed to stop oxygen from being sucked into the room and feeding the blaze, broke the glass on the fire alarm outside the door and punched the button.

Nothing happened. Whoever had started the fire must have taken the time to disable the alarm system first. Angie swore beneath her breath, then hollered.

Gatreaux appeared beside her, followed by Hazel.

Gatreaux reached up and tugged on a wire that was almost as ancient as the building itself, and which was now probably highly illegal. "The cable's been cut." With a grunt, he yanked the two loose ends free of the small metal clips that held it in place and touched them together. Simultaneously the alarm and the sprinkler system came on.

Water drenched Angie. "Oh, great." Most of the evidence was stored in paper bags. What hadn't gone up in flames was now being turned to wet mush.

Within minutes the fire was out. Gatreaux checked inside, then peeled off his wet shirt and tossed it on the ground.

Hazel whistled. Angie fanned herself and looked away. Her hair was a mess, her evidence store was gone, several cases would now be in serious jeopardy—it was possible that one or more of the Laurent brothers and their gang would walk—but the day was finally looking up.

Toussaint exited the plane and immediately walked to the flight counter, flashed his badge and made his request. A few minutes later, after fielding a minor official and a lengthy explanatory phone call, a copy of the passenger manifest for the flight Myra Waltham had been on was faxed through.

He scanned the sheet. Waltham, being near the end of the alphabet, was one of the last names listed. His gaze shifted upward, to the first names on the list and immediately settled on the D's. *Dexter, S,* leaped out at him.

Toussaint slammed into his car and reached for his cell phone as he accelerated out of Royal Street and turned right down Canal, searching for an on ramp to Interstate Ten.

Jane's phone rang, then switched to voice mail. He left a brief message, then dialed again.

"Pick up, dammit."

He tried Gatreaux's number, then reception, with no success, then finally managed to get Miller.

Surprise, surprise, there had been a fire in the evidence room. The fire had messed with the wiring and the electrics, and their landline and radio were presently out. No one was hurt, but Boulet and the public were going crazy. Someone had broadcast the fact that communications were down on a local radio station, and a mini crime wave had already started.

"By the way," Miller said, "Angie's been trying to get hold of you. That print on the microfilm came back, but it didn't have Butler's print on it. The print belongs to an FBI agent, which is why it took so long to identify. It wasn't in any of the state systems."

"Stephen Dexter." Toussaint turned onto the Interstate. "I just found his name on Myra Waltham's flight to Washington." With the cover-up that had happened twenty-five years ago and the gradual destruction of evidence, nothing else made sense. "Has he been picked up?"

"Negative. He's on leave."

On vacation in Lassiter. "Then get Jane."

"I'm on my way there now. I've been trying to raise Marc, but he's not answering."

Toussaint's jaw clamped. "Then Dexter's got her. I'll be there in thirty minutes. Start at the old Dexter farmhouse."

When he still couldn't raise a reply from either Gatreaux or Hazel, Toussaint set the phone back on the seat beside him and drove.

* * *

When Toussaint reached his house, Miller and Gatreaux were there, along with an ambulance. Marc and Lewis were both still unconscious but stable. The consensus seemed to be that while they showed no signs of waking up, they weren't in any great danger.

Miller brought him up to speed. "No wounds or contusions, but they're out. Looks like they've taken something. They had a pizza delivery. We're checking on that."

Miller's phone buzzed. He picked up the call, spoke briefly, then hung up. "That was the pizza place. They had a delivery here about two hours ago. They've lost their truck *and* their driver."

Toussaint raced out to the old Dexter homestead, which was now lost in a subdivision and the back end of an industrial area. Slowing, he studied the houses and the sheds. There were plenty of garages and carports, but all of them looked as recent as the houses. There was no sign of the barn that Charles had talked about.

He stared at the neighborhood, urgency winding him tight. He was close enough to the river to smell the water, far enough away that the view was blocked by houses.

A copse of old, gnarled oaks tugged at his memory. The farm had been on the outskirts of town, but it had been overtaken by Lassiter's urban sprawl, cut up and parceled out as sections. The farmhouse, which was in the process of being searched, was still standing and was situated on Erman Crescent, which was nearby. The main highway was just beyond.

Events began to come together in his mind.

Jane had been hit on Sugar Hill Road.

From the few comments that Etienne had made, he knew that all his uncles had spent at least a portion of their childhood locked in the barn Charles had talked about, courtesy of an abusive stepmother. Eloise Dexter had beaten all three of the Dexter children, but most especially Charles.

A comment Etienne had once made about Charles and Charles's reference to the barn, along with the seemingly aimless struggle he had at dawn, abruptly made sense.

It had been beneath his nose all the time.

Charles had been digging tunnels.

He had probably started as part of an escape fantasy then he had simply kept going, creating a warren beneath the ground.

Taking a turn onto the industrial site, he drove past a marina complex and a storage facility. He caught a glimpse of the back of the Dexter house and braked. The storage facility was a newish complex, but it was close enough to the house that it might occupy the site where the barn used to stand. He drove into the storage facility and saw the nose of a station wagon parked at the rear. His pulse rate accelerated. Sliding his weapon from its holster, he checked the load, chambered a round, then exited the car. The vehicle was a rental, which fit. Why perpetrate a murder in your own vehicle, when you can rent one under a false name and make an evidential mess in someone else's car?

He called Gatreaux and finally got a reply, gave him the car's registration number and requested backup. He also gave him the name and address of the storage facility. If he didn't miss his guess, it belonged to Stephen Dexter. When the farm had been sold, the proceeds had been split three ways. Toussaint was willing to bet Stephen had invested his share, and probably Charles's, in purchasing this lot and constructing a new building over the old, therefore preserving what lay beneath it.

He studied the ground, which was covered in fine blue-chip gravel. A chill went down his spine when he discerned what could be drag marks. He checked the door and tested its strength. There was no point in trying to either shoot out the lock or kick it in; the door was made of reinforced steel.

His cell phone rang. It was Gatreaux.

"The storage facility is owned by Stephen Dexter, and guess what else? So is the sugar mill."

Toussaint stepped around the corner of the storage building and checked out the mill. It was so much a part of the landscape that he had hardly noticed it. Years back it had been owned and operated by the Dexter family.

As he studied the mill, something clicked in his mind. The production of sugar required the use of large quantities of water. If Charles had dug tunnels, it was conceivable that he'd eventually connected up with the storm drain system beneath the mill, giving him access to a whole rabbit's warren of tunnels.

And Stephen must have known about it.

Suddenly the way the man he'd followed from the fairground had seemingly disappeared into thin air in a blind alley made sense. The alley had backed onto the sugar mill. There had been no way out but down. The man had been Stephen, and he'd gone underground.

Twenty-Eight

Jane became aware of movement. She lifted her lids with difficulty, the pull of whatever drug had been used to knock her out was still strong enough that she was having trouble just opening her eyes.

She was being dragged in darkness; her hands were tied, but not her feet. The hiss of a tarpaulin or a trunk liner scraped on hard ground beneath her; the chill of dank soil struck through her clothes. A pebble caught beneath the tarp, dug into her spine for a short distance, then skittered away.

She tried to orient herself, but the darkness was absolute and a chill dread grabbed hold deep in her stomach. They were underground.

Her captor stopped, adjusting his grip and resting for a moment. In the darkness, the sound of his breathing was amplified, along with the hollow drip of water.

With an abrupt motion, he resumed his forward movement, and Jane forced herself to stay awake and keep her eyes open. As long minutes ticked by, she waited to see something—anything—that would give her some clue to where she was, but the darkness remained total. She had to wonder how *he* could see. Then she remembered what Toussaint had said about night vision equipment.

He stopped once more, and her skin crawled. She couldn't see him, but she sensed he was staring directly at her. For long seconds she remained still, keeping her breathing even; then, with another jolting tug, he continued on.

He had drugged her with something that left a bitter aftertaste and a heavy feeling in her head. Her guess would be a sleeping pill of some kind, which would account for the bitter taste of the coffee.

To knock her out like he had, he must have used an enormous dose. After years of operations and pain management, her tolerance for most available drugs, including sleeping pills, was huge. It took almost enough anesthetic to knock out a horse before she went under.

Without meaning to, she let her eyelids slide shut again.

* * *

The next time Jane opened her eyes, she was stationary and lying on a table. For a moment she floated, neither asleep nor awake, caught in a half-way place. She realized she must have slipped back into unconsciousness.

Reddish flickering light filtered through her lids, and for a moment she was caught in a powerful sense of déjà vu.

Memories flooded back, fragmented and painful. She remembered surfacing from her coma as her leg was removed from traction, the pain of the procedure enough, finally, to jolt her out of the void and re-engage her mind. She remembered the face of the surgeon, staring down at her from a great height, and with unexpected clarity, she remembered her mother.

An ache started in her chest and spread to her throat. Moisture burned in her eyes as, rapidly, image overlaid image.

A tired movement as Emily hung up an apron after waiting tables, her dark hair pulled back in a knot, the line of her neck graceful. Emily in jeans, a pack on her back, her hand holding Jane's.

They had worked and traveled, traveled and worked, staying in this town for a few weeks, another for just a matter of days, a seemingly endless succession until they had hit Lassiter. Because it had been summer, she hadn't had to enroll in school. She'd simply helped Emily out while she'd cooked and cleaned at the Dexters' farm and looked after John.

Her mother's name had been Emily Mathews.

A faint sound disrupted the flow of memories. Stiffening, Jane turned her head far enough to finally see who was in the room with her. The reddish light came from a lamp shining off walls that had been painted red, and for a moment the distorting glow made her head swim and obscured the features of the man who was bent over mixing some concoction in a bucket. When he turned his head slightly, his profile came into sharp prominence. A heavy ache started at her temples, a crushing pressure in her chest, and abruptly she had it all.

Tears stung her eyes and burned at the back of her throat. Experimentally, she moved the fingers of one hand, gauging just how sluggish her movements were, the pressure building in her chest. Stephen Dexter, older than she remembered but still recognizable, approached the table, his gaze locked with hers, and with a choking cry, she exploded, launching upright. Her forehead drove into Dexter's jaw. Light exploded in her eyes, and her head spun darkly. Sucking in a breath, she managed to retain consciousness. If she let herself pass out, she would die.

Steadying herself against the table, she ran her eyes around the room, looking for something, anything, to use as a weapon. Picking up a lump of plaster the size of a melon, which she realized he'd used to cast a mask, she staggered toward where Dexter was lying. Swaying, she lifted the mold and brought it crashing down on his head.

The plaster cast came apart, crumbling into pieces. Jane wobbled, went to her knees and began to pass out. Her hands swung out and landed on Dexter's chest. His chest lifted beneath her palms, and, with a sound that was more animal than human, she reared back.

She crawled to the table, then pulled herself to her feet and began searching the small, grotesque room. In a knapsack, she found a knife. Fumbling until it was reversed, she began to saw at the thin nylon rope binding her wrists. As soon as the ropes parted, she shoved the knife in the waistband of her trousers and began collecting the masks that decorated the walls.

She stumbled, still dizzy from whatever Dexter had drugged her with, dropping masks and throwing them. The masks were rudimentary and grotesque, most lacking any color to the wax, some sporting garish touches of lipstick and eye shadow.

As she searched for her mother's face, blank-eyed features stared at her. Faces that had belonged to women who had had lives, husbands—maybe even children. He had stolen them away from the people who loved and needed them, taken their lives, their dignity and their femininity. He had taken their hair.

Enraged, Jane swept the paraphernalia that littered the table onto the floor. She found plastic bags of plaster of Paris stacked in a corner, and systematically slit them open and emptied them. White powder filled the room like a fine mist as she picked up a canvas shopping bag that had been folded neatly beneath the bags of plaster of Paris and loaded it with masks, the knife and Dexter's flashlight.

Bending, she pulled the gun from his shoulder holster, kicking herself for not doing that right off. She studied the gun. She knew a little about them— enough to shoot occasionally at a shooting range and write a crime thriller—but nothing about weapons had ever made her comfortable. This one was a Glock, a very light nine-millimeter pistol. With a shudder, she placed the gun in the canvas bag, took the lamp off its hook and walked out the door.

She had taken his weapons, the lamp and his flashlight, but she couldn't kill him. Even after all he'd done, something in her held back from the finality of taking his life.

Jane studied the tunnels and randomly chose a

direction. She had no idea where she was, or if she would ever get out, but even if she didn't survive, she would scatter enough evidence that someone would find something eventually. And Dexter would have a hard time disappearing this time. She was willing to bet his fingerprints and DNA would be on every mask.

After just a few yards, the tunnel split into two. Jane decided to start by going right, then, if the tunnel branched again, left. That way she would have more chance of moving in a straight line and putting maximum distance between herself and Dexter.

She continued to walk for several minutes, counting every step to keep herself from panicking. She wasn't claustrophobic, but small dark tunnels weren't exactly her favorite places. Every time she reached one hundred, she threw a mask at the dirt wall, destroying another abomination and adding to the trail of evidence.

Rounding a corner, she stopped. Her flashlight picked out something light on the ground, and her heart sank. Somehow she had walked in a circle and ended up almost back where she'd started. Turning on her heel, she stumbled back in the direction she'd come, looking for the last turn she'd taken. When she reached the intersection, she directed her light down one tunnel, saw the pale glimmer of another mask and chose the other direction. Bending almost double, she started down the much narrower tunnel. The rabbit hole only ran for a few yards, intersecting with a much larger tunnel that sported the luxury of seeping concrete walls.

Tears dripped off Jane's chin as she walked, but they were largely in reaction to what had happened and a healthy kick of anger and fear; she didn't have room for grief yet.

She threw the last mask. It hit the tunnel wall and fragmented, and a raw shudder swept her as wax and hair dropped into a puddle of water and floated. Jane stopped, transfixed, as the remains moved ahead of her, propelled by what must be a slight downward slope. She shone the light around. She must be in an old set of storm drains. Logic dictated that they had to empty into something, and that something would be the Lassiter River. If she followed the flow, she would find a way out.

Dexter's eyelids flipped open, his ears ringing, his mind sluggish.

Ignoring the vicious ache in his lower jaw and the spots that danced in front of his eyes, he bent and retrieved his ankle weapon. He checked the load on the gun, then began feeling around for his knapsack. His fingers bumped into the rough canvas. Opening the flap, he removed his night vision goggles and put them on. Instantly the room took on a pale greenish shape and form.

As he pushed himself to his knees, he spat out blood and the fragment of a tooth, then grabbed for the edge of the table and hung there, waiting out the sickening throbbing in his head. Running his tongue tentatively around the inside of his mouth, he swore. One of his front caps was gone.

He fingered the swelling on his jaw, and the goose egg that bulged on his forehead and extended down, closing one eye. He spat again, ejecting more blood and another shard of tooth. The bitch must have hit him again while he was out.

Using the table as a support, he dragged himself to his feet. He hadn't felt like this since he'd been on the high school football team and been stiffed in a tackle. He'd gone out like a light and woken with a concussion, but that had been more years ago than he cared to remember.

Blinking, he tried to force his left eye open, but the swelling was too far advanced. Cursing beneath his breath, he took stock with his one good eye. The room looked like it had been hit by a hurricane. Masks had been knocked off walls and lay scattered on the ground, his equipment was wrecked, and plaster of Paris was strewn over everything, but even taking the chaos into account, something felt wrong.

His head turned to the table. She had taken his flashlight—and she had taken his gun. The niggling feeling of wrongness grew. He began to take inventory, and the hammering in his head exploded on a kick of adrenaline.

She hadn't just destroyed the masks; she had taken some with her as evidence.

The clever bitch was going to indict him.

Fury pumped through him. Back as far as he could remember, he had never been enough of anything to satisfy Eloise. The standards she had set had always been beyond his reach, and she had pushed him until he'd moved from bedwetting to an ulcerated stomach. But he had been clever, and he'd won in the end. He had outsmarted both Charles and Etienne.

Despite the fury and the throbbing pain, he smirked, transfixed by his own cleverness. He had even outsmarted Eloise.

Etienne thought Charles had killed her, but he hadn't. He had simply handed Etienne the pills that Stephen had placed in the cupboard. When Eloise had died, Charles had tormented Etienne by telling him they had both killed her, but as twisted as Charles had been, even then, he hadn't been interested in killing Eloise. Maybe if he had, that would have been healthier. Instead, he had seemed addicted to the abuse.

Kicking aside a crumpled lump of wax, he lurched for the door and started for the tunnels, following the faint traces of plaster of Paris that had clung to her shoes. He checked the luminous face of his watch. By his calculations, she had a twenty-minute start on him, but that could easily be cancelled out by the fact that he knew where he was going and she didn't.

As he walked, he noticed chunks of wax and hanks of hair—the remains of masks. His fury mounted. The collection had been destroyed.

Jane was a lot stronger and a lot smarter than he'd given her credit for, but she had made a basic mistake. She should have killed him while she had the chance.

He reached the storm drain system and stopped, putting his ear to the wall. He could detect a faint, regular vibration. Someone was in the tunnel up ahead. Settling the goggles more securely in place, he moved forward in the darkness.

Twenty-Nine

Rain spattered Jane's face as she pressed her palms against the metal bars of the grill and shoved. Metal grated against concrete, shifted a fraction of an inch, then settled back in place.

The rain grew heavier. Water began to pour down on her head and stream down her arms, soaking her. She shivered, abandoning the attempt. This was the third grill she'd tried to budge. She was tall enough to reach the bars, but not tall enough to pop the heavy grills from their concrete seating. What she needed was something to stand on, anything to give her a few more inches of leverage. Once she removed the grill, she would be able to lever herself up and out.

Wrapping her arms around her middle to conserve warmth, she started back down the tunnel and passed yet another manhole entrance that had had the ladder removed. Her teeth began to chatter. Dexter had been thorough.

She'd toyed with the idea of yelling through the grills in the hope that she would attract someone's attention, but the likelihood that Dexter would hear and be able to pinpoint her position was stronger than the possibility that anyone would hear her through the muffling sound of the rain.

A skittering sound over and above the trickle of water sent her heart slamming against her chest. A family of rats, Mom, Dad and the kids, streamed past, brushing her ankles.

Jane swallowed a bubble of hysteria. Normally she would react to rats, but, trapped beneath the ground with a ruthless killer, the rats seemed as harmless and comforting as domestic cats. Jaw clamped to still the chattering, she followed in the wake of the rats, moving as quickly and soundlessly as she could through the growing stream of water. Something had sent them running. Maybe it was the fact that the drains were filling—or maybe it was something else. Or some*one*.

A faint sound behind her made her halt. Ears straining, Jane peered back in the direction she'd come. Dim light shafted through the grate, along with a steady runnel of water, obscuring her vision. If anyone was there, she couldn't see him.

Moving ahead cautiously in the near darkness, she tried to listen above the sound of running water. Reaching into the canvas bag, she found the hard metal shape of the gun. Gritting her teeth against the sound it would make, she pulled the slide back. With a clicking noise that reverberated, the round slid into place.

Jane flattened herself against the tunnel wall and lifted the gun in a two-handed grip. Her hands tightened on the weapon, her knuckles stiff and swollen from hitting Dexter. She heard the sound of a splashing footstep.

A metallic taste filled her mouth, and she realized she had bitten her lip.

Another footfall echoed. The grayish light from the manhole dimly outlined a masculine shape. For a split second Jane was certain it was Dexter; then the familiar gliding step and the shape of his shoulders registered. Toussaint.

Relief shuddered through her.

There was something about Toussaint—something not quite mortal. He had walked into her worst nightmare and found her, and for the first time since she'd realized Dexter had drugged her food, Jane decided everything was going to be all right.

Lowering the gun and putting it back in the bag, she stepped into the center of the tunnel.

Toussaint gripped her arms and pulled her into a hard clinch. He felt wonderful, warm and reassuringly masculine, and he smelled like heaven: male musk and sweat with a dash of cologne. She realized how important the simple animal comfort of touch and smell had become in the short time they'd been together.

Toussaint's mouth came down hard on hers; then he set her away from him. "Where did you get the gun?"

"Dexter."

Slipping an arm around her waist, he propelled her toward the grate. When they reached it, he examined the wall where the ladder used to be. It had stopped raining, but water still dripped. "Speaking of Dexter," he said softly, "where is the man of the hour?"

Without warning, the metal grate crashed down. Toussaint stumbled and fell, the grate lying at a drunken angle on his back. A dark shadow dropped through the hole, his face swollen, one eye completely closed.

Dexter gestured with his gun and smiled ghoulishly. "I'm here. Turn around."

"Not in this life." If he was going to shoot, she would rather see the bullet coming.

She backed away from Dexter, wondering if there was any way she could retrieve the gun from the canvas bag, and hoping to draw him away from Toussaint, who was lying frighteningly still. Dexter followed her, one step, then two.

Her foot turned on something—a small rock—and her balance went. She registered the short, sharp swing of Dexter's arm, the jolt when his fist connected with her jaw. Then everything went blank.

When Jane came to, she was being half floated, half dragged, helped along by the shallow stream of water that flowed through the drain.

Her jaw was stiff and sore, and her ears were ringing, but her head was reasonably clear. Dexter had knocked her out, but she'd been on her way down when he'd hit her, which had effectively pulled his punch.

"Down you go."

The grip on her wrist was relinquished. A boot caught her on one shoulder, pushing her forward; then she was sliding downhill in a large pipe, her head submerged. Water filled her nostrils and mouth, and leaked into her lungs. Clamping her jaw, she fought the urge to cough. If she opened her mouth, her lungs would fill and she would drown.

Abruptly, the solid shape of the pipe beneath her disappeared and she was in the air. Her body jerked in reflex, her arms flinging up to protect her head; then the ground came up to meet her and all the air was punched from her lungs. For long seconds she was unable to breathe; then her chest convulsed and oxygen punched in. Coughing and gasping, Jane rolled, ending up face down in the puddle of water gathered around the outflow pipe.

Mud and water streamed down her arms as she pushed herself to her knees. A footfall made her freeze. Fingers wound in her hair and jerked, and cold metal dug into the flesh of her throat. "Get up. Walk."

Jane stared into Stephen Dexter's face. Dark bruising mottled the swelling on his jaw, temple and the left side of his face. The puffiness extended to his nose and part of his right eye. From the way he kept blinking, he must be having trouble focusing out of his one good eye, which meant, aside from his vision being impaired, he was concussed.

If he was concussed, she had a fighting chance.

"Don't try it," he said softly.

Jane almost retorted, "Why not?" Mentally unbalanced or not, Dexter was hurt, and his judgement had to be impaired, despite the fact that he had managed to knock Toussaint out.

The thought of Toussaint was like touching on a wound, and rage swelled in her chest.

Her mind worked feverishly. Dexter was going

to kill her, stow her body somewhere safe, then go back and clean up his little party room before Toussaint's backup came looking for him and discovered what Stephen Dexter did in his spare time. When he'd packed up what was left of his trophies and sanitized the area, he would dispose of her and Toussaint's bodies and leave town, mission accomplished.

Coldly, she stared back at Dexter. Either he didn't want to pull the trigger here, because someone might hear the shot and investigate, or he was worried that after coming through that outflow pipe, the gun might not fire.

"Get up," he repeated.

"You'll have to help me," she said flatly. "I'm hurt."

Thirty

Toussaint stirred. The heavy weight on his shoulders shifted. With a groan, he twisted, and the object—a metal grate—slid to the ground.

Levering himself to his feet, he touched the base of his skull and winced. His fingers came away wet, and it wasn't water. He searched for his cell phone and pager, and came up blank. Dexter must have removed them along with his gun and the flashlight.

And Jane.

He would have to go for assistance. It was a judgment call, but without a flashlight, communication or a weapon, he was more of a liability to Jane than an asset.

He levered himself up and out, wincing as his

head throbbed. For a moment he stayed on his knees; then he pushed himself upright and got oriented.

Dexter jerked Jane to her feet. "Move."

Make me.

Deliberately, she swayed, favoring her leg. Dexter knew plenty about her, and since he was the one who had run her down, he had to know just how badly that leg had been hurt. "Which way?"

Dexter jerked his head, then winced, his right eye blinking, but the gun was still steady. Reluctantly, Jane began to limp along through the muddy trickle of water, heading toward the river. As they rounded a small headland, the peaked roofs of buildings around and behind them came into view. Beyond a thick line of trees, a large storage facility occupied most of the ground, and beside it lay a swampy reclamation site that was deserted.

Dexter pushed her in the direction of the storage facility. The pilings of a wharf appeared, and Jane's heart began to race. His car must be parked somewhere near.

An outcropping of rock forced them onto the narrow shale beach that edged the water. Her feet sank in, and she staggered, going down on one knee. Dexter jabbed her in the back with the gun.

Her fingers closed around a rock. "I need help."

He jerked her to her feet, keeping his distance, the gun still aimed at her. Deliberately, Jane stumbled off balance again, her shoulder forcing his aim wide. Lifting the rock, she brought it crashing down on his head. Dexter sagged, his eye glazed, blood trickling down his temple, and she swung again, this time catching him on the jaw.

Pain exploded up her arm as his head snapped sideways. His hand shot out as he stumbled, off balance on the shifting surface. His fingers closed around her upper arm, digging into her flesh as he toppled into the shallows, dragging her with him.

She stopped trying to fight his strength and shifted tactics, going with him instead, and Dexter went under, his head fully submerged.

Almost immediately, he surged upright, hand still locked around her arm, and Jane stepped into him again, pushing him off balance and deeper into the river. The current swirled, dragging the shale from beneath her feet, and she stumbled. Dexter swore, spitting blood and water, then abruptly dropped beneath the surface, pulling her under with him.

Jane had a split second to fill her lungs; then muddy water closed over her head. Dexter continued to pull her down, grinning, relishing the fight. The current slewed them sideways and upward, to where the sun struck the surface in an oily swirl. A piling loomed, and next to it, the long shape of a boat's hull.

Dexter kicked upward, but Jane surfaced first. As she grabbed another breath, she used her free hand to shove Dexter's head against the piling. Maintaining her grip on his shirt, she dived, kicking off from the hull. His fist caught her a glancing blow on the side of her jaw, but, cushioned by water, it lacked stopping power. Jane arrowed downward, hampered by Dexter's resistance, but she didn't have far to go, and she had the element of surprise. That was Dexter's problem; as smart as he was, he just couldn't think outside the box.

Her shoulder hit the encrusted piling. Blood misted around her face. Grimly, she hooked her free arm around it, then both legs, and clung, anchoring Dexter just inches beneath the surface. His hand tightened around her arm, fingers tearing at her skin. His foot lashed out, thumping into her ribs, and she lost air. His face loomed, abruptly close to hers; then her throat convulsed as his fingers clamped around her neck. He squeezed, and silvery bubbles burst from her mouth, drifting upward. He leered at her, and Jane closed her eyes, refusing to panic. He had her by the throat, but he was running out of air and could only squeeze for so long, and she could hold her breath for longer.

Her fingers, wrapped in a death grip in Dexter's shirt, went numb. Her lungs burned, and she swallowed to distract herself from the need to breathe. The pressure around her throat eased, then disappeared, and the resistance finally went out of Dexter. Head spinning from lack of oxygen, she held on for a count of ten, then released him and kicked to the surface.

Seconds later, her feet hit the edge of the steep gravel bank, and she half-stumbled, half-crawled from the water. Coughing and sucking in air, Jane studied the river, following the flow of the current where it disappeared around a bend. She thought she caught a glimpse of Dexter's shirt floating further downstream, but it was difficult to judge. With the tropical bursts of rain that Lassiter seemed to get on a daily basis, the river was full and opaque, the current fast.

Letting out a breath, she shoved the wet hair from her face and winced as her hand stung. "Big mistake, Dexter," she muttered, eyes skimming the fast moving surface of the water again. "When half the bones in your body have been broken, what do you get to do? Swim."

Telling herself that he couldn't have survived, she trudged toward the outflow pipe and Toussaint. Ten minutes later she had found Dexter's flashlight and the knife, but there was no sign of either gun. Pulling herself up the grassy bank, she went in search of the manhole cover Dexter had used to get into the underground system. At a rough estimate, twenty minutes had passed since he had dropped the drainage grate onto Toussaint. In that time, she didn't think it had rained. If Toussaint was alive...

Her jaw clenched against the possibility that he had died. No. That couldn't happen. Not now that she had finally found him.

Peering into the hole, she saw the grate lying on the floor in a pinkish puddle, but no Toussaint. Relief warred with worry. Toussaint had survived, but she had no way of knowing he was all right. There was only one thing that would make water pink like that, and that was blood.

The best case scenario was that he had found a way out and gone for help, the worst, that he was still in there somewhere, maybe concussed and unconscious.

Jane did a quick search of the immediate area, found the rusted ladder that fitted into the grooves of the wall, descended into the drainage system and flicked on the flashlight.

Studying the floor, she began to walk, measuring her paces. She passed another manhole cover, then continued on until she came to an intersection. Rounding a corner, she came face-to-face with Dexter.

His face was swollen and mottled, his arms full of fragments of masks. She shone the flashlight directly into his eyes as she backed up, in the hope that the beam would spoil his vision and increase her chance of escaping.

Gruesome pieces of masks showered into the shallow water pooling around his feet. A gun materialized in his hand. He lifted his arm, and Jane realized that, this time he wasn't going to bother with rituals or keeping quiet.

A footfall echoed, momentarily distracting him.

Another footfall sounded, and all the hairs at the back of her neck lifted as Dexter's aim shifted.

"Hey, Uncle Stephen." Toussaint's gaze locked with Jane's. "Down."

Obediently, she dropped to the ground, wincing as her bad leg protested. The flashlight slipped from her fingers, the beam strobing on the seeping walls. Simultaneously, a shot snapped through the tunnel, the concussion deafening. Panic exploded. For a wild moment she thought Toussaint had been shot, and more than once, because the roar of the gunshot was still bouncing off the walls. Ignoring Dexter's grotesque form, she launched herself to her feet, grabbed the flashlight and swung the beam on Toussaint.

He was still standing, staring through her as if she was invisible, his gaze fixed unwaveringly on Dexter. A shiver ran down Jane's spine. Once, when visiting a game park, she had seen lions stare like that when they fixed on their prey—cold and direct and lethal.

A choking sound jerked her head around. She realized that the only reason Dexter was standing was because the wall was supporting him. With a sound like a deflating balloon, he crumpled and slid to the ground.

Toussaint stepped past her, and it was then that she saw the gun. He'd had it in his hand all the time, but in the confined quarters, she'd been in the way. He kicked Dexter's gun away and holstered his own. Then, with a convulsive movement, he gripped her shoulders and jerked her close. "You're crazy, do you know that?"

Jane wrapped her arms around his waist and buried her face against his throat. "And you're just plain scary." He had stood there staring at Stephen Dexter as if he was invincible, almost giving her a heart attack.

"I was just buying Gatreaux an angle."

"Do any more 'buying' and I'll shoot you myself."

"With this?" With a slick movement, Toussaint had her knife.

Jane looked at the gleaming blade and shuddered. Dexter had been going to cut her with it. She was squeamish, she didn't like blood, but this time—for Toussaint—she would have used it. "I didn't have a gun," she said flatly.

"Are you telling me you got out and then came back in?"

"I thought you were in here."

Gatreaux appeared, a rifle in his hands, which explained the explosive sound. Dexter hadn't been shot with a handgun. Gatreaux shook his head. "You've been here six months, you finally get a woman, and look what happens."

Toussaint looked over Jane's head. "Thanks Gatreaux."

"No problem." Gatreaux stared at Dexter and shook his head. "You shouldn't have to shoot a family member."

Twenty minutes later, the site was cordoned off, Miller was trying to contain Brady—unsuccessfully—and Angie and Roland were setting up to go in.

"Does it have to be down a hole?" Angie muttered, shrugging into coveralls and pulling her hair back with an elastic band. "I've got a thing about holes. I hate them." She started down the ladder then waited for Roland to pass her bag down.

"Hey, Toussaint! Why couldn't you arrange to shoot him someplace convenient?"

"Like where? Hawaii?"

Angie suppressed her instinctive terror of small dark places and walked toward the body. At least they'd gotten some lighting. The place was lit up like a subway station. "I could be good with that. A first class ticket, a little champagne, a swim at the beach afterwards."

She stared at the body on the ground, and a shiver ran up her spine. He was older, but lean and muscular. His face was puffed and swollen and resembled nothing so much as a rotting potato.

She glanced at Gatreaux, who was being put through the third degree by Boulet. She caught Gatreaux's eye. "I heard you put a bullet in him. You've got that date."

Startled, Gatreaux looked at the pugnacious expression on Angie's face. His chest rose, and he tried not to grin.

Jane stared at the two holes punched in Dexter's chest. At first she'd thought Toussaint hadn't fired, but he had. It was a moot point who had actually killed Dexter, because either shot would have done the job, and in the end, it didn't matter. Dexter was dead.

Minutes later, the tunnel now definitely crowded, Jane climbed out into daylight. After the dim dankness of the tunnel, the sunshine was impossibly brilliant.

Toussaint's arm came around her. "No pictures."

Tyrone was sitting on the hood of his car, uncharacteristically quiet. "I wasn't going to, although you could say this is the story of my life, too, since I was in it practically from the start." He looked at the shadowy hole. "I'm not working today, I'm here for Arnold. I heard Dexter's dead."

At Toussaint's nod, Brady pulled two cans of beer out of his pockets, set one on the hood of the car and opened the other one. He tilted the can in a toast, lifted it to his lips and took a sip. "This one's for Arnold. Figured he'd like someone to see this finished."

A brisk breeze blew off the water, whipping Jane's hair around her face as she eased into the passenger seat of Toussaint's car. Her hair was a tangled mess, her clothes had dried to her skin, along with streaks of dried mud, and the stink of the tunnel still clung. She needed a shower, and she needed some more clothes. Lassiter was hard on clothes.

Toussaint slid into his seat and started the car.

Jane stared at his profile, noticing the crusted blood where the metal grate had caught him just behind the ear. That was the second time she'd thought he'd been killed. The first time had been when Charles Dexter had run them both down with his car. For a bleak moment she relived the panic she'd felt when she thought Dexter had killed him. Once should be enough in a lifetime. "By the way, I remembered my name."

Toussaint braked. The car slid to a halt on the damp grass. "What is it?"

"Jane."

Epilogue

It took several months to find and catalogue all the
evidence. The fact that most of the masks had been
broken, some shattered completely, didn't bother
anyone—not even the purists. There was more
than enough evidence to convict both Charles and
Stephen Dexter—and to add another chapter to
the textbooks. No one with a claim to a balanced
mind wanted to look overlong at what pleased a serial killer and, besides, there was the overriding
issue of dealing correctly with the human remains.

Where the remains could be identified and the
families contacted, what was left was returned for
burial. In some cases, the tiny fragments supplied
were all the family had of the deceased victim, because the body itself still hadn't been located.

Two weeks after Dexter was shot, a grave was

located on a piece of reserve land that bordered the old sugar plant, and which had once been part of the old Dexter farm. Six bodies were recovered in all. Jane found her mother, and Toussaint found his. Surprisingly, Eloise Dexter's remains were also identified. Eloise had originally been interred in a crypt in the Lassiter cemetery, which meant Charles or Stephen had, at some point, removed her body and transported it to its new grave.

In all, forty-three separate sets of remains were identified, and six bodies recovered. Of those, twenty victims were located through missing person files, and Etienne finally got his closure.

Charles Dexter was moved to a high security prison, into a hospital ward for the criminally insane, although with his general ill health, he wasn't expected to live long.

After the scientists had finished collecting their samples and doing their research, Stephen Dexter's body was cremated and his ashes scattered at an undisclosed destination. Because media curiosity was so intense, Etienne had wanted to put paid to the curiosity and the publicity that a grave would generate.

With the help of Jane and Etienne's testimony, and the work of profilers, psychologists were able to piece together what had gone so terribly wrong in the Dexter family that two out of three brothers had evolved into fully-fledged psychopaths.

The answer was in their personalities, their environment and, predictably, Eloise Dexter. Charles had been highly strung and a handful at school and at home, while Stephen had been abnormally concerned about trying to gain approval.

The main inciting event for the psychopathy had been the death of Burton Dexter and Eloise's subsequent control of the three children. When she had put the key to "the pit" in Stephen's hand, the pattern was set. Charles's already violent tendencies and fantasies of revenge had begun to take form, and Stephen experienced his first taste of power. While Charles later expressed his rage in the most grotesque way, through murder and mask-making, Stephen directed his into civilized channels. Wanting to experience more of the power of authority, he became a cop.

Using the newly formed psychological profiles, the experts had come up with a likely sequence of events. When Stephen had discovered that Charles was a serial killer, he had been both terrified that his own career would be ruined and fascinated by the power Charles had exerted over other human beings. Furious that Charles was stupid enough to actually commit a murder at his own residence, endangering Stephen and his career, Stephen had beaten Charles senseless, then had finished killing Emily Mathews. He had then gone after Jane and

John, running Jane down and leaving her for dead, and injuring John.

The reason he hadn't killed John was still up for debate, although it seemed reasonably clear that Stephen had known that while he could convince Etienne that Emily and Jane had unexpectedly "left town" without any forwarding address, there was no way he could get away with explaining John's death, as well. In the end, he had settled on the fiction that Charles had taken John for a ride in Stephen's car and hit a tree, putting them both in hospital. That way the dent in the vehicle was explained, and so were all the injuries.

Shortly afterward, the Dexter property was sold, but Stephen made sure to retain the barn and the old sugar mill, and Charles's secret tunnels, so he could hide the trophies and the evidence, and prevent anyone from digging up any remains. The best guess was that at first he must have planned to dispose of the evidence, and "sanitize" the whole property once the furor over the killings had died down. But as time passed and the case was closed, he had apparently changed his mind, contenting himself with gradually destroying caches of evidence around the country, destroying files, and keeping the storehouse of trophies intact.

Twenty-five years after that first fateful night, when Stephen had picked up Jane's book and discovered that the only witness to his killing was alive after all, he had finally stepped over the line and decided to kill again.

Always fascinated by the ritual and the detail of what Charles did, now he finally had both an excuse and an opportunity to indulge his fascination. He stepped easily into the role of copycat killer.

The final question, as to why Etienne had remained immune to Eloise's influence, when both Charles and Stephen hadn't, was answered with remarkable simplicity by the psychologists. Sometimes, they claimed, people were just born a certain way, and from a young age, Etienne was absorbed with building and creating, not destroying or taking away. That, combined with his own innate self-containment, had been enough to invalidate Eloise's influence.

When the full extent of the investigation was finally revealed, the major tabloids had a field day, but that was one story Tyrone Brady was no longer interested in writing. A major news syndicate offered him a large amount of money for an investigative expose, but, after years of mostly writing the kind of laid-back news that the people in Lassiter enjoyed reading with their morning coffee, he no longer had the stomach for hard reporting. Besides, to write the story, he would have to write about Arnold, and no way would he offer any kind of disrespect to his friend.

When the case was finally wound up, Toussaint and Jane moved to Beach Haven.

He'd gone to work for the Beach Haven PD, and Jane had gotten on with her next book.

Five months later, a registered package arrived. Curiously, Jane studied it. It was from Angie. Inside were a letter and a second, wrapped, parcel. Jane opened the letter. Angie was still going out with Gatreaux. He was a little young and impulsive, but he was growing on her; she was even thinking of allowing him to move in with her.

She picked up the second package. It was small and light, and seemed to consist mostly of bubble wrap and tissue paper. Gently, she began to unwrap the layers. When she peeled off the last layer, for a moment she was afraid to breathe.

Inside was her missing jewelry, and not one charm bracelet, but two. Heart squeezed almost perfectly tight, she held the second bracelet cupped in the palm of her hand. It was made of silver and tiny, sized for a child's wrist, with seven charms dangling from a delicate chain.